FAMILY BONDS- GRACE & LINCOLN

AMORE ISLAND

NATALIE ANN

Copyright 2024 Natalie Ann

All Rights Reserved

No part of this book may be used or reproduced in any manner without a written consent.

❀ Created with Vellum

AUTHOR'S NOTE

Author's Note

This is a work of fiction. Names, characters, places, events and incidents are products of the author's imagination or are used fictitiously. Any resemblance to actual events, locales, organizations or persons, living or dead, is entirely coincidental.

ALSO BY NATALIE ANN

The Road Series-See where it all started!!

Lucas and Brooke's Story- Road to Recovery
Jack and Cori's Story – Road to Redemption
Mac and Beth's Story- Road to Reality
Ryan and Kaitlin's Story- Road to Reason

The All Series

William and Isabel's Story — All for Love
Ben and Presley's Story – All or Nothing
Phil and Sophia's Story – All of Me
Alec and Brynn's Story – All the Way
Sean and Carly's Story — All I Want
Drew and Jordyn's Story— All My Love
Finn and Olivia's Story—All About You
Landon Barber and Kristen Reid- All Of Us

The Lake Placid Series

Nick Buchanan and Mallory Denning – Second Chance
Max Hamilton and Quinn Baker – Give Me A Chance
Caleb Ryder and Celeste McGuire – Our Chance
Cole McGuire and Rene Buchanan – Take A Chance
Zach Monroe and Amber Deacon- Deserve A Chance

Trevor Miles and Riley Hamilton – Last Chance

Matt Winters and Dena Hall- Another Chance

Logan Taylor and Kennedy Miles- It's My Chance

Justin Cambridge and Taryn Miles – One More Chance

The Fierce Five Series

Gavin Fierce and Jolene O'Malley- How Gavin Stole Christmas

Brody Fierce and Aimee Reed - Brody

Aiden Fierce and Nic Moretti- Aiden

Mason Fierce and Jessica Corning- Mason

Cade Fierce and Alex Marshall - Cade

Ella Fierce and Travis McKinley- Ella

Fierce Family

Sam Fierce and Dani Rhodes- Sam

Bryce Fierce and Payton Davies - Bryce

Drake Fierce and Kara Winslow – Drake

Noah Fierce and Paige Parker - Noah

Wyatt Fierce and Adriana Lopez – Wyatt

Jade Fierce and Brock James – Jade

Ryder Fierce and Marissa McMillan – Ryder

Fierce Matchmaking

Devin Andrews and Hope Hall- Devin

Mick McNamara and Lindsey White- Mick

Cody McMillian and Raina Davenport – Cody

Liam O'Malley and Margo West- Liam

Walker Olson and Stella White – Walker
Flynn Slater and Julia McNamara – Flynn
Ivan Andrews & Kendra Key- Ivan
Jonah Davenport & Megan Harrington- Jonah
Royce Kennedy & Chloe Grey- Royce
Sawyer Brennan & Faith O'Malley- Sawyer
Trent Davenport & Roni Hollister- Trent
Gabe McCarthy & Elise Kennedy – Gabe
Ben Kelley & Eve Hall – Ben
Dane Grey & Sloane Redding – Dane

Paradise Place

Josh Turner and Ruby Gentile – Cupid's Quest
Harris Walker and Kaelyn Butler – Change Up
Philip Aire and Blair McKay- Starting Over
Nathan Randal and Brina Shepard – Eternal
Ryan Butler and Shannon Wilder – Falling Into Love
Brian Dawson and Robin Masters – Mistletoe Magic
Caden Finley and Sarah Walker- Believe In Me
Evan Butler and Parker Reed – Unexpected Delivery
Trey Bridges and Whitney Butler – Forever Mine
Dylan Randal and Zoe Milton- Because Of You
Cash Fielding and Hannah Shepard – Letting Go
Brent Elliot and Vivian Getman – No More Hiding
Marcus Reid and Addison Fielding- Made For Me
Rick Masters and Gillian Bridges – The One
Cooper Winslow and Morgan Finely- Back To Me

Jeremy Reid and McKenna Preston- Saving Me
Christian Butler and Liz Carter- Begin Again
Cal Perkins and Mia Finley- Angels Above

Amore Island

Family Bonds- Hunter and Kayla
Family Bonds- Drew and Amanda
Family Bonds – Mac and Sidney
Family Bonds- Emily & Crew
Family Bonds- Ava & Seth
Family Bonds- Eli & Bella
Family Bonds- Hailey & Rex
Family Bonds- Penelope & Griffin
Family Bonds- Bode & Samantha
Family Bonds- Hudson & Delaney
Family Bonds- Alex & Jennie
Family Bonds- Roark & Chelsea
Family Bonds- Duke & Hadley
Family Bonds – Carter & Avery
Family Bonds- Egan & Blake
Family Bonds- Carson & Laine
Family Bonds- Grace & Lincoln
Family Bonds- Kelsey & Van

Blossoms

A Love for Lily – Zane Wolfe and Lily Bloom
A Playboy For Poppy- Reese McGill and Poppy Bloom

A Romantic For Rose – Thomas Klein and Rose Bloom

A Return For Ren – Ren Whitney and Zara Wolfe

A Journey For Jasmine- Wesley Wright and Jasmine Greene

A Vacationer for Violet – Violet Soren And Trace Mancini

A Hero For Heather- Heather Davis and Luke Remington

A Doctor For Daisy- Daisy Jones And Theo James

An Investigator For Ivy- Ivy Greene and Brooks Scarsdale

A Date For Dahlia- Dahlia Greene and Hugh Crosby

A Surprise For Sage- Sage Mancini and Knox Bradford

Looking For Love

Learning To Love – West Carlisle and Abby Sherman

Love To The Rescue – Braylon Carlisle and Lily Baker

Love Collection

Vin Steele and Piper Fielding – Secret Love

Jared Hawk and Shelby McDonald – True Love

Erik McMann and Sheldon Case – Finding Love

Connor Landers and Melissa Mahoney- Beach Love

Ian Price and Cam Mason- Intense Love

Liam Sullivan and Ali Rogers - Autumn Love

Owen Taylor and Jill Duncan - Holiday Love

Chase Martin and Noelle Bennett - Christmas Love

Zeke Collins and Kendall Hendricks - Winter Love

Troy Walker and Meena Dawson – Chasing Love

Jace Stratton and Lauren Towne - First Love

Gabe Richards and Leah Morrison - Forever Love

Blake Wilson and Gemma Anderson – Simply Love

Brendan St. Nicholas and Holly Lane – Gifts of Love

ABOUT THE AUTHOR

Sign up for my newsletter for up to date releases and deals. Newsletter.

Follow me on:

Website
- Twitter
- Facebook
- Pinterest
- Goodreads
- Bookbub

As always reviews are always appreciated as they help potential readers understand what a book is about and boost rankings for search results.

BLURB

Lincoln Harrington knows what it's like to be used. To feel as if he's not good enough or he'll never measure up. His emotional wounds as a teen burned worse than the flesh ones. As an adult, he knows what to look out for and how to safeguard his heart. He's made a promise to himself to never get in that position again...except for once in his life, he might not be able to keep that promise.

Grace Stone doesn't have the Bond last name, but everyone knows she is an heir to her grandfather's billion-dollar fortune. Her entire life has been judged and based on what she'll get or have rather than who she is. As a result, her trust issues tend to push many away. She gave up on men a long time ago, but one keeps catching her eye. She decides it's time to make her move. But the joke is on her, as his trust issues will keep him from getting close. The question is whether the two of them can move past their history and open themselves up to a future.

PROLOGUE

"I want you home by eleven!"

Lincoln Harrington was sitting in the passenger seat of his girlfriend's Mustang. Lara's grandparents had given it to her for her sixteenth birthday two years ago. Lara was eighteen. A few months older than him. He didn't care all that much.

He felt he was the luckiest dude in the school dating this hot chick that most wanted and she wouldn't give the time of day to anyone but him.

"Sure!" Lara yelled back and she slid into the car. "Not likely. They are so controlling. I can't wait until we graduate in two months and then I'm out of here."

"Have you told them yet you aren't going to college?" he asked.

Lara's parents had her on a short leash most of her life. At least from what she'd said. It wasn't until recently that her mother convinced her father to let her have some freedom since she'd be going off to college soon.

Or so they thought. Again, words from Lara's mouth.

"No," Lara said. "I've got time before they have to put the

money down. I'm getting away from here and them. Then it's just the two of us and no one to answer to."

He leaned over and kissed her while she started the engine and it roared to life.

The muscle car had been a huge argument in Lara's family. She'd told him all about it. Repeatedly in the eight months they'd been dating.

Lara's father thought it was too dangerous. Lara's mother told her father to lighten up, you only lived once.

Lincoln was going with the second, but he had to admit that Lara was a little reckless at times. More than he was, and for a guy entering the Air Force with the goal of being a fighter pilot, that was saying something.

"I want you with me," he said. His heart had been long gone the minute he found out she was a virgin. "But it won't be right away. I've got to go through basic training, then figure out where I'll end up. You know you can't live with me unless we are married."

"I want to get married," Lara said excitedly. "You can take me away from here and care for me right?"

"Always," he said. Though he had doubts he could give her the life she was used to. She insisted it wasn't a big deal, but her words and her actions never lined up.

He was middle class. His parents had stable jobs and they had a decent well-maintained house.

He'd never wanted for much in his life, but it's not like his parents bought him a car for his sixteenth birthday.

He had a job and he put half in and his parents put the other four thousand in. He thought it was awesome, but it wasn't the car he was riding in now and never would be.

Lara's parents made it a point to rub that in their daughter's face all the time too.

That Lincoln wouldn't or couldn't give her what she deserved and that she could do so much better.

He'd overheard her parents talking one day that she'd find someone better suited for her when she was in college.

She argued that she loved him and didn't care about those things.

Yet they never went places in his car and she always was asking him to take her out, him using most of his paycheck on that rather than putting money away.

"Then that is all I care about," Lara said. She hit the gas hard when the light turned green and he was sucked into the seat.

"What are you going to do when I'm in training?" he asked

Every time he brought this up she'd avoid answering. He'd always been a man with a plan. He couldn't live by the seat of his pants. It just wasn't his way.

Could be he didn't have anything to fall back on like Lara did.

"I'll figure it out," she said. "If I have to start college for a semester, I'll do it. Doesn't mean I have to finish."

He cringed. He didn't care how much money her parents had, that was just wasteful to him.

Unless she changed her mind and was going to end things with him.

He tried not to think that way. It was going to be what it was.

It's not like he was changing his plans. This had been his dream ever since his parents took him on vacation and he got to look at old fighter planes and helicopters. The helicopters drew him in more, but he was willing to give them both a try.

His parents always knew what he wanted and they supported him even through their fears.

Lara found it exciting and sexy. The night he'd told her what he was going to do after graduation was when she told him she was ready to go all the way. That was a month after they'd been dating.

It fed his ego that she was supporting his career choice, and from that point on, she'd bragged to many at the same time she'd tried to show him how much she needed speed.

He wouldn't say he ever had a need for speed like she did.

Not when she took a turn fast enough to have him grabbing the door.

"What is your rush?" he asked. "We're only going to the movies."

"I've got this car, might as well drive it like it's meant to be."

He'd told her all the time to let up on the gas. She'd let him drive it a time or two, but that was it. He didn't ask, she'd offered. He didn't want her to get in trouble if her parents found out.

"If you abuse it too much it won't last that long," he said. He took care of what was his.

"It will be fine," she said, laughing, her hair blowing in the breeze with the sunroof open and the windows down.

That was her answer to everything.

Lincoln knew he'd have to learn to accept that if they were going to be married. No two people were the same or perfect.

They got to the mall, went in and grabbed a quick burger at the food court, then were in the theater with five minutes to spare. They spent more time in the back making out, his hand sliding under her shirt and even down her pants, than they did watching the movie.

When it ended a little after nine, they walked around the mall before closing and were back in her car at ten.

"What do you want to do for an hour?" he asked.

"I'm not going to be home at eleven," she said. "It's lame. It's Saturday night and I'm eighteen. You don't have a curfew."

Only because he knew she did and his parents were fine with that. When he got home late, it worried them and he'd apologize left and right, but they knew he was at the mercy of Lara if she was picking him up and dropping him off.

He'd offered to get her, but she always wanted to be out in her car. Since it was a sweet ride he couldn't complain much about it.

He didn't have a chance to dispute her comment when she pulled out in traffic with another car coming not that far away.

"Lara!" he shouted, but it was too late.

The truck hit them in the driver's door, throwing Lara's body like a rag doll in a washing machine toward him only to have it snap back by the seatbelt.

His last thought was this was going to end up being his fault. He knew it.

He didn't remember anything else before his airbag went off, knocking him unconscious.

1

WORTHY OF ME

Seventeen Years Later

"Hey, Grandpa," Grace Stone said, walking in the back door of her grandfather's home on Amore Island.

Steven Bond, one of the last remaining of his generation. He came from Edward's side of the family and had three children.

"There is my girl," her grandfather said. "What's in the bag?"

"Food," she said, wiggling her eyebrows. She was always laid back and carefree with him.

"I figured that much. But what kind of food?"

"Stuffed shells," she said. "Plus a loaf of bread that I baked this morning."

Her grandfather's house wasn't that big. Maybe twenty-five hundred square feet. It was a two story with a primary on the first floor for easy living for him in his elder years.

Not that twenty-five hundred square feet was small for homes, but considering his billion-dollar wealth, most would expect something much more grand.

That was her grandfather's house in Boston. The one that was too big and lonely for him. In the nicer weather he spent more time on the island, but she knew he wouldn't get rid of the mansion that had been in Edward's side of the branch for years.

"It's your day off and you're still cooking. Not that I don't appreciate it."

Her grandfather had gotten up and followed her into the renovated kitchen. Not that it was anything up to her standards, but it would do.

"I can't help the fact that what I do for a living I need to do daily anyway," she said. "You're keeping me company on my day off."

Her grandfather snorted. "If you weren't single you wouldn't need your grandfather to keep you company."

She didn't want to hear this again. It felt like it was all she heard lately.

More than half of her cousins were now married or getting married. Some had kids on top of it.

If she could get past the walls she'd put up over the years, maybe she'd have a shot with someone, but the fact she was always looking for someone's motive just kept her locked in her single-girl status.

Most got sick of her doubts in the end and walked.

She couldn't help who she was though. If they didn't want to stick it out, that was on them.

"Who has time?" she said. "I work weekends and nights."

"Not every night," her grandfather argued. "You run the

kitchen, you can take some more time off or at least rearrange your schedule."

She sighed. "Grandpa. Since you still have some controlling shares of The Retreat, you know it's the wedding destination of the Northeast for those with big bucks."

She was rubbing her fingers together with a grin.

Sure, her grandfather didn't do much more than sit on the board of The Retreat. Even her Uncle Charlie did the same. Right now, her older cousin, Hunter, ran it. That stupid antiquated clause that only a male Bond could run it.

Better Hunter than her. She wanted no part of any of it. Never did and never would.

She liked going to work and doing her job and not having the responsibility and liability of running the business.

Which was stupid really because she ran the kitchen. She hired and she fired and trained, but she was given a budget. She didn't worry about any of those other pesky details.

"It is the place to be," her grandfather said proudly. "And someday I hope you get married there too."

Grace rolled her eyes, and when the oven beeped, she stuck the shells in there. "Not on my radar."

"You're thirty-one years old. When are you going to settle down?"

She might be small, but she was mighty.

She had a loud voice and let it be heard.

Not just by the sounds coming out of her mouth either.

She put her hands on her hips. "When I find a man worthy of me is when I'll consider it. But on this island, the pickings are slim."

More like trustworthy, but she'd never say that.

"It's your choice not to go to Boston."

"I grew up there," she argued. "I was meant to be here. It's what I always wanted out of my life. I'm happy and that should be good enough."

Besides, she hated the hustle and bustle of the bigger city.

She might not have the last name of Bond, but it seemed more knew her there than here.

Between her mother's organization and her father's job, the Bond name and her tie to Amore Island, all the men she'd come in contact with in her life wanted a part of *those* things.

It didn't feel as if anyone wanted to get to know her.

Not even friends in school. At least she hadn't felt that way.

"Of course we are thrilled you are happy," her grandfather said.

She pulled out the bread and cut him a slice since he'd been eying it on the counter. "You want a piece of this, don't you?"

"Is it still warm?" her grandfather asked, moving closer and sniffing the air.

"I just took it out of the oven on my way out the door," she said. "And since I'm spoiling you with an early dinner, don't you think we can talk about anything else other than my personal life?"

"Sure," her grandfather said. "It's not like you've got a dating life."

She wanted to grind her teeth but wouldn't. He was just picking on her like he always did.

The middle granddaughter and the baby of her family. She was closer to him than her cousins. At least she felt she was.

She'd never say she was the favorite, but at times it seemed it.

That was why once a month she brought him dinner. She'd do it more often, but he wasn't always around when she had a day off.

"And I like it that way," she said. "How long are you on the island for?"

Mid-March was early for her grandfather to be here for long periods, but he had business ventures all over the island, Boston and Cape Cod. More that she didn't know about and didn't care.

She may be an heir to that fortune, but it was so far down the line, it wasn't even funny. There was a generation before her anyway. Her mother, her uncle and her aunt.

"I might stay the week," her grandfather said. "I flew over this morning. With Egan's baby coming soon, I know they are pretty swamped. So I scheduled my flight back rather than calling last minute knowing that they'd squeeze me in." Her grandfather reached for the slice she'd cut, then the butter, and slathered it on.

"I hope I can catch my flight tomorrow with him on baby watch," she said. "Mom will kill me if I don't make it."

"You won't have a problem," her grandfather said. "They will get you there regardless."

"It's nice they've got three helicopters now and the extra pilots. Not that I use the service much, but I don't want to ride the ferry and sit around waiting. I'd rather just get there and back."

"Your mother is thrilled," her grandfather said. "She's been trying to get you to do this for years."

She cut a slice of bread for herself. There was nothing better than fresh warm bread in her eyes.

"She kept having this on Friday or Saturday night," she

argued. "It's not easy for me to get that time off. Even if planned, if there is an event or wedding at The Retreat, that has to come first."

"You always make it come first. That is your choice."

Grace stuffed her mouth full of the yeasty warm bread and said around a mouthful, "I hate public speaking."

"Finally some truth out of your mouth."

She chewed and swallowed. "I always tell the truth. What do you think I'm lying about?"

Her grandfather stared at her. "Why you're single."

"Grandpa," she said sternly. "I'm going to leave if you keep it up."

"Will the stuffed shells stay though?"

She couldn't help but laugh. "Nope. I'll take them with me."

"Then I'll stop. I promise."

"You won't," she mumbled.

"I heard that."

"You hear everything even though you complain your hearing isn't great. I think it's all a ruse."

Her grandfather laughed at her and continued to eat his bread.

When they were sitting at the table eating dinner, she thought for sure the topic had finally been dropped, but she was wrong.

"What do you think about me introducing you to someone?"

"Someone?" she asked. "As in a date or work?"

"Could be both. Maybe you need someone that does the same work as you."

"Nope," she said. "Been there and done that."

The guy didn't like she was the boss. Didn't like she got more attention for her cooking either.

The last thing she needed was someone who turned a relationship into a competition.

"I didn't know that," her grandfather said. He reached for the casserole dish and got himself a second serving. It did her heart well to see him eat her food.

She'd been cooking for him since she was a child when she visited. She'd joke that was why he always wanted her to come visit.

She didn't care. Grace had known what she wanted to do from a young age and since he owned and ran The Retreat, he was the one to tell her what the expectations were.

In her mind, the more he loved her cooking, the easier it would be for her to work there.

Just because her family owned it didn't mean it was guaranteed she'd end up with the job. There were plenty of other hotels with restaurants in the family she could work at.

No way. In her mind it was The Retreat or nothing at all.

"I don't tell you everyone I date," she said.

"When was the last time you were on a date?"

"I don't remember," she said. "I don't even care."

"Do you even try? Do you have your eye on someone and maybe you are waiting for him?"

This was too close to the truth. She didn't want to lie and say no, but if she said yes then he'd ask more questions.

She'd thought she'd done a really good job keeping this to herself for years.

"Do you think I'm the type of person to wait around for someone?" she asked, laughing.

"Never," her grandfather said. "That's the thing about my daughters and granddaughters. They don't let anything hold them back or stop them from going after what they want."

"Nope," she said. "We don't."

She reached for the spoon to get another shell even though she wasn't hungry. If she was paying attention to the food maybe he wouldn't notice her aversion to this topic.

Because the truth was, she had her eye on a sexy pilot she didn't get to see often, but when she did, he never bothered to be any different than how he was with anyone else.

The last thing she wanted to do was put herself out there with one of her cousin's employees, and his best friend, to be rejected. Nor did she want anyone to feel sorry for her either if that happened.

For now, she'd just continue to keep this little secret to herself.

2

HIGH CLASS

Lincoln shut the helicopter off on Amore Island. It felt as if he was running like crazy today, but they were all pitching in knowing this could happen.

If it wasn't for the fact that he knew his clients would be early and waiting for him, he wouldn't have been able to squeeze in what he was doing right now, but everyone was willing to work it out.

Before he even could climb out, he saw Grace Stone come walking in her brisk stride toward him.

He always found her name a contradiction.

She wasn't graceful at her five-foot one-inch frame. She was more than a foot shorter than him and maybe weighed a hundred pounds. It was probably an exaggeration, but even her bone structure was small.

For someone who made a living in the kitchen, it didn't seem as if she ate a lot.

But that was just him guessing because with his love of food if he had someone cooking for him, he'd be fifty pounds heavier and would easily give up his fast food addiction.

Then there was her last name.

Stone.

He knew right away she was hard as her last name when it came to her career and those who worked for her.

Not that he'd seen her in action, but he knew the Bond family members took their careers seriously when none of them even needed to.

He could appreciate that character trait.

More so since he'd had to work to get where he was.

Everything he had he earned and would continue to do it and liked surrounding himself with like-minded people.

"Thanks for working around the schedule," he said when Grace hopped into the helicopter. "I'm shifting things all over today."

"Not a problem," she said. "Everything okay?"

"Egan's been at the hospital with Blake since this morning. No false alarm this time, but baby Bond is taking his sweet time coming out."

"That's exciting," she said. "I'm sure Blake will be thrilled to be holding her son."

"She will be," he said. "Egan more so."

Lincoln always felt that huge pang of jealousy when he saw his best friend and boss putting his mouth to his fiancée's belly and talking to their son.

He supposed Egan's laid-back nature was perfect for a new dad because Blake seemed more nervous.

"I bet he's got some crazy name picked out," she said. "Still no idea?"

He knew but was sworn to secrecy. "They said they need to lay eyes on him before they decide to know if it'd fit or not. Besides, I think he's worried there was a mistake with the ultrasound."

Grace laughed, her long black hair that was floating past

her shoulders swished around while she put her headset on and buckled in.

Once she was set, Lincoln started to flip switches and get the bird up in the air.

Grace didn't talk again until they were flying toward Boston. He could do both, talk and fly, but he liked that she gave him time to get set.

"Is Egan worried that Blake might make him paint the room pink before the baby can go in there?"

"No," he said. "He said he's keeping it blue even if it ends up being a girl."

"Just like if he painted it pink, he'd keep it if it was a boy?" she asked. "I could see Egan doing that."

"Yeah, he'd think it was funny and it'd drive Blake nuts."

He'd heard all about how Egan won the room color when Blake wanted to keep it neutral. Some silly competition of who could get a squirrel to take a nut out of their hand first.

There were some things he just didn't ask because he didn't want to know the answers as to why it was even happening.

"With any luck they don't have to worry," she said.

"Most likely not."

"With everything going on, I hate that you've got to fly me back in a few hours."

"No worries. It worked out. As soon as we land, Blake's dad should be waiting for me. I'm going to grab him and bring him back here. They waited to let him know until she was further along."

"How long has she been in labor?" she asked.

"No clue," he said. "I just know Egan brought her at five this morning when she finally told him she was having contractions."

He was sure Egan wasn't thrilled about being kept in the dark. He knew he'd be pissed off if it were him.

"Hopefully there will be a baby soon," she said.

"Not too soon since Conrad wants to be there."

He'd do everything he could to make that happen for his best friend.

He'd known that Blake didn't have the best relationship with her father when she moved here over a year ago. The fence had been mended and Egan said he'd run to get Conrad himself to make it happen.

No way he was letting his best friend leave Blake's side for anything.

Between him, Roxy, their other full time pilot, and, Rob, their part time one, he'd managed to get all the flights covered for the rest of this week. Egan wasn't allowed to show up at the airstrip until Monday.

Six days with his wife and child. Orders from his mother.

When Janet Bond put her foot down, everyone listened.

Himself included. She'd told him she'd hold him responsible if Egan attempted to work.

He was as scared of her as he was his own mother.

"Knowing you," Grace said, "you'll get him there on time. Maybe I'll be one of the first to know about the birth by the time you get me later. Sorry about all the going back and forth."

"It's fine," he said. "Otherwise I'd just be sitting around. You said you'll be back to the docks by eight?"

"That is the plan. I'll let you know if I'm late. I've got your number."

She did now because he pulled it up to text her to come an hour earlier.

"Just text me if you're running late," he said. "I'll be at the docks anyway."

"Oh, remind me when we land I've got something for you."

"You do?" he asked, turning his head. "What's that? Is it food?"

She grinned. "I've heard more than once how much you like to eat. That maybe you eat a lot of fast food?"

The appalled look on her face said it all. "I'm on the go a lot."

"I know. It's made the rounds that some people give you food when you fly them places."

"We always appreciate food," he said. It was usually family that fed him. Grace was considered family. Well, she was family to Egan. Just a different branch.

The only other billionaire branch.

Maybe he'd thought she was sweet on the eyes the first time he saw her.

And that he enjoyed talking to her and knowing she'd be the type to throw back a beer with the guys and not get all fussy and fashionable on him. He didn't do well with high-maintenance women.

He had too many demons in his past with women who were in a higher class than him.

Not that he thought Grace would give him the time of day for more than a beer and some jokes.

Which was how it would be better to think of her anyway.

"I've been in a bread-making mood," she said. "There is half a loaf there and a container of stuffed shells. I made them yesterday for my grandfather and had extra."

"Do you hear that thumping over the blades?" he asked.

"No," she said, looking panicked. "What is it?"

"It's my heart racing over having dinner. I know what I'm eating once I get Conrad here and am back at the docks waiting for you."

She reached her small hand out as if she was going to swat his arm, but she couldn't reach him. "Not funny in the least."

"Sure, it was," he said.

She liked to crack jokes with him in the past; he was only doing the same. Though she wasn't smiling so maybe he wasn't as funny as he thought he was.

It's not as if he saw her often. Just flying back and forth when she needed a lift or at a family function they both were attending. She said she didn't have enough time to wait and board the ferry. He'd have to say he agreed, but he was spoiled and didn't have a reason to ever ride it.

When Egan got married in a few months, he'd see Grace again too.

He'd have a lot of eyes on him as the best man and would have to be doing his part that day too.

Grace had a smile on her face when he landed twenty minutes later so at least he didn't scare her too much. They'd been joking about anything he could think of.

He shut the helicopter off and watched as she climbed out. He wasn't positive about what she had going on tonight, but she was dressed up.

Not in a dress but in black pants with a longer brown jacket that covered her hips. He got a glimpse of some sexy black pumps. He didn't think she was going on a date but didn't or wouldn't ask. It wasn't his business.

"See you in a few hours," she said.

"You forgot your bag?"

"Oh crap," she said, going back over to get it.

He beat her to it and climbed in and then handed it over.

"Actually," she said. "Can I leave it here? I just need my purse." Which she pulled out and put on her shoulder. "The rest is food for you."

"In that case," he said, reaching for it, "you're good."

"Thanks," she said, moving fast toward the parking garage. He was sure her family had cars stored there for anyone's usage just like Egan's did.

He often took Egan's Range Rover when he needed to, as his truck was on the island.

Lincoln half jogged to the offices. He didn't have a jacket on and it was low forties for mid-March. Not cold enough in his mind to put a coat on that he'd have to take off while flying. He hated to have any bulky gear on.

When he opened the office door, he saw Conrad Baldwin standing there looking anxious.

"Give me a minute to put this away and we can leave," he said to Blake's father.

"Take your time," Conrad said. "Egan has kept me updated that she's still not fully dilated."

He tried to hide his shiver. He didn't want to think of those things. Some stuff was better left out of his brain.

He'd seen enough injuries and death in his life. Not just in the Air Force either.

Once he had the food stored in the fridge in Egan's office that the two of them shared, he went back out to see Conrad standing by the door.

"Let's get you to see that grandson being born," he said.

"Let's do that," Conrad said. "I'm not sure why I'm so nervous. I wasn't this nervous when my kids were being born."

Sometimes it felt like he was a therapist to people too. Imagine that.

"She's tough," Lincoln said. "She's marrying Egan, so she has to be."

"Good point," Conrad said.

The older man didn't laugh, but he did crack a grin. He'd take that for now, then he could go back and enjoy Grace's food until he got to see her again.

He was becoming a pro at watching people from a distance.

3

POKE IN THE EYE

"You're early," Melanie Stone said. "I wasn't so sure that would happen."

"Lincoln texted me to get an earlier flight. Blake's in labor and they were rearranging the schedule. It worked out."

"That's exciting," her mother said. "Maybe someday I'll have a grandchild."

Grace wanted to let out a big sigh but decided not to. She'd be truthful instead. "Did you and Grandpa talk this over so that I was getting double-teamed on it?"

"What?" her mother said. "No. And you look lovely. Give me your jacket. I didn't think you'd wear a dress. But you look appropriately like you."

Her mother was in more of a formal dress, but it wasn't Grace's thing. It's not like this was her event. It was her mother's and she was just a guest speaker.

"Thanks," she said. "My feet are already hurting, but I'll be fine."

"You know I appreciate you doing this. You'll get home late though."

She laughed. "Mom. I work until ten or later on Friday and Saturday. I'll be back on the island before nine."

"And then have thirty minutes to drive to your place."

She lived on the south end of the island closer to The Retreat, but she wasn't on the furthest tip either. Port to port could be almost an hour depending on traffic.

The airstrip wasn't quite in the middle of the island, but it was closer to the north end. When her grandfather made comments about her going to Boston, she almost always went to Plymouth when she was going off the island.

That port was closer and the ferry ride was slightly less. She wasn't one to take the helicopter places unless she was pressed for time.

But it wasn't like she needed to leave the island much either. Everything she wanted or needed was there or she ordered it.

Another thing she couldn't get men she dated to understand.

Just one more thing to deal with when it came to dating. Someone who didn't want or care for island living and she wasn't going anywhere.

Maybe that was another thing that was appealing about Lincoln. He lived on Amore Island and seemed content to stay, from what she'd heard. He'd been there for years.

She'd even broken down and brought him food to see what reaction she'd get out of him.

Maybe her grandfather's words were like a nudge to her. Or a poke in the eye for her to do something.

It didn't seem she made up much ground though other than putting food in his belly.

And got a couple of smiles out of him.

Enough that she almost left her purse in the helicopter

and that wouldn't have gone over well with her notecards in there for her speech.

"Which is nothing, Mom. You're starting to sound old."

"Don't even think about that," her mother said. "Come and let me introduce you to a few of the other speakers that are here tonight."

She let herself be dragged away.

Her mother started and ran a not-for-profit geared toward empowering women in the workforce or getting back into the workforce after motherhood or any type of situation where they'd been out of work for years.

They didn't just serve low income, and events like this brought out big donors.

The Bond family name helped also.

Her cousin Hailey had spoken at this event before. So had her cousin Emma who was a Romantic Suspense author.

There were a lot of women with careers in the family that could speak, but this was the first year Grace had done it.

She stood there while her mother introduced her to a few women who had returned to the workforce after being in domestic violence situations and were thriving in their lives and careers.

It made Grace wonder what she was doing here.

Many would say she was born with a platinum spoon in her mouth and another in her hand.

She worked hard for her job, but she could have had any job in the family given to her.

She could have her own restaurant right now too, but it was not what she saw herself doing.

At one point she knew she'd settle down and have a

family. Having to run a business and not just a kitchen would make that harder to do.

It's not like she'd be the type of person to push responsibilities off on other people either.

Her mother was running around and checking on everything and she noticed her father off by the bar and decided to join him. There were still forty minutes at this point before the event started. It wasn't the end of the world that she got here an hour earlier than she planned.

"How come you aren't calming Mom?"

"She thrives in this atmosphere and you know it," her father said. "And she appreciates you doing this."

"I know. It worked out well with being my day off."

"You do know she purposely planned it this way so you couldn't say no."

Grace did know that, which made it impossible for her to come up with some excuse to get out of it.

"She'd get more in attendance on a Friday or Saturday," she said.

"She would, but it's not about that," her father said. "Though your mother said the same amount of tickets were sold again."

"I'm glad," she said. That made her feel somewhat better.

"What do you want to drink?"

"Just a seltzer with lemon," she said. No reason to have a glass of wine as she wanted. She could get that when she was home later.

She got her drink and then found her table and sat with her father. She didn't want to be paraded around as Melanie Stone's daughter. She just wanted to be known as Grace Stone. Not someone's granddaughter or daughter, not even niece.

Just her.

She was pretty sure it'd never happen and wasn't so sure why she was hung up on it all the time either.

She had a great life and no complaints and had to get over it.

And two hours later, she was the first to speak. That was worse in her eyes.

She got up there and talked for five minutes. That was what her mother told her she had to do.

All she said was she'd had a dream for years and knew in her mind it was what she was meant to do. And if she was going to do it, she wanted to be the best she could. Work the hardest and get to that place.

Chefs were predominantly men. The percentage of women head chefs was even lower. Being good wasn't good enough. You had to be great. But it was possible with work, determination and a helping hand.

When she was done, she talked about mentoring youths in the summer. Something that was her idea and her mother loved it and made it work. She'd been doing it for years and didn't brag about it.

That wasn't her reason for doing it. To her, she just wanted to give back.

She held one clinic in Plymouth and then another in Boston. Both were at family-owned hotels and restaurants. That was how she spent two weeks of her vacation each year. Another week, she'd take for her, and though she had more time, she rarely used it. At least in weekly increments.

"That was beautiful," her father said.

Grace felt the heat fill her face. "Thanks. I didn't know what to say."

"You said what should be said. Everyone here knows your background and you came at the angle that nothing is free and you still worked for it. That's a powerful message too."

She never thought of it that way before.

But those words were still in her head when she parked her parents' car in the parking garage and raced to the charter office, whipping the door open three minutes before eight.

"Slow down," Lincoln said. "You're going to break an ankle."

"I probably will," she said. "I can't wait to kick these things off. I miss my work shoes."

Nice sturdy black sneakers that weren't lookers, but her feet thanked her.

"Just like Egan," he said. "Are you another one that would be barefoot all the time if you could?"

"Yes," she said. "Just not possible in my job. I'm ready if you are."

"I am," he said. "Here are your dishes back. Washed and all."

"You ate it all?" she asked. She thought there were at least two servings there.

"Most of it," he said. "I transferred the rest to a container here. This way I don't have to worry about getting it back to you."

Which had been the plan and he didn't seem to get it.

Damn it.

This passive-aggressive approach went right over his head.

Unless he wasn't interested. That was a possibility too.

Then she thought of the other three speeches she'd heard today and realized that hard work didn't just get localized to careers but also to personal lives too.

"I'm sure you're tired after flying all day," she said when they were walking to the helicopter.

"I'm used to it," he said. "I sleep more and better on the island than I did anywhere else in my life other than where I grew up."

Thoughts of him lying in bed with no shirt on, maybe nothing at all, filled her brain and she started to feel a little flush under her jacket.

"I love it there," she said. "I'm right on the water where I always wanted to be."

Her grandfather's home was near her on the island. Her parents had a place close by with a water view but no beach.

She wanted a beach.

She wanted to lie out in the sun and feel the heat on her body in the warmer months.

Watch the sunset over the ocean from her deck or her bedroom balcony.

Those were the things that relaxed her after long workweeks. She did her best thinking there too.

"I don't have a water view or anything from my place," he said, "but I see it multiple times a day."

"You must have seen so many beautiful things in your life," she said.

He started the helicopter and then lifted up. It was five minutes before he answered her. She did the same with Egan. Let them do their job, and once they were set, she'd talk again.

"Not all beautiful, but they did help wipe out some of the nastiness in the world too."

It was then she remembered she'd heard he was an attack pilot in the enemy territory. He was on rescue missions too.

So yeah, not all of his job was pretty or had a happy ending.

"Sorry for saying that," she said.

"Don't be," he said. "It's the truth."

"I need a drink," she said.

"Tough night?" he asked.

She realized now he didn't know what she had going on. She'd never said.

"I had to do a speech at one of my mother's charity events. I've found a way to avoid it for years but not this year."

"I'm sure you did great," he said.

"Why do you say that?" she asked. He turned his head and she was mesmerized by his deep dark eyes and brown hair. Short on the sides and a little longer on top.

He had a full beard that needed a trim. He didn't always have one. This might be the fullest she'd seen it, but it had a sexy mysterious vibe going on too that she liked.

He had jeans on that were fitted to his body but with enough stretch to show he had some muscles going on. His Bond Charter long-sleeved shirt wasn't baggy either, tighter on his arms. Yeah, he had more muscles than she realized.

"Because everything about you screams confidence. Even if you don't feel it, you won't let anyone else see that. So you would have practiced and made sure you did a good job. No, not a good job. A great job."

Twice now she'd been told complimentary things.

Things to push her to do what she'd been sitting on for longer than she cared to admit.

"How would you like to get that drink with me?"

"What?" he asked, turning to look at her again.

"I asked if you wanted to get that drink with me. Or if

you have an early day, which you probably do with Egan out, then maybe another time."

"I can do a drink," he said, smiling. "It beats having a beer alone."

"Great," she said. "Oh. I forgot. Is there a baby yet?"

"Not yet," he said. "But I'm sure it's going to be soon."

"Then maybe I'll be the first to know in my family it if happens while we get that drink."

It was now or never.

She put it out there. He accepted.

Man up and find out what his thoughts were once and for all.

Then she could move on.

She just hoped it wasn't her moving on alone.

4

ZEN SPOT

"What do you want to drink?" Lincoln asked when they got to a small bar that he came to often. It was off the beaten path and had more regulars than not. Back in the day he thought this was someone's house that changed over to a small cafe and then a bar.

Grace looked around at the place. She didn't wrinkle her nose at the stained paint on the walls, the old scarred wood floors, or the stools at the bar that looked like they belonged more in a diner than a bar.

"Whiskey," she said. "Neat."

He laughed. He shouldn't be surprised. He'd thought she'd be the type to throw a beer back with the men, but whiskey was even better.

"You heard the lady," he told Jason the bartender. The old man was missing a few teeth and had a crooked grin when he did smile. In the summer you could see the old faded tattoos showing off his years in the service. "Make it two."

Lincoln waited until the drinks were on the bar, then picked them up and nodded to a booth in the corner.

Grace followed along. "I didn't know this place existed," she said. "I know most of the places on the island."

"I'm sure you do," he said. "This is my personal Zen spot."

She put the glass to her lips and took a sip, not flinching over it either. It wasn't expensive fancy shit she was probably used to tasting or drinking, even cooking with.

"I like that," she said. "That is what I think of the water. Even in the winter, I'm at peace sitting in the window seat looking out over the ocean. Mother nature is a bitch but beautiful at the same time. You just have to know what it is you are looking at or when."

Lincoln smiled when she said that. In all his years on the island, he hadn't talked to her much like this even though he noticed her plenty.

He wasn't quite sure what they were doing now either, but he'd always been known to go with the flow.

"I've lived a lot of my life that way," he said. "Take it as it comes and make the best of it."

Even if he hated to live it that way, but in the service, sometimes you had no choice.

Now he had a choice and that was to plan things out better.

Put away for rainy days and make sure you've got something to show for all the work you've done.

Pride. He took pride in everything he did.

"So that is what you're doing with this drink?" she asked, frowning. "I didn't know it put you out."

"Having a drink with a pretty lady is hardly being put out," he said. "Don't think that. Just surprised you asked is all, but then I got thinking you looked like you needed it. Why don't you tell me why?"

"Like a therapist?" she asked, smirking.

"You'd be surprised by the things people say to me in flight."

When people were nervous, scared or excited, all sorts of things slipped between their lips. He'd heard it all in the service too.

A tiny bit of excitement mixed in with a bushel of nerves. Him being the one doing the flying, he was paying more attention to going into enemy territory than contributing to those talks.

Nothing was worse in his mind than flying home injured or dying buddies. Confessions came out to ease their guilt and he tried to pretend he didn't exist while they rambled but couldn't do it.

There were just some things that would never leave his brain when it came to those dying last words.

That last breath of someone you know and even love.

He'd experienced it way too many times in his short life.

"You're probably right," she said.

"So tell Dr. Lincoln what's bothering you tonight," he said.

She laughed. "Dr. Lincoln?"

"It works with your cousin."

He'd said it to Egan enough in their years of friendship to get his best buddy to open up. Lately it'd had more to do with Egan's relationship and impending fatherhood.

More good than bad, that was for sure. That was what he wanted to hear in life too.

Grace shook her head. "Nothing much," she said. "I'm not much for public speaking. I've put this off for years though my mother has wanted me to do it. I just felt that it wasn't for me."

"Why?" he asked.

"Because she runs a not-for-profit to empower women or help return them to the workforce after long absences. Most of the clients they serve are low-income or coming out of hard situations. That isn't me."

"So?" he said. "You said most but not all. I'd think seeing a young woman dominating her field and talking about it would be a good thing regardless of their background. Maybe in spite of it."

"Meaning what?" she asked, sipping her drink.

He saw the confusion in her eyes. He didn't want her to think he'd insulted her.

"I'm sure everyone there knew you were your mother's daughter, correct?"

"Yes," she said.

"Then they know your background. They know that, like Eli, Egan, and Ethan and all the other Bond family members, you could have coasted through life doing nothing but sitting on the beach and looking out over the water."

She laughed. "True."

"But you didn't. You've got a career that takes sweat and determination in a field that is run more by men. You could own your own restaurant and work when you wanted and issue commands sitting back and cooking when you felt like it."

"I'd never do that," she said indignantly.

"That's right, you wouldn't any more than your cousins or your mother did. So in speaking to this group, you show that it doesn't matter where you come from, hard work is the key to success, not luck or landing in the right spot in life."

Though there were times he thought luck was what landed him in Boston and this job.

"You make a valid point," she said.

"So it stands to reason that is why your mother wanted you there. And maybe it was to get you out of your comfort zone. Though if I was to be honest, I don't mind you in the kitchen."

She lifted her eyebrows at him. "Excuse me?"

He laughed and lifted his drink to his lips. "I'm not sexist thinking that a woman should be in the kitchen. I'm just saying you've got one hell of a talent. I was going to eat that entire dinner but figured you'd think I was a pig. Ever pick up a cereal bowl when you're done and drink the milk?"

"Of course," she said. "Doesn't everyone?"

"No," he said. "My mother always dumped the milk. I thought it was crazy. But she ate fiber cereal so maybe no one wants to drink that."

Grace laughed. "I wouldn't. Give me Cocoa Puffs and the milk is the best."

"Captain Crunch," he said.

"We could debate that, but that can be another conversation."

"Back to your dinner. I wanted to lick your container clean. I mean pick it up and stick my face in it and lick it like a dog would until every last drop of sauce was gone. But I would have picked you up with sauce in my beard. Talk about embarrassing."

Grace was laughing so hard and even angled her head to check his chin out so he twisted it for a better look. "That is what the bread was for."

"And there isn't one crumb of bread left," he said.

"Good," she said. "I should have given you a whole loaf."

"I'm stuffed and don't care. I'll eat the rest tomorrow on

one of my breaks between flights. It will save me from fast food again. I get a lot of food delivered to the docks."

It was easier than leaving. He'd order and they'd drop it off and he'd eat when he got back from a flight. If he was just transporting products and not people, he'd eat a sandwich or something while flying.

"I suppose you do what works for you. I have a hard time eating out. Not that I don't enjoy it."

"But you're used to a certain quality of food," he said. "I don't blame you. I'd never order out again if I had your food daily."

"Thanks," she said. "I appreciate that. And you only had one simple dish."

"I'm sure there isn't anything about you that is simple," he said.

The conflicting thoughts in his brain didn't normally take up much space anymore.

He was a champion at pushing those thoughts away that he didn't or couldn't deal with.

Being attracted to a woman he could never see himself with was sure the hell up there high on that list.

"You'd be surprised," she said. "At least I think I'm simple but guess too many times in my life I'm judged for where I came from."

He snorted. "Don't I know that."

She took another sip of her drink. "So tell me," she said. "Where are you from and how did you land on Amore Island working for my cousin? I know you were in the Air Force but not much else."

"Just conversation during our drink or don't you want to go home yet? Still trying to unwind?"

He wasn't sure what this whole night was about, but

having a drink with a sexy woman wasn't something he'd ever say no to either.

"That and some more," she said. "Maybe I'm curious about you."

It was the grin that told him there was more going on, but he wasn't one for playing games with women out of his league.

Been there and done that and wasn't about to put himself in that situation again. Once was enough and the amount of guilt on his shoulders still weighed him down more than carrying two hundred pounds through mud.

"I can be an open book," he said. "Know how I'd said luck doesn't have you landing places?"

"Yes," she said.

"Well, it did me."

"I've got to hear this," she said.

"I was visiting a friend in Boston after getting out of the service. It's not like I had much going on, I was still trying to find a job."

"Where are you from?" she asked. "You didn't say."

"Scranton, Pennsylvania. I was staying with my parents at that point. I wasn't tied to staying in the area but needed a landing spot for the short term."

"Parents are good like that," she said.

"So, the night I was with my friend in Boston, we decided to hit this bar up on the docks and had taken a wrong turn. Rather than drive in circles, we pulled over and I walked into Bond Charter. I'm not beyond asking for directions if I'm lost."

"Says not a lot of men," she said, laughing.

"Very true, but we wanted that drink. I figured it was a Charter company, I'd fit right in talking to someone. There was Egan talking to his father about needing another pilot soon. But before they could buy a second helicopter they needed more business, but in order for that, they needed another pilot."

"Wow," she said. "That is lucky. Or fate. As I'm sure you know, this island is known for that."

"When it comes to love," he said, laughing. "Though we all know Egan gets picked on for being lucky. Blake tells him that all the time. But I bust his ass how lucky he was I walked in that night."

So yeah, sometimes luck happened and it happened to him too.

"Egan could always step in crap and smell like an apple pie."

"Before I could say why I was there, I'd said I was a helicopter pilot and looking for a job."

"What was their reaction?" she asked. "I never heard this story."

The two Bond men turned and looked at him, Egan the first to start firing questions off, Mitchell standing there shaking his head.

He'd later learned that was Egan's nature, not to plan it out, and he'd been given an interview on the spot while his buddy walked in and wanted to know what was taking so long to get directions.

"I had an impromptu interview right there. My buddy came in after ten minutes wondering if I was the one lost in a building. Egan ended up joining us at the bar and the interview continued."

Before they left for the night, he'd given all his information to Egan and was told if Lincoln was serious they'd run a background check and get references and get back to him.

He was more than serious and said to go ahead, then he could look into housing.

"Typical Egan," she said. "Did he have shoes on when you met him? Unless it was cold out."

"He had sandals on. It was June. I didn't know who the Bonds were. I thought they were looking for a pilot in Boston and found out it was the island."

All that came out a week later when Egan called him with the job offer.

He should have spent more time looking into Bond Charter but didn't think anything of it. Part of him didn't think it'd pan out and he hadn't even told his parents about it.

The fact they only had one helicopter told him he wouldn't be flying that much but then learned all sorts of cargo needed to be brought back and forth and he was working nights for that, then days that Egan could take off to get a break.

Within months, a second helicopter had been purchased and business started to boom.

"How hard was it for you to find a place to live?" she asked.

"I stayed with Egan until an apartment opened up. He was renting a house at that point. I was struggling to find a place and then I asked if I could just keep his rental when he moved into his place if he didn't mind me staying there until his house was ready."

Egan's home was being built. They'd lived together for about six months and he took over the lease and had stayed there ever since.

He'd been terrified he wouldn't be able to afford it but surprisingly the place wasn't that bad.

He'd later found out it was a property owned by Mitchell, so he was sure the rent was adjusted for that reason. He never asked because he didn't want to know. It's not like it was crazy low, but he was positive not as high as they could get with someone else.

"Then it all worked out," she said.

"It seems it has," he said.

She was eying him now and he couldn't figure out what was going through her mind.

His drink was gone, hers too, but since it was a weekday night and close to ten at this point he was guessing she'd want to go home.

"I'm assuming you've got an early day tomorrow," she said. "Thanks for indulging me with conversation."

"Never a problem," he said.

They stood up and walked out together, the cool night breeze picking up some.

"Thanks again," she said, almost hesitating, then she walked to her SUV and climbed in. Lincoln got in his truck once he knew she was safely on the road and went home to his lonely place.

5

FACT OF LIFE

"Grace, there is someone here asking for you."

Grace turned to see one of the front lobby staff coming into the restaurant three weeks later. It was Wednesday morning at ten and she was in her office rather than the restaurant.

She was off Monday and Tuesday most weeks. Wednesday was spent doing orders, scheduling and other paperwork or appointments as needed. She normally didn't work in the restaurant unless absolutely needed on that day and was out by dinnertime.

Thursday through Sunday she'd come in around noon and work until the restaurant closed and the dinner service was cleaned up, though the kitchen stayed open until midnight for those who wanted room service. They'd open again at five in the morning for room service, the restaurant serving breakfast at seven.

Certain times of the year were busier than others, but this was spring break week and though the weather wasn't that warm on the island for the first week of April, they were still pretty packed.

"Did they give a name?" she asked. "I don't have anyone scheduled."

Vendors came in a lot to speak with her. Sometimes those wanting to plan weddings here would come for food tasting and selections, but that was normally set up in advance.

Not that it couldn't be last minute and she'd be as accommodating as she could.

"No. They are young. Almost like a kid. I feel bad, but she said she'd stay until you were available. I get the feeling she'd sit out in the lobby all day and I don't want to do that to her."

"A kid?" she asked.

"A teen maybe. I could be wrong. She looks a little...down and out. But she asked for you by name. She showed me your card. I'm not sure how she got it."

Hmmm, that was odd. "Okay. I'll be out in a minute."

Grace finished up what she was doing and pushed back from her desk in her office off the kitchen.

She had a big window that allowed her to look out to see the action. She ran a tight ship and they knew it, but when she wasn't in there next to people, she knew things tended to slack some.

She went through the halls and into the lobby, saw the person who had come to get her and followed her head nod. It was horrible she didn't know her name, but there were so many staff on site and they changed all the time, Grace was lucky she could keep track of those that worked for her directly.

A young woman was sitting by herself in a chair on her phone, her head down. By her attire, though she was clean, she wasn't someone that had a lot.

Jeans that appeared to be faded more from wear than

fashion, older sneakers on her feet and a black fleece jacket over that.

The long brown hair was straight and combed but had no style, just a part in the center and hanging past her shoulders.

"Hi," she said, walking closer. "I'm Grace Stone and you are looking for me?"

The young woman's head snapped up and she stood up fast. She liked that move. A respectful one.

"Thank you for seeing me. My name is Tracy Gingham. You might not remember me. I took one of your week-long classes two years ago in Boston one summer."

Grace didn't remember everyone that came to those classes, but she did enjoy doing them. Though she did remember Tracy now.

Quiet and shy, but when she cooked you could see her willingness to learn and a hidden talent that had to be nurtured and brought out.

That one week she could give the kids wasn't enough and she knew that.

"I do remember you now," she said. "What can I help you with?"

"I was there on a scholarship from one of the local organizations," Tracy said.

Her mother's organization. There were always a few sponsored along with those that paid. That was how they were able to run those clinics at little to no cost. Her mother did all the work. Or had staff that ran it.

"Yes," she said. "I remember."

"I'm looking for a full-time job. I saw that you have a line cook opening."

She frowned. "Are you eighteen?"

"I'll be eighteen in two weeks. Ummm, is there a place we can talk privately?"

"Of course," she said. "Why don't we go to my office."

Normally she wouldn't give time to someone that was looking for a job and showed up like this. They'd send in their application and she'd weed it out that way.

But there was a desperation in this young girl she couldn't turn away.

She might have been told more than once she was as tough as her last name, but that was in the kitchen.

She expected perfection.

This...this was something different and she had too much of her mother in her to not find out what was going on and see if there was some way she could help.

"Thank you," Tracy said, still standing when they entered.

"Please sit. If you're not eighteen, I'm going to assume you're still in high school?"

Manners and professionalism that you didn't see with a lot of kids this age. She was impressed.

"Yes," she said. "But when I turn eighteen in a few weeks, my foster family doesn't have to keep me. I don't think they will. I need to get a job. I thought maybe if I had a job and offered to pay rent I could stay until I put enough money away."

This broke her heart. "Do you live on the island?" she asked.

"No. I took the ferry over. I'm in Plymouth. I was in Boston with another family two years ago when I took your course. Then I returned to my grandmother but went back with another foster family when my grandmother passed. I've got a friend that is here on the island. We were in a home together before and have kept in touch. She said that maybe I could live with her family and pay rent. I guess I was hoping for that but don't know."

"And you need a job first," she said. Her head was spinning right now. "Were you planning on finishing school? I need someone to work days and weekends. It's a full-time job."

Tracy put her head down. "I want to finish school, but I don't know what else to do. I don't want to be on the streets either."

Tracy was trying to be strong, but her eyes were filling with tears. This was just pulling at Grace and almost making her ill at the same time.

She wouldn't ask if there was anyone else Tracy could live with. She was positive the answer was no.

"Why me?" she asked. "Why here and not somewhere else?"

"Because this is what I love to do. What I want to do. Where I live now, they like it when I cook because they don't have to. I just feel...at peace in the kitchen. I don't know that anyone would hire me for more than washing dishes. If that is what I have to do, I will, but I don't have the means for culinary school and I thought, if I could learn here, it'd be like learning from you. Learning from the best. And I know it's hard to find employees on the island too."

She didn't think Tracy was feeding her ego, but it felt good to hear.

"There is a procedure for people to get hired here," she said. "And experience required."

She had high standards. The only experience that Tracy had seemed to be that one-week course two weeks ago and then cooking at home.

"I know," Tracy said. "I'd be willing to do anything needed. I didn't expect to be hired as a line cook."

There was so much going through her mind and how she could get this to work. In her heart she couldn't turn this girl away, but the obstacles were enormous.

"When you turn eighteen you have nowhere to go?" she asked. "I can verify this with your case worker?"

Tracy nodded her head. "I can give you her name." Tracy was pulling her phone out of her pocket. "I've got her number too."

"Why don't you give me that information," she said. "I can't guarantee you anything. If I can find work for you here, there are conditions. One of them is you have to finish high school. You can transfer here to the island. You need a place to stay, a home where you're taken care of. You might be eighteen in two weeks, but you're still a kid."

A kid that seemed to have a rough life and one she didn't know much about. Which of course she'd rely on Griffin to take care of. He did most of the security checks for the family businesses.

"I'm independent," Tracy said. "And I'm a hard worker. I just need a chance. I can prove it to you."

"Let's go in the kitchen," she said.

She stood up and went to a far corner of the kitchen where it wasn't busy. "Do you want me to cook for you?"

"I do," she said. "You tell me what you like to cook. What types of foods."

"I like breakfast foods," she said. "And I cook dinner every night too, but it's simple things."

Grace imagined that was the case. But she could always use someone here on the weekends cooking breakfast. Even after school or at night doing just room service-type meals.

That could be a good starting point.

"French toast, pancakes and eggs are ordered the most for room service," Grace said. "Easy enough things. I'm going to have you make me a few different kinds of eggs. Then we'll move to pancakes and French toast."

"Really?" Tracy said. "I can do that. I learned from you two years ago and haven't stopped."

She smiled. "Then show me what you've got."

An hour later, Tracy was walking out the door with a full belly and a bunch of leftovers from what they'd cooked and a promise that Grace would get back to her in a few days. That she had to make some calls.

Time she didn't have either, so she called the one person that she knew could help her.

"Hello, Grace," her mother said. "What can I do for you since you don't normally call me during the day."

She filled her mother in on the situation. "What are my options if any? I don't know if it's possible to get her on the island, then find housing. I'm thinking more along the lines of a foster home and if the county won't pay the monthly fee maybe there are funds available for that with your organization?"

Grace would pay it herself if she had to but didn't want to go that route right yet. Sometimes it was neater to keep things official through an organization.

"There are," her mother said. "That isn't an issue. You're talking three maybe four months while she finishes school and gets on her feet?"

"I was hoping more along the lines of to the end of the year. If we could find a family to take her in, one that has been vetted obviously. She'd be living there free from her end. She'd be working part time with me, finish her schooling, then move to full time if it works out. By the end of the year I will know if it's going to work and that will give her time to figure things out. Or us to reassess the situation."

"I'll make some calls," her mother said. "She's still a minor."

"For two more weeks. I can't imagine her being on her own."

"It happens more than we know," her mother said. "It's sad but a fact of life. I don't have as many contacts in Plymouth as I do in Boston."

"They will hear your name and talk to you," Grace said.

Her mother laughed. "Most definitely. Does Tracy have the ability to work there or did she just touch a soft squishy part of you?"

"Both. I've got a meeting with Hunter in twenty minutes to let him know."

"You run the kitchen," her mother said. "Do you think Hunter is going to tell you no? It's just a part-time employee who is of age."

She sighed. "I know. I just feel as if I should inform him."

"Because Kayla was in foster care and you know he's going to want to help too," her mother said.

Hunter's wife, Kayla, had been in foster care most of her life. The two of them met when Kayla applied for a job in the lobby, then caught Hunter's eye.

"I didn't realize it at the time, but I think Tracy reminds me of Kayla or how she'd be at that age."

She loved her cousin's wife. Visited with her when Kayla came down with the kids or wanted some food. Oftentimes Grace would deliver it to Hunter's penthouse and visit with Kayla on her break.

She'd have to say she didn't have a lot of friends in life. Not ones she would consider close friends and it was nice to have that with Kayla.

It's not like she had much of a dating life.

She'd even put herself out there with Lincoln weeks ago

and he didn't seem to be biting what she'd been throwing out.

Maybe if it was food he'd bite more.

Which got her thinking, but that had to be put on the back burner right now.

"Then you're probably making the right decision," her mother said. "Email me the information you've got and I'll make some calls."

"Thanks, Mom," she said and hung up.

She typed up what she had plus her thoughts for her mother and sent that email off, then went to see her cousin in his office on the floor below his penthouse.

"He's waiting for you," Hunter's secretary said to her.

She walked in like she always did. "Did you bring me food?" Hunter asked.

"Sorry," she said. "You should have said something."

"It's fine. I'll get something later."

It was close to lunch. She knew he ordered at the restaurant or went and had lunch with Kayla and his sons.

"So I've got somewhat of a situation. Not bad. Could be good. But I wanted you to know."

Hunter listened to everything she said about Tracy and what her mother was doing. "You hire your staff," Hunter said. "That's your domain."

"But it's not my hotel," she said. "You should know something like this. I'll cover my bases. Chances are most of the living costs will come through funds my mother has."

"Listen, Grace. We all know how stupid that clause was in the will and it's changed."

"You've got two sons," she said, smirking.

"I do, but if they don't want anything to do with The Retreat, that is their choice. Maybe one will be a lawyer and go bug my sister."

She laughed. "Hailey would take Ben in a heartbeat."

"I know she would," Hunter said. "Jack, on the other hand. He's the wild one of the two."

She smiled thinking of Hunter's two kids. "I think I've got a soft spot for Tracy. I see some of Kayla in her."

"Which is why you're here. If your mother can't make it work, we'll figure it out."

"Thanks," she said. "It's not a money issue. I'm more concerned about finding her a place to stay."

"If she has to stay in an extra room here for a bit," Hunter said, "we'll sort it as best as we can. She'll be eighteen; legally it's not an issue. Don't stress about those things. One step at a time."

"Thanks," she said.

"You're not as mean as everyone says you are," Hunter said.

"Don't tell anyone. I don't want them to think they can walk all over me in the restaurant."

"No one will *ever* think that," Hunter said, laughing.

She left after that and went back to her office.

Maybe that was why she was still single.

She had all these walls up because of her family history and no one could break them down.

Not even when she tried to give a man a hammer to start chipping away, he still didn't seem to understand what to do with it.

6

LIKE A DATE

"What is that?" Lincoln asked when Grace walked into the hangar on the island two weeks later.

"You come across as a rustic kind of eater," she said. "This is my mashup of a chicken pot pie and a shepherd's pie."

"Oh my God," he said. "It's a damn good thing Egan isn't here. I'm not sharing."

She placed the container on the counter. "It's still a little warm, but you can put it in the fridge and then heat it in the microwave."

"Or eat cold," he said. "Some foods are just as good cold as hot. You want to cringe, sorry about that. No insult to your talents. Don't suppose I can get a taste now."

She pulled a fork out of her back pocket. "I've come prepared."

He grabbed it out of her hand and stuck it in the flaky crust. No reason to slice it. He wasn't sharing.

"Is that mashed potatoes?"

"It's pie crust. Homemade."

"I didn't expect any differently," he said.

"Chicken, bacon, peas and gravy. Topped with mashed potatoes and then another layer of the crust on top."

He was going for a second mouthful and stopped. "I stopped listening after bacon. I don't care. I want to bathe in this."

She laughed at him. "Good. It was something I thought up over the weekend."

"So this isn't something you've made before?" he asked, going for a third bite. Damn, he could eat the whole thing now and just might rub it in Egan's face. The gut ache would be so worth it.

"Nope," she said. "I like to try new things on my days off."

"It's not much of a day off if you're doing this," he said.

"Sure, it is," she said. "Everything I cook isn't for the restaurant. I've got a weakness for rustic foods myself. I made two of them. One is for me."

He smiled at her. "Did you eat it like I am?"

"No," she said. "I cut a slice. That doesn't mean I might not finish it the way you are though. Midnight snack and all."

He took one more bite and then wrapped it back up. That would hold him over until later. No reason to be a pig in front of her. "So I'm not the only one eating at midnight?"

"Most likely not. It's not that I'm waking up to eat," she said. "I might not get home and unwind until then. I don't have a chance to sit and eat while I'm working. I taste as I go but don't get much of a meal. I eat when I get home most times."

"I'd be eating nonstop if I had your job," he said. "Be right back."

He brought the pie to the mini fridge in Egan's office and then came back.

"People say that all the time, but once you do it for so long, you don't think much of it. It's tasting for seasoning, not eating for pleasure or enjoyment."

"Like me almost moaning over those five bites I just ate."

"Exactly," she said.

"If you're ready, we can leave," he said. "You've got a flight back in four hours, right?"

"I do," she said. "I just need to take care of a few things in the city. Best to do it this afternoon and get back before dark. I don't care to go to the city much and this is twice now in about a month. If I need to get off the island I'd rather go to Plymouth."

"The island is pretty sweet," he said.

They went to the helicopter and got in. He started it up and was soon in the air and taking off.

"How is Kaden doing? Has Egan been getting any sleep?"

"Baby Kaden Oliver has an appetite bigger than mine from the sounds of it and wants to eat every hour."

"I'd heard he was a big baby," she said.

"Over ten pounds," he said. "Blake is still cursing him, but boy is he a cutie."

He'd never thought he was a baby person, but seeing his best friend's son and how Egan was with him made him think about his own life.

His future.

If he could find someone who liked the island living and wouldn't mind his hours.

That seemed to be a bigger issue in the past few years.

He supposed he could easily move to Boston and fly out of there. It wasn't a big deal.

Roxy and Rob were doing it. It'd be workable, but it was not where he wanted to be.

"I don't even want to think of it," she said. "It's a fact of life and though I want kids at some point, the way to get them out isn't something that sounds like a lot of fun."

"Nope," he said. "I wouldn't want to be a woman."

"That's kind of a sweet thing to say," she said.

Lincoln felt his face flush when he didn't normally have that reaction over anything.

"Do you make sweets too?" he asked. Might as well turn this around if he could.

"I do, but pastry isn't my thing."

"It seemed it with the crust on what I just ate," he said.

"I can do just about anything, but I've got cuisine I'm better at than others," she said. "Just like most people."

He nodded and they continued to talk about the island and other mundane topics. He landed and then went into the offices as Grace took her leave to go to the garage and get a car.

"What are you doing here?" he asked Egan when he saw him at the desk.

"I got back early. My client was done faster than they thought and we returned. I've got two hours before my next flight."

"I'm leaving as soon as I load up the helicopter," he said. "I've got to get back to return your cousin but can squeeze this in easily."

He was going to bring some private art to a collector in New York City. That would take up three hours of flight time round trip. He figured Grace wouldn't be complaining if he was a little late but didn't think that would happen.

"She'd wait for you," Egan said.

"Yep. She said she would," he said.

It'd come up while they were chatting. He didn't know what she had planned for her time in Boston and didn't ask.

"Grace doesn't normally get rides on the helicopter," Egan said. "That's two now in a month."

He shrugged. "I guess. I don't pay much attention. For all I know she's ridden with you."

"Not often," Egan said. "She always rides with you."

He looked at Egan's smile. "So?"

"And she brought you food a month ago."

"So?" he said again.

"You had a drink with her after the flight," Egan said.

He'd told Egan about it. Just in passing and nothing more. "Not a big deal."

"Did she bring you food today?" Egan asked.

"Yeah. But I'm not sharing." He smirked and ran his hand over his belly.

"Asshole," Egan said. "What did she bring you?"

"I'm not saying and if you eat any I'll know. I weighed it before I left."

Egan was laughing even harder. "If I had a scale in the office I'm sure you would have. You've always been greedy with food."

"You haven't had to eat some of the shit I did in the service," he said. "And you do have a scale in the office. The postage meter."

He saw Egan's smile drop, which told him that his buddy was going to try to sneak some of his food.

Egan had done it before when others had brought him food. He knew and never said a word. It'd be a bite here and there as if Lincoln wouldn't know.

He knew everything.

"Jerk," Egan said. "What is going on with you and Grace?"

"Nothing," he said. "I flew her over and she brought me food."

"Twice in a month," Egan said. "And she asked you to get a drink with her. Like a date."

"Nooooo," he said.

"Yessssss," Egan said. "You can't be this slow."

Guess he didn't know everything. "She was being friendly."

"Grace Stone. My cousin Grace Stone? She's not a friendly person to many."

"Sure, she is," he argued. "I've never seen otherwise."

"I haven't either. Not to family. She's upfront and snarky at times. Just like my wife and we know how much I love that."

"I don't know that Grace is just like Blake."

"And you're thinking about it, which means you've talked to her enough to wonder," Egan argued.

"What are you getting at?" he asked.

"That my cousin is throwing all sorts of darts your way and hasn't hit the bullseye once."

"I'd think that Grace was a straightforward enough person that if she wanted to ask me on a date, she would have."

"Idiot," Egan said. "She did."

"Fuck!"

"What is that reaction?" Egan asked. "What's wrong with my cousin?"

It must be the appalled look on his face that had Egan frowning. "Nothing is wrong with her. She's stunning."

Grace had jeans on today. A pair of baggy ones that were more for comfort than fashion he was guessing. She had a fitted cotton shirt tucked into her tiny waist. She didn't have a jacket on but was carrying one on her arm. There were fashionable sneakers on her small feet and he watched her ass as she had her fast walk to the parking garage.

"Then go on a date with her."

"I did by your explanation," he said. And he felt a little like a fool for not seeing this before.

"Why not ask her on another?" Egan asked.

"I'm not positive the first was a real date," he said, scratching his chin. He'd shaved yesterday and now that it was all growing back it was driving him nuts. He wasn't sure why he didn't just keep it trimmed.

He was playing some of that night back in his head. It did have all the makings of a date. All but a kiss and an exchange of numbers or the plan to set another up.

They did have each other's numbers though.

"I think it was," Egan said.

Which made something else pop into his head. "How come I ended up with Grace's flight today if you're just sitting here?"

"I didn't plan on sitting here," Egan said. "You know that. I don't make the schedule. My client got his business done fast."

"But you can change it whenever you want. You did it before when you wanted to be with Blake."

"Then consider this one of those fate things my cousin might have been hoping for," Egan said, grinning.

"I think you're nuts."

"That's been said to me a lot of times," Egan said. "But I'm not."

"I've got work to do," he said and left to get the art and load it on the helicopter.

It'd give him a few hours to think this through in his mind.

Before he could climb in and take off, Egan said, "Don't talk yourself out of things because of who she is."

If anyone knew about his life, it was Egan. He'd shared more than he had with anyone else.

Most of it was over a beer, but plenty was when they lived together.

Egan just had a way of getting people to talk without you even knowing.

Griffin, Eli's best friend, complained that Eli had the same trait. Had to be a Bond thing.

"But she can't change who she is any more than I can," he said.

"And you should know by now that my family is the last group of people that thinks about those things," Egan said.

Pretty strong parting words that he couldn't argue with.

7

SOME KIND OF ATTENTION

"This is nice," Grace's mother said to her an hour later when they met up for lunch.

"It is," she said.

She'd asked her mother to meet today. She was trying to think of any excuse to go to Boston and get a flight. First thing to do was book the flight.

Second was hope she got Lincoln to fly her over.

Third was to make some food. The old saying about the way to a man's heart...

She didn't know if she was looking for his heart at this point. She just wanted some kind of attention.

Maybe acknowledgment.

She wasn't sure what else she could do to get him to see what she was trying short of being blunt.

That might be the next step.

Once the flight was lined up, she decided to see if she could meet her mother for lunch. It wasn't as if she had much more to do in four hours, but she'd do some shopping while she was here.

"How is Tracy doing?"

"I think she's settled. She is going to start work on Saturday. Today is her first day of school and I want her to figure everything out and get caught up. How did you find housing?"

Her mother patted her hand. "I remembered the Weatherbys. They moved to the island about ten years ago after they retired. Their kids and grandkids aren't close by. They are lonely, and they'd done some work with my organization and had foster kids in the past."

"But you said they aren't fostering her, right?" she asked.

Her mother had said she'd found an apartment for Tracy. Though she wasn't sure that was the best setup, the caseworker and her mother assured her it was. Tracy was even excited.

"They aren't. They've got a studio apartment over their garage. It's for visitors to stay, but they don't get much. I talked to them and they loved the idea. We are covering the rent until the end of the year. They didn't want anything at all, but I told her that was silly. I have programs to cover housing for situations exactly like this."

Grace hadn't realized that and should have. "So she's on the property but by herself. She doesn't have a car though."

She knew this because Tracy was only half a mile from The Retreat and said she could walk to work and she'd be taking the bus to school.

"No. Marissa Weatherby said that they'd help her get her license. We have funds to get her transportation when the time comes. For now, she needs to focus on school. Her housing is being paid for along with food vouchers to keep her supplied. She'll be working for you and making money for anything else she needs."

"But there could be more," she argued. "Not just a roof

over her head and food. What about clothing or activities or personal hygiene items?"

"Grace," her mother said. "I've got it covered. Tracy will be fine. There is money for incidentals. She didn't want anything. She's been working part time and has her own cell phone already. Her utilities and internet are part of her rent. She'll have money from her job and she was assigned a case manager within my program. She will have to meet with that person every two weeks and Tracy has someone to go to if she needs anything."

Grace let out a breath. "Okay. I need to stop worrying."

"I find it commendable that you are. The question is why are you so focused on someone you barely know?"

She should have figured her mother would see through things.

"I think it's the right thing to do when someone is in need," she said. "You'd know that firsthand. You've made it your mission to do that."

Her mother never wanted any part of The Retreat and her grandfather gave both of his daughters large settlements. There were other businesses in the family that her mother and aunt, her uncle too, had a say in or even some controlling interest, but they'd never get a part of the legacy of The Retreat due to that stupid clause.

Her mother took her settlement and founded her organization, her grandfather helping with donations over the years, but now there were all sorts of state and federal funding too.

"I have," her mother said. "But you've never taken that big of an interest in my career."

"I'm sorry about that," she said. "I should have."

Her mother smiled. Their lunch was brought out and she dove into her burger. The first bite, she knew it wasn't as good as hers, but she didn't expect that. But it wasn't horrible either.

"No," her mother said. "You can't force someone to like something you do."

She frowned and then let out another sigh. "So I'm learning."

"What's going on, Grace? Talk to me. Do you have boy troubles?"

She laughed. "I haven't dated any boys in a long time."

"Man troubles?" her mother said, grinning.

"It's nothing."

"It's something. You've been single for a long time. You say you like it, but I don't think you do. Is it that all your cousins are finding people? Hunter and Hailey are married with children. Roark got married a few months ago."

"That's right," she said of one of her other male cousins. Roark French was the son of the other daughter of her grandfather. Melissa French, who was a mystery writer under the pen name of Steve Spencer. The world thought her aunt was a man. Only close family knew otherwise.

It drove her mother insane that her sister didn't shout to the world she was a woman and made it big and to prove she might not have gotten the notoriety if she had written under her own name.

"But you're not the only one single," her mother said. "Much to my frustration, your brother is too."

Her brother, Skyler, was older than her by four years. He should be the one in a relationship or married by now, but it seemed like this generation was waiting until they found the right person. It seemed some of them kissed a lot of frogs along the way.

At least she felt as if she had.

"And so is Emma," Grace said. Emma was Roark's younger sister. "And she lives in a world of romance."

"And drama and violence too," her mother said. Emma was a Romantic Suspense author.

"She'll never find someone because she is too used to writing about her perfect man and they don't exist."

"No one is perfect," her mother said. "But it seems to me you might have your eye on someone and he's not looking back?"

She could lie but hated to do that.

"Maybe."

"Are you going to tell me who it is?" her mother asked.

"Only if you keep it to yourself."

"I can't tell your father?" her mother asked.

"You can and he won't say anything."

"So this is someone I know by the sounds of it," her mother said.

"Oh, you know him. I think he's blind or not interested."

"Who is it?"

"Lincoln," she said and then took another bite of her burger so she didn't have to talk.

"Lincoln, who works for Egan?"

"Do you know another one?" she asked.

"No. I had no idea. Fill me in so I know what is going on. Maybe I can help."

Since it's not like she felt as if she could tell anyone else, she told her mother about her flight last month and then this one.

"He likes my food," she said, shrugging.

"Everyone loves your food. Did you stop to think that maybe he's confused?"

"What is there to be confused about?" she asked. "I asked him for a drink a month ago. I brought him food twice. I thought for sure he'd have to contact me to return the plate and didn't."

She was hoping this time it might happen. The food was on the island and as far as she knew, Lincoln was in flight right now and then returning to Boston to get her.

"I think for someone who is always upfront and in people's faces, for once you're not. I'm not sure why. I can see where he might not see what you're doing."

"Come on," she argued. "He's a smart guy."

"I'm just saying he might be unsure and because it's his boss's cousin, it's not like he would be willing to assume anything and risk offending you."

She hadn't thought of that.

"So you're saying I should be more blunt? Like ask him out again?"

"It can't hurt," her mother said. "He could say no."

"Or he could say yes out of pity because he doesn't want to hurt my feelings." Jesus. Now *she* was confused.

Her mother shook her head. "I don't know that you've ever been this insecure in your life. You're talking yourself out of something rather than into it."

"I know," she whined. "I never do that."

"Nor do you get this frustrated either over anything that isn't related to food."

"I guess I just have to man up on this. The worst that can happen is he says no. The best, he says yes."

"He could say yes, you could get some dinner or you could cook for him. Lots of things. Then you could realize you don't connect. But you won't know any of that if you can't be honest."

"Fine," she said. "I'll see what he says when he picks me up. Now I've got a few hours to kill."

"You mean you've got no plans in Boston?" her mother asked. "You came here for lunch?"

"I set this up a few weeks ago. I was hoping it was Lincoln flying me over."

Her mother laughed. "And if it was Egan then what would you have done?"

"No clue. So I have to not lose this chance. I think I'll go get some things for Tracy. She'll need them for work. A good pair of sneakers. I already ordered her two uniforms."

Everyone got uniforms at work. That was how they kept a strict dress policy.

"That's nice," her mother said. "Do you know her size?"

"I was hoping since you got her some things, maybe you did? Otherwise, I was going to guess, which isn't smart, but I did try to look. Her feet are bigger than mine."

Her mother pulled her phone out and was texting something. "I just sent a message to Tracy's case manager. She'll know those things. It's part of the information they collect so that we can gather what might be needed. My guess is we purchased some clothing or shoes for her anyway."

"Thanks," she said. When the bill came, her mother reached for it before her and put her card down.

"It was going to be my treat," Grace said.

"I can spoil my kids as long as I want. The fact you came to me and got some advice just made my day."

She didn't often call her mother for much.

"Glad I made your day. Maybe mine can be made too."

"You know you're going to have to keep me posted."

"I will," she said.

Grace left the restaurant shortly after and went shopping, keeping an eye on the time. Lincoln had said he might be running late, but that was fine. She wasn't on a timeline.

When she got to the docks she didn't see any of the helicopters there, least of all the one she flew over in with Lincoln.

She parked the family car that was left there and got her bags out of the back. She ended up buying good sneakers for Tracy and another pair for herself, then a few more items of clothing. It's not like she needed much when she wore a uniform daily.

When she was walking to the offices, she heard the helicopter coming in and knew it was Lincoln. Rather than go inside, she went toward it and waited until he landed and shut it off.

"I'm not late, am I?" he asked, jumping down.

"No," she said. "I'm early. I didn't know if you had to go inside for anything."

"Nope," he said. "Let's go if you're ready."

She climbed in, put the headset on and got comfortable while he lifted them in the air and they took off for the island.

She kept trying to think of things to say and everything sounded stupid to her so she didn't talk at all.

"You're quiet," he said.

"Sorry. Shopping tires me out."

"I can understand that," he said. "Looks like you had a successful day."

"I had lunch with my mother and then picked up a few things rather than ordering them since I was there. Are you done for the day now?"

It was going to be a little after four once they landed.

"I wish," he said. "I'm going to get that pie you brought me and have some dinner and then I've got to bring a few people on the island back to Boston within two hours or so. Then I'll be done."

Which meant she couldn't ask him to dinner tonight.

But she had tomorrow off too.

"How late are you working tomorrow?" she asked.

He turned his head and smiled at her. "I have Tuesdays off."

"You didn't a month ago when you brought me to Boston."

"That was different. Blake was in labor. But that is my one day off. I normally work another light day if I can't get it off fully."

"I have Tuesdays off too," she said.

"So you said," he said, grinning at her.

"How would you like a nice home-cooked meal fresh out of the oven?" she asked. Might as well go all in.

"Are you asking me on a date?" Lincoln asked.

He looked a little confused but not as much as she'd thought.

Maybe her mother was right. She wasn't clear enough.

This couldn't be any clearer.

"I am," she said. "But if you don't want to, don't worry. I won't be upset. I'm not trying to make this awkward or anything."

"Not awkward," he said. "Dinner would be great."

"I've got your number," she said when they were starting to land. "I'll text you tomorrow."

"I'll be around," he said.

She got out of the helicopter when it was shut off, grabbed her bags and walked to her SUV.

She turned after a few steps. "See you tomorrow."

"Yeah," he said. "See you then."

8

FEEL NEEDED AND WANTED

The next day Lincoln found himself pulling his truck in front of Grace's two-story house.

He wasn't sure how he ended up on what would now be considered the second date with her when he hadn't realized they'd had a first.

She'd been quiet on the flight home and he thought maybe Egan had been wrong. But then the Grace that everyone knew and talked about in terms of being bold appeared and asked him to dinner.

He had to admit there was part of him that wanted to say no.

That knew the two of them had no future so why waste their time?

But the other part had Egan's voice in his ear to get over it. That Grace wasn't like that. No one in the Bond family was.

He didn't believe it but didn't want to put it to the test either.

Or maybe he had a slight bit of hope for something he was chasing and never could catch.

Did he want to set himself up for that kind of pain again?

Not really.

Yet his feet walked him right to the front door and up the porch where he rang the bell.

He wasn't sure the type of house he was expecting.

Maybe something bigger and flashier than this was.

It was still a beautiful house. Nicer than anything he'd lived in, but it wasn't billionaire-status housing.

But Grace would have a part of that fortune.

He knew beyond a doubt she had to have a trust fund like the rest of them.

"Hi," she said, opening the door. "Come in."

The scent of cooking food hit him hard and almost made him think of those cartoon characters that were lifted in the air by the cloud of aroma beckoning them toward the kitchen.

"Damn, it smells good in here."

"Thanks," she said. "Beef Wellington."

"I know what that is," he said. "Fancy."

"Yes and no. Beef and pastry for the most part. I've got some green beans too. Didn't know how you were about vegetables."

"I eat just about anything," he said. He'd never been fussy about food. "My parents have a small farm. My mother grows all sorts of vegetables and we've got some chickens and pigs."

"I didn't know that," she said.

"That's not their job. It's just they live on farmland and my mother likes growing her own things."

"I'd love to have fresh vegetables, but I don't have the time nor the space for it."

"I don't know where my parents find the time either, but I guess it's her hobby."

"What do your parents do?" she asked. "If they aren't farmers."

He followed her through the front living room. It looked nice but didn't have a TV in it so he was guessing it might not be used much.

There was an office on the other side. Down the hall he walked into a big open room. The house didn't appear to be brand new, but it was nice and open and modern inside.

When he saw the size of the kitchen to the right and the setup he realized the reason.

"No way this house had a kitchen like this when you bought it."

"No," she said, laughing. "I had it all redone. There were a few rooms back here. Kitchen, dining room and living room. Now it's all open. I wanted a massive island and that is where I eat most of the time."

The island looked almost like a table with stools on one side and each end. Looked like eight by his count. Two on each end, four along the side.

There was a big dining table off to the side of the kitchen, then her living room on the opposite side.

A TV to die for on the wall over a fireplace, comfortable leather furniture and a gorgeous view of the ocean past a patio.

Who was he kidding? This house was worth a few million by the view alone.

"It's stunning," he said. "I don't think I'd leave this spot though."

He was looking out over the glass doors. Four of them that he bet all opened up like an accordion.

"I spend a lot of time on the patio. With a coffee or glass of wine. If it's cold I've got the fire pit going."

He saw it with some chairs surrounding it. Nice and cozy.

"We can sit out there later if you want," he said.

"I'd like that. You didn't answer my question, but you can tell me it's none of my business if you want."

"Huh? Oh, what my parents do. My mother is a teacher's aide. So she gets out early and has the summers off. That is why she loves to garden. Guess it gives her something to do in the summer. My father is a welder."

He wasn't going to be embarrassed over his parents' careers. Brice and Katy Harrington were great people and wonderful parents.

"And you went into the Air Force," she said. "Is that always what you wanted to do?"

She didn't say anything else about his parents' careers. He wasn't sure what he expected. She didn't look down on them or make some comment about their working-class status.

Guess he'd built things up in his mind there from the past when he didn't need to.

"It is," he said. "I didn't see myself going to college. It wasn't for me. I got through school because it was expected, but that was about it. My mother has a two-year degree, my father trade school. They tried to talk me into doing something like that."

"They must be proud of your career," she said. "Proud of your service to our country."

"They are," he said. "I'm an only child. They just wanted to make sure I was settled. I am."

"Do they miss you not living close by?" she asked.

He laughed. "I'm ninety minutes away by air. I take one of the helicopters home when I visit."

"That's nice of Egan, but I'd expect no differently."

"In the past if I was gone it'd just be sitting there anyway. But now with four pilots and three aircraft, I'm not so sure that will always be possible."

"I'm pretty sure Egan wouldn't have a problem with it," she said. "Not with his best buddy."

"He still has a business to run," he said.

"Can I get you a drink?" she asked. "Dinner will be ready soon."

"Sure," he said. "Do you have beer?"

"I do," she said. "Help yourself to what you like. There are a few in there."

He walked into her kitchen and opened the large stainless steel fridge, saw the variety of beers and reached in to get one.

"Do you want one?"

She took it out of his hands and opened it, then poured it into a glass and handed it over. "I'm going to have wine."

He saw the wine fridge under the island. "I could have had a glass of that," he said.

"Have what you want. It won't go to waste. If I don't drink it all, then I'll cook with it."

He wanted to make some comment about her cooking with expensive wine because he knew beyond a doubt she didn't drink anything that he'd be buying.

Or what he would have bought years ago.

He made more money now than he ever thought he would.

Egan hired him at over six figures years ago. He'd gotten raises in that time and bonuses quarterly. He had no complaints at all and Egan told him nonstop that he couldn't run the business the way he did without Lincoln as his pilot.

It was nice to feel needed and wanted.

He took a sip of his beer and she poured her glass of wine.

"If we've got time why don't we go on the patio and chat," he said.

He wanted to clear the air. There was no way he was going into this blind and wanted to understand where her head was and what she was looking for.

"We can do that," she said. "Then you can tell me what is on your mind because something is."

Guess not only could he not see things but people were able to see through him more than he ever thought before.

"What are you looking for?"

"Meaning between us?" she asked, her hand moving back and forth.

"Yes," he said.

"Do you ask that of all the women you go on a date with?"

"I think this is date number two," he said. No way he was going to admit that Egan had to point that out to him.

She grinned and her eyes lit up. "Well, if you knew the last one was a date, then I've got to wonder why you didn't reach out again. Did you only say yes to this one because you didn't want to offend me by saying no? Did I put you on the spot or something?"

This wasn't going as well as he thought it might.

He ran his hand through his short hair. "No. I'll confess I didn't realize the first time was a date until yesterday. I just thought you didn't want to have a drink alone."

"I didn't," she said. "But I also wanted to have it with you."

He nodded his head. He liked how she answered directly. "That is why I said yes to today. But it's not like we don't have some kind of family connection."

She lifted an eyebrow at him. "I'm not sure it's a family connection. You work for my cousin. It's not like Egan and I are that close. We aren't in the same branch, not that close of relations either. It's not like my parents work closely with Mitchell like Charlie and Hunter Bond do."

She had a point. Hunter, who was first cousins with Grace, was much closer with Egan, Eli and Ethan. They did business together too. Charlie and Mitchell owned businesses together as well.

But Grace didn't fall under that umbrella as others did.

"You make a good point," he said. "But you know, I don't have your...lineage."

She started to laugh. "You're joking, right?"

"No," he said seriously.

She frowned. "I'm not sure what I can say to you to make you believe I don't care about those things. How about the fact that I can take care of myself and don't need a man to do that for me."

"I never thought otherwise."

"Then you're worried people are going to think you are only with me for my name and what I can bring to the table? Money?" Her eyes were slicing through him like a hot knife through butter.

He'd pissed her off. He wasn't expecting that.

He'd be honest. "It's happened to me before," he said.

"We can circle back to that another time. I'm not sure you want to talk about it."

"I don't," he said.

"Then I'll tell you that my family doesn't care about

those things. Hunter married one of his employees who grew up in foster care."

"I'm aware," he said.

"Roark married a woman who came from a single mother who didn't even want to raise her other daughter."

"I know that too," he said. Roark's wife, Chelsea, worked for Hailey Bond and had been in the service as military police prior. She was raising her teenage younger sister on her own when she moved to Amore Island.

"Then I'm not sure why you think I or anyone in my family would believe what you're saying. And I'm only talking about my branch right now. I haven't even gone into the other branches, but you know as well as I do it's the same there too."

He did know that and started to feel like a fool.

"You've put me in my place," he said.

"I don't think I've even begun to put you in your place, but now isn't the time either," she said. "I need to go check on dinner." She marched to the kitchen, her little body almost vibrating with her frustration.

Well, that didn't go over so well and now he wondered how the rest of this date was going to go and if there would even be a third.

Guess it was best to know now and he could tell Egan that his boss was wrong. Fate meant nothing and it wasn't meant to be.

9

FRUSTRATING AND IRONIC

Grace had a short fuse and she needed to walk away from Lincoln before it caught fire and blew up in his face.

She couldn't believe this was what was causing him to not look at her like she was him.

And how did you change that?

More so the fact that she'd had men only want her for that reason and now the one she wanted felt just the opposite. Or something like that.

Talk about frustrating and ironic at the same time.

She checked on dinner, pulled it out and then set it aside to rest. She went back to the patio and started to laugh. It felt like the only thing she could do.

"I didn't think you'd have that reaction considering you looked ready to bite my head off a minute ago."

"Let's say I went in to cool down and take a breather and had a realization."

"What's that?" he asked.

"That the reason you are staying away from me is the

same reason most men wanted me. I can't win no matter what I do."

She downed her wine and shook her head. She should have done that in the house so she could have filled her glass back up.

"Excuse me?"

"You heard me," she said. "I've had the hardest time finding a man that I didn't have to worry about only wanting to be with me because of what I could bring to the table. Even friends, I struggled there too. I think most in our family did, which is why a lot of us are so close because we had each other and understood that."

"I didn't think much of that," he said. "But I sure the hell want nothing from a woman that has to do with money. I can take care of myself too."

"Exactly," she said. "I thought, here I'm going to make the first move. Someone who knows our family well and has met me. You're well-liked and respected by many members of the family. That means your character is strong. So yeah, that worry I had is gone. And then now you're telling me in your eyes I'm pretty much off limits for what my fear was."

"Shit," he said. "How long have you been attracted to me?"

Might as well air it all out. "A while. That was looks. Then I've talked to you and heard about you and thought, hmmm, I wouldn't mind getting to know him. You didn't seem to get the hint though."

"I've never been considered slow before," he said, scratching his chin. She thought it was a funny movement and liked that his full beard was gone and in its place was just a nicely trimmed one. "But I just told you why. I wasn't looking at you because of that reason."

She wasn't sure what to make of that.

"If I wasn't part of the Bond family, would you be interested in me?"

"You are part of the Bond family and that can't be changed," he said. He held a hand up when she went to talk. "But I am here so I'd say that means I'm interested in you."

"Prove it," she said, lifting her chin.

"What?" He looked confused again.

"Prove to me that you are attracted to me. Or interested in me."

He set his beer down. "Not sure what you want me to do, but this is all I've got." He yanked her hard against his body, his mouth crushing hers.

Oh yeah.

This was exactly what she'd been thinking of. No, dreaming of. For months. Maybe years.

Her arms went up and around his neck. She had to get on her tiptoes for that but didn't care.

And didn't care that she was getting a calf cramp a minute later holding that pose while they continued to make out, their tongues dueling, their bodies pressing against each other, sweat rolling down her back as her heart rate raced faster than ever before.

When her watch started to vibrate on her wrist, she pulled back thinking it was the worst time for a call.

When she looked down and saw it was an alert of a high heart rate she started to giggle and then laugh so hard she was bent over with it holding her waist.

"I'm not laughing at you," she said, wiping a tear from her eye.

"Since I'm the only one in the room right now it's hard to believe that."

She showed him her watch. "Look. You should be proud of yourself. How is that for proving to you what I feel?"

He grabbed her wrist and started to laugh. "Damn. That's a first."

"For both of us. Can we wipe the slate clean now?"

"Not sure what you mean by that," he said.

"I know you're not interested in my bank account."

"Hell no," he said.

"So that relieves both of our minds on that. I want nothing from you other than you...well, maybe another kiss like that before the end of the night."

"I can handle that," he said. "You're feeding me and all."

"I am doing that. It's almost ready too. How hungry are you?"

"Very," he said, his eyes looking her over.

"Good," she said. "You're not getting much more than a kiss. Though I did make you dessert too."

"I'll take it," he said. "Where are your plates?"

"What?"

"Your plates. You cooked, I can set the table. Or aren't I allowed to touch anything in your kitchen?"

She smiled. "I am territorial about my kitchen but not for that. In the cabinet to the left of the sink."

He moved back into the house with her following and grabbed two plates. "Silverware?" he asked.

She pointed to a drawer not that far away as she sliced the Wellington. Her beans were done with bits of bacon and almond slivers mixed in. They were just warming. Normally she would have made them very fresh but wanted to have time to talk to Lincoln.

She was thrilled she'd come out and said what she had, but something was telling her that he was still holding back.

There had to be more to it than what he'd said about his reasons for not approaching her.

Just like there was more to her too.

Maybe if she brought it up a little more he'd understand. She could share enough and hope he opened up too.

Once they were seated at the island, him on the corner, her next to him on the side so they could see each other, he filled his plate.

"How is it?" she asked after a minute of eating.

"Sorry," he said. "Me stuffing my face isn't compliment enough?"

"I love watching people eat my food," she said. "It's very rewarding."

"I love anyone cooking for me. My mother is a good cook. She feeds me well when I visit. She'd send me packages but couldn't send me food she'd made when I was in the service. So when I came home on leave she'd feed me like crazy. All my favorites were there nonstop."

"That's great," she said. "I'd do that. What are some of your favorites?"

"I'll eat just about anything," he said. "But I don't want you to think I'm only with you for your cooking."

It was the boyish grin on his face that had her laughing. She was relieved they'd gotten to this point. "That doesn't bother me. I enjoy it and it's a skill I've earned, not something I was born with."

He tilted his head. "I like that."

"Thank you," she said. "I'm proud of what I do for a living. I've worked hard to get here. I've struggled to get men to understand that or accept that it comes with negatives."

"A lot of time and effort goes into it," he said. "With my job, I don't work traditional hours. I can go in at the crack of dawn and get home in the middle of the night. Or get called out in the middle of the night if there is an emergency and someone needs to get off the island."

She knew that. That Egan was contracted with the State Police and the hospitals if other helicopters weren't available.

"I work nights and weekends. It's hard to have a relationship with those hours. I'm not a clingy person and have no expectations because I can't make promises." Which was kind of a lie because she did have expectations but not in terms of the time spent with someone as much as their honesty.

"The same," he said.

"Then we understand each other there."

"Seems it," he said.

He wasn't saying all that much but was still eating and smiling at her.

"I know a lot of people think I shouldn't work that much."

"It's your choice. What I know of your family is none of you live off of what you're born with."

"Remember that," she said firmly.

He turned to look at her and held her stare, then nodded.

"You've been burned," he said.

"Probably as severely as you," she said.

"No," he said. "Not even close."

"You're not going to share, are you?" she asked.

"No," he said. "Not right yet. There is no reason for it now."

That was debatable in her mind, but they'd gotten further than she thought and would let it go.

"Do you like lemon?"

"I do," he said. "Did you make a lemon dessert?"

"This is a rich dinner and I thought something light and citrus would clean the palate."

"Yeah, my brain doesn't work that way. I just know what I like," he said, grinning.

Her hand reached over and wrapped around his neck to pull him closer for a kiss. "Me too!"

10

COMMON GROUND

"How did it go?" Grace's mother asked her the next morning. She was up early and getting ready to go to work. Since it was her day in the office and not really in the kitchen she showed up when she wanted and did the same at the end of the day.

Most times she was there longer than she had to be. She took pride in her job and her work and she was thrilled that Lincoln understood that about her.

"It was good," she said. Her mother knew she had a date with Lincoln. She'd told her how the flight back went on Monday. It felt like she needed a girl to talk to and her mother was it. Kind of sad in a way, but her mother seemed to be enjoying it.

"Wonderful. Are you going to fill me in on some details?"

Grace let out a big sigh. If it was someone her own age she would, but with her mother it was hard. She did need some advice and her mother knew her the best.

"He's noticed me but never thought of me as someone he could date."

"Why?" her mother asked. She heard the confusion in her mother's question the same as she'd had.

"Because of my background and history on the island."

"You mean because you come from Edward's side of the family? Did you ask him if you came from William's if he would have felt differently?"

Damn it. She didn't think of that. She should have.

"I'm positive it's that and not just the Bond family. It's the money," she said. "That much was clear."

"So he was afraid you'd think he only wanted to be with you for that reason?" her mother asked. "That is insulting to you both."

"I should have said that too. I was pissed. I actually walked away from him and took a moment to gather my thoughts and then I just started to laugh. You see how ironic this is, right? It's the one thing I've worried and stayed away from for years and yet he is staying away from me for the same reason."

"I guess it could be funny when you say it like that. I'm assuming you told him that?"

"I did. He didn't know what to say. He made some comment about being burned worse than me, but I didn't ask for details. I got the impression he wouldn't have told me anyway."

"It will come up again if it matters," her mother said.

"That is my thought. But then I started to doubt his reason for coming for dinner. I asked him to prove to me he was attracted."

"I don't know if I want those details," her mother said drily. "But you need to control those doubts. You know that. It's what burned you more than once."

Her mother wasn't telling her anything she didn't know.

Sometimes she'd had friends or boyfriends that weren't

after her for her money or family name, but her doubts and accusations pushed them away when they got sick of having to try to prove themselves.

Which again proved the point that she needed someone else to talk to other than her mother. There was only so much she'd say and maybe she didn't want to hear all her faults either.

"He kissed me," she said. "Nothing more than that. More than once too. Dinner went well. I learned some about him. His parents are hard workers and they live on a farm. His mother has summers off and has a huge garden and loves to cook with her freshly grown vegetables and herbs."

"You would love to have that," her mother said. "Something in common."

"I did say that," she said. "I wish I had the space and the time to do it here. He's the type of guy that loves food. Nothing fancy, but he'd eat fancy. I pegged him for rustic and so far am winning him over that way."

"If you need to win him over it's not meant," her mother said.

Grace laughed. "I know that. I just love to cook and he loves to eat. It's a common ground and you know I find so much pleasure in feeding people. He said when he'd come home from the service his mother had everything he loved loaded in the house for him. When he visits she sends him back with lots of food frozen to heat up."

"Oh my God," her mother said. "He's dating his mother."

Her jaw dropped. "Stop that."

"I'm just kidding. It's a good thing. When we are with someone we care for we find traits from other people we've cared for in our lives. There is probably a big part of that for him. If that makes him feel more comfortable around you and what he thinks might be something to keep your backgrounds apart, then go with it."

"Thanks. I need to hear that. I've got to run now, but I'll let you know how date number two—well, three, goes when it happens."

"You didn't set it yet?" her mother asked.

"No. He has Tuesdays off and then his schedule is crazy. I know that. I work nights and weekends too. We'll figure it out or it will be next week at the same time. Not much more we can do about it."

"You can sneak over to the hangar and drop him off some food when you know he might be there," her mother said. "Before your shifts."

"Good point. I'll think about it."

She hung up after that and left for The Retreat. Rather than go to her office, she went right to the penthouse floor and knocked.

Kayla opened it up. "Hi, Grace. I didn't know you were coming by."

"I hope I'm not interrupting anything."

"Just play time," Kayla said.

Ben and Jack had toys spread out all over what used to be a formal living room but now was a play area.

"Grace," Ben said, running toward her. "Did you bring me food?"

"No," she said. "What do you want?"

"Cookies," Ben said.

Kayla snorted. "He always wants cookies. I told him we'd bake some this afternoon. Ashley has been letting him make things when she babysits and now he wants to do it all the time."

Ashley was her cousin Roark's stepsister-in-law. She was a senior in high school and had expressed interest in cooking too. She'd spent some time talking with her and they'd convinced Ashley to go away to culinary school for two years.

Maybe Tracy and Ashley would get along well.

"Before I tell you the real reason I'm here, when are you going to see Ashley again?"

"This weekend," Kayla said. "Hunter and I have to go to some dinner thing in Boston. Why?"

She filled Kayla in on what was going on with Tracy. "Do you think you could mention something to her to seek Tracy out and introduce herself? I think if anyone can understand what Tracy might be going through it's Ashley. I don't have her number. I could get it from Roark, but you know, my working time is when Ashley is doing schoolwork."

"I'll absolutely do it," Kayla said. "I think that is wonderful you are helping Tracy out. I would have loved something like that as a child. Just someone to even talk to."

"I know," she said. "Which brings me to something else. Not quite the same thing but a little bit of it. Can I trust you to keep this quiet for now? I don't know what may or may not come of it."

"Of course," Kayla said, grinning. "What's going on?"

"I went on a date with Lincoln last night."

Kayla's eyes lit up and she pulled her toward the kitchen. "This calls for coffee. Talk."

"I don't have much time but can manage a cup," she said. She filled Kayla in on what had been going on and how she'd had a crush on him for a while and that it seemed Lincoln did too but why he'd kept his distance.

"And you wanted to know my advice since I felt the same way when I started to date Hunter?" Kayla asked.

"Yes. How did you relax? What did Hunter do to get you to do that?"

"It took a lot of time," Kayla said. "He kept assuring me no one cared, but it came down to meeting Nicole and Hailey. They made me realize I was looked at as a person first."

"But Uncle Charlie felt otherwise," she said.

She knew her uncle wasn't thrilled and thought people would judge Hunter. Uncle Charlie was pretty reserved and old school. Stuffy was more like it.

"Hunter stood up for me, and Hailey and Nicole were in my corner," Kayla said. "Getting pregnant didn't help any. I felt like now he'd judge me for that, but it wasn't my fault."

"No," Grace said. "It was Hunter's for knocking you up. Do you think he did it on purpose?"

"Stop laughing," Kayla said. "It all worked out. Charlie is great with me and the kids. I guess my point is, even having that obstacle we were still able to move around it."

"Because Hunter had patience and stood by your side," she said. "Patience isn't one of my better traits."

"Then you better learn to get some," Kayla said. "I thought my pride was big, but I'm guessing a man's might be more. Lincoln comes across as a protector."

Grace let out a sigh and took a big sip of the coffee set in front of her. "Yep. I think so too. Right now I'm trying to wear him down with my cooking. My mother said I shouldn't have to wear him down."

"Sure, you do," Kayla said. "If you know in your heart that he might be the one for you."

"I don't know that," she rushed out to say. Though she had this island in her blood she wasn't so sure she felt the lore and legend.

"Yes, you do," Kayla said. "But you don't have to admit it. Just think about the fact of how you've felt for years. You say you have no patience, but that is some right there."

Kayla had a point. "Okay. I still don't know much more than I think he's hot and that we had a good time on the date once we got past that conversation."

"That's a good first step. Hunter had to convince me to even go on a date with him. And then after that first one do it again and again. I'm surprised he didn't just throw in the towel."

"I hear what you're saying. I don't think it will be that way."

"Your mother and I are the only ones that know about this date?" Kayla asked.

"That I'm aware of. My guess is Lincoln will mention something to Egan. I hope he does. Egan will be on my side."

"See, you need backup. That means you want this to have a chance and work. It's in your heart," Kayla said, grinning over the rim of her cup.

"Snot," she said. "I'm taking this with me to my office." She picked her cup up. "I'll bring it back later. With cookies for Ben."

"Yay," Ben yelled. She'd said that loud enough for the little guy to hear her.

Jack came running in next and slid on his knees on the floor, stopping at her feet. He was the wild one and she loved it. "Do I get cookies too?" It was cute listening to him. He would be two in a few months, but his speech was pretty good.

She put her coffee down, then picked Jack up and tossed him in the air. "Of course you do." She kissed him on the cheek and set him on his feet, but he was bending his knees so she put him down that way. When the two women were alone she said quietly, "When do they get another sibling? I know Hunter wants more."

Kayla closed one eye at her. "Don't get on Hunter's side."

She laughed. "Okay, I need you on mine, so I'll stay out of it."

Grace left feeling a lot more confident than she had when she got up this morning, which was saying a lot because normally she was a confident person and hated that this was mixing her up in the head.

11

FORM OF ACCEPTANCE

"You went on a date with my cousin?" Egan asked Lincoln on Wednesday afternoon. The two of them had a layover in Boston before their clients came in and he figured he might as well fill his boss in.

"I did," he said. "Do you have a problem with it?"

"No," Egan said. "How come I'm just hearing about this now? Why didn't you tell me yesterday?"

"I was off yesterday," he argued.

"So," Egan said. "You could have texted. You tell me everything else. I don't know why you didn't tell me Monday when I saw you at the end of the day either."

Because he wasn't positive he was still going to show up but didn't want to admit that.

"I wanted to wait and see how it turned out," he said.

"I'm sure it was fine," Egan said. "More so if she cooked for you. You're pretty easy to win over. She has you like putty in her tiny hands if she puts a bowl of tuna noodle casserole in front of you."

He started to laugh. Egan had all but gagged when he'd heated up a dish of that. But his mother had sent him back with it on one of his visits home. Comfort rustic food. Just like Grace had pegged him for.

He hadn't been home in a few months, but when his mother sent him back with that again, he wouldn't bring it to work.

Or maybe he would, just to watch Egan gag over the smell of microwave tuna. The guy complained about how bad Kaden's diapers were and had no problem changing them but couldn't handle the smell of microwave fish.

"She's multiple steps up from tuna noodle casserole," he said.

"Tell me about it," Egan said.

"Not much to say."

"Of course there is," Egan said. "She put you in your place, didn't she?"

It was the smirk on his buddy's face that had him giving in. "She did."

"Told you," Egan said. "What did she say?"

"Is this a therapy session? I thought I was the doctor between us."

"I can dish it out too," Egan said. "More so when I think you're being an idiot."

"Hardly an idiot and you know why," he said.

"You were a kid. A teen. Misplaced love and it wasn't even love and you know it. It's not the same thing."

"Whatever," he said. "It doesn't change what happened and how I've carried that guilt for years."

"Not your fault," Egan said. "I didn't know you back then, but what I know of you and the person you are, you got sucked into someone else's drama and they locked you in that place. Even to this day. Don't carry that shit with you. Grace isn't that way and neither is our family."

Lincoln knew that, but it was hard to break out of the place he'd been locked in.

His parents still felt it from time to time too.

"I know," he said. "I'm getting there."

"So what is the next step after Grace gave you shit? Did you tell her why you are the way you are?"

"No," he said. He wouldn't tell Egan that he let it slip that he'd been burned worse than her. It didn't matter. "It didn't seem the place for it."

"Did she tell you about her?" Egan asked.

"What do you know you aren't saying?"

"Nothing," Egan asked. "We all felt the same pinch at times. It's hard to find someone with our last name or heritage. I think that is why my family is so accepting. If you put stipulations on things you narrow down your dating pool to begin with. The fact that those who live on the island full time don't want to live anywhere else already narrows things. This life isn't for everyone."

"No," he said. "I've learned that too. I know I could move to Boston and still keep my job."

"Of course you could," Egan said. "But it's not what you want. Or is it?"

"Fuck no," he said. "I like the pace of living here. I like my little rented home. The city isn't where I want to be."

"Because living on the island reminds you of living back home?" Egan asked.

"Scranton is a big city but nothing like Boston. I like being in the country. Riding my four-wheelers and snowmobiles."

"Nothing you do here," Egan pointed out.

"No. I can do that when I go home." And he did. If he went home for more than a day, which didn't happen often.

Family Bonds- Grace & Lincoln

His mother had been asking him to take some time. A vacation even. Come home and relax.

He'd been thinking of it.

But with Kaden's birth he didn't want to put his boss in a bind. He'd think about taking his vacation soon though. Even if it was a long weekend.

He never wanted to forget where he came from and didn't think he ever would.

Too much was keeping him locked there anyway.

"When are you going back again?" Egan asked.

"No clue. We are going to get into our busy season soon," he said.

"So? I've got more pilots. You can figure it out and take some time."

He'd have to drive though if he went for a few days. No way he could take the helicopter that long and wouldn't even think of it. Not when someone else could be flying it.

"I'll think of it. Maybe before Memorial Day weekend when it will pick up more."

"Fine," Egan said. "But you need to take a week's vacation at some point too. So plan that. I'm going to force you to do it at some point. You need a break. I don't think you've gotten one in a long time."

"When have you had a week off?" he asked.

"I took a week off when Kaden was born. I'm taking a week off for my honeymoon now that Blake realized Kaden will be fine without us for a week."

He started to laugh. "You mean she had to convince you that Kaden would be fine without *you* for a week?"

He knew Egan hated leaving his son. He could understand that too.

"Whatever," Egan said, waving his hand in an exaggerated fashion. "My mother is in heaven having her grandson for the week. I know Kaden will be fine."

"He will," Lincoln said. "I'll go over and spend time with him. I'll convince him to love me more than you so when you come back he comes to me first."

"Asshole," Egan said, laughing. "It won't happen, but I know you'll try. Why don't you use that energy for the new chick you're dating."

"Did you just refer to your cousin as a chick?" he asked with his eyes wide. "I can't wait to tell her that."

Egan smirked. "You like her. I know you do. It's the first thing you thought of just now. Running to her and ratting me out."

He sighed. He couldn't believe how he fell for that.

"Fine," he said. "I like her. But we both have busy careers and I'm not sure when we are going to have time to see each other."

"You'd have that problem with anyone. The fact she is in the same boat means she won't be demanding. Did you stop to think that is a weight off her shoulders too to not worry about?"

"No," he said. He wasn't sure why he didn't think of that.

"And you both have Tuesday off," Egan said. "We can work your schedule so that you can have lighter days on Mondays or even Mondays off. You don't need to work six days a week anymore."

"Thanks," he said. "I'll let you know. I don't think either one of us is ready to be spending that much time together."

Egan laughed. "You're talking yourself out of things rather than into them, but I'm not going to get on your case about it. It's your life."

"Gee, thanks," he said, laughing. "*Now* it's my life."

"It's always been your life, but as your best friend I'm not going to sit by and let you throw something away either. Then again, on this island, fate and all, I don't think you need my help."

"Ass," he said and walked out listening to Egan's laughing.

His best friend did give him a shit ton to think about though and he could appreciate the fact that Egan was being flexible to allow him to spend time with Grace.

Lincoln supposed that was a major form of acceptance in the Bond family. Though it wasn't the extended family he was worried about getting the acceptance from.

He'd had bad experiences with the parents of a woman he was in love with and that was all he was concerned about now.

He'd never put himself in that position again where he wasn't accepted and had to spend so much energy to fight for something that ended up not being worth fighting for in the end.

12

THE VICTOR

"Good morning," Grace said, walking into the hangar on Friday morning. Egan and he both looked up at the sound of her voice.

"Hey," Lincoln said. He looked at his watch. "It's seven thirty, what are you doing here so early?"

"Breakfast," she said, lifting up the dish in her hand. She moved over to the counter, pulled the brown bag that was sitting on top of it off and took the lid off the dish. "French toast bake." Then she opened the brown bag. "Bacon and egg waffle sandwiches. They are still hot but not for long. Figured they'd travel better since you'll be in the air soon."

Egan all but elbowed him out of the way as if it was the World Cup soccer match and he was going for the ball, then grabbed the bag out of his cousin's hand. "You've never brought me food before. How come?"

Grace laughed as Lincoln wrestled the bag out of Egan's hand, the two of them almost on the floor at this point as they were body-blocking the other and slapping hands in a game of flag football. Only the flag was this delicious scent of food that he was supposed to be getting.

Lincoln came up the victor. He had moves that could bring a man to his knees, but he wouldn't do that to his best friend. Or his boss.

Or maybe he would for some food.

"You don't kiss me like he does," Grace said.

"Eww," Egan said. "We are cousins."

"That's right. Maybe I should have said that first and you would have let go of the food. But no worries. Here is yours."

She pulled one out of her large purse and handed it to Egan.

"Thank you," Egan said, kissing her on the cheek. "That doesn't count though does it?"

"Not likely," she said.

"I appreciate the food," Lincoln said, opening one of the perfectly wrapped breakfast sandwiches. This was like when he'd brought Laine home and her father's chef had food ready for him too. This job had a lot more perks than he'd ever thought it would.

"How about a kiss for it?" Grace said. "I got up real early to make it. I'm not due into work for another few hours."

He cringed around a mouthful that she'd gotten up and come out of her way, and moved closer, then kissed her on the lips. Not the kind he'd like to do.

Egan cleared his throat. "That is not much different than the one I gave her on her cheek. It sucks he's getting more food than me."

"He's sexier than you," Grace said.

She had a smirk on her face and Lincoln felt the heat fill his. Then it rushed over his body fast enough that he now knew what a hot flash felt like.

"You two are gross," Egan said. "Here I thought you might have come here for a ride."

Grace wiggled her eyebrows. "Another time. Another place than here too."

There went a second flush of heat in his body. He had no idea she could do that to him.

"Grace, you're making Lincoln blush. I didn't know that was possible."

She laughed. "Neither did I. I find a little food goes a long way."

"It's not the food," he said around a mouthful. "It's the words."

"Okay," she said. "I'll say them in private next time. Maybe mixed with some others. Come give me one more kiss. And you shouldn't need syrup with the casserole, it's flavored enough."

"Thank you," he said, leaning in to kiss her one more time. This time she put her arms around his neck and held him there a second longer.

"Yum. I taste bacon."

She moved out of the hangar after that.

"Dude," Egan said. "That was hilarious to watch."

"Not much funnier than watching Blake walk all over you with her snarky wit."

"It's sexy," Egan argued. "I love it. But she made you blush. What the hell is that about?"

"It's your cousin," he said.

"So?" Egan said. "Other women have done and said worse things than that to you around me."

"It's not the same," he mumbled.

"For someone who fought this for so long, two dates or so in and you're acting like a long-lost fool."

"Not likely," he said. He wasn't about to let himself go to anyone. And if he did, it was going to take a lot more time than a week.

"You do realize that she got her ass up early to bring you breakfast."

"Hard to miss," he said, finishing off his last bite. "I didn't even know there was such a thing as a waffle breakfast sandwich."

"Tell me about it," Egan said. "I'm going to be encouraging this relationship hard if this is going to be how we start some mornings. I expect you to share too."

He snorted. "I'm not using her that way."

"It's a joke," Egan said. "There was a time you'd laugh along with me. Make a crack back. You know, like a few weeks ago you'd do that."

He wasn't sure why he was so defensive about it now.

No, he knew. He didn't want anyone to think he was with Grace for anything other than her.

Even something as simple as food.

"I'm a little out of practice," he said.

"From what?" Egan asked.

"Dating."

"You date," Egan argued. "Maybe not that often or at least from what I can see."

"I date without the intention of it turning into more."

"Ahh," Egan said. "But with Grace you don't want that mentality?"

"No," he said. "It doesn't seem right. I mean we talked and all. We know the other's schedule. I'm just taking it as it comes."

"Then what is the problem?"

He shrugged and then walked into the small kitchen and came back with two forks. If Egan stuffed his face with more food maybe he'd stop with all the questions.

"I don't know," he said. "It's different."

Egan took a forkful of the casserole and popped it in his

mouth. Lincoln did the same and his eyes almost rolled back in his head over the taste.

"Jesus," Egan said. "Suck it up to get fed like this. Or figure it out. Don't blow it."

He knew his boss was joking this time and laughed. "I'll try."

The two of them had a few more mouthfuls before he put the top on. No way he was sharing the whole thing. This was going home with him and he'd be eating it for breakfast before work.

"Do you have another sandwich in that bag?" Egan asked, looking at the bag that wasn't deflated. "You got two?"

"I kiss better," Lincoln said. "And that one is for the air."

Egan grinned. "There is the guy I know and love. Loosen up and have some fun with this."

"I'll try," he said again. He could understand why his best friend was confused because he sure the hell was too.

Egan moved over to the computer and started to type a few things in. He assumed his boss was checking the schedule for today and the weekend.

"Rob told me he's available on Mondays after ten."

"So," he said.

"You can bring Rex and Hailey back to Boston in the morning and then take the rest of the day off."

He frowned. "If I leave the helicopter there for him, how am I getting home?"

Normally he left it there on Monday nights and flew back with Egan or Roxy. They worked it out daily, that way there were two left in Boston for his day off on Tuesday that Rob worked.

Egan was pushing some more buttons. "There is a cargo shipment scheduled for Monday morning back here, he can bring you when he delivers it. Then the bird is left."

Family Bonds- Grace & Lincoln

On Wednesday he normally flew over with Egan to Boston to get it and he assumed that would be the plan again.

He didn't mind sharing his helicopter. When it was just the two of them, they swapped them out at times but Egan always had the bigger and better one.

With the business's latest purchase, Egan was the only one that was driving that beauty, and he'd gotten Egan's older one and Roxy was flying his.

On Egan's day off, Lincoln was the only one allowed to fly the new helicopter if needed.

It all worked out and it's not like he could lay claim to anything.

"Why are you doing this?" he asked.

"So that Grace can get that ride that she is looking for."

He threw his fork at his boss's smirk, but the two of them laughed. "Asshole."

"Just helping my family out."

"What if she has plans on her day off?"

"The fact she got her butt up early to cook for you tells me that she'd change any of her plans to spend some time with you. I thought for sure you were smart enough to know those things."

"Guess not," he said.

He grabbed his phone and sent her a text to see if she had plans before Egan started to even rearrange things. No reason to at this point, as he'd rather work.

"I'm going to start scheduling you Mondays and Tuesdays off," Egan said. "We'll work it out as it goes, but you should have two set days off. We are always on call on the island and you know it."

"Yeah," he said. He was taking more of them now

because Egan was trying to help out with the baby and not always getting a ton of sleep.

"Then don't argue with me. I sign your paycheck."

"I didn't think you'd go that low to help a family member out."

Egan winked. "I'd think I'm helping you out just the same, but again, you're family too."

That put him in his place more than anything else in this conversation.

13

LOVE LANGUAGE

"What did you bring me to eat?" Emma French said to Grace thirty minutes later when her cousin opened the door.

"French toast casserole," she said, laughing. Since she was making it for Lincoln she made another for her cousin.

"This isn't your style but totally mine. Yum. Are you going to have some with me?"

"I had breakfast this morning," Grace said. Her cousin had asked her to come over to answer some research questions for her next book.

Guess Emma's main character was a chef who was going to end up the prime suspect in a murder that happened in his kitchen. Grace was always willing to help her family out.

"How about coffee?"

"That I'll take," she said.

She followed Emma to her kitchen. Her cousin was a recluse barely leaving her home let alone the island.

"Pick a flavor," Emma said, pulling out a drawer of pods for the one-cup coffee maker. "Or I've got others in here."

A cabinet was opened and there had to be at least ten large boxes not even opened.

"What the hell, Emma? Do you plan on being locked in or something? Don't tell me you actually drink that much coffee and that is only a few weeks supply?"

"No," Emma said. "But you know I stock up. I only go to the store about once a month. Maybe twice. Creamer doesn't always last that long."

Her cousin opened her fridge and she saw the four containers of creamer in there and rolled her eyes.

She didn't think she could live like this. Where you hardly saw anyone. She wondered how often Emma talked to people.

"How do you do it?"

"Do what?" Emma asked, popping the pod that she'd picked out into the machine.

"Live like this? I know you don't like to see people much, but do you ever talk to anyone?"

"I talk to my characters all day long. My brain gets confused and clogged. I don't need to talk to actual people."

"That's scary."

Emma laughed and handed her over the cup. "Not really. You know I've never been one to hang out in large groups. This works for me."

"You're not lonely?"

Emma shrugged. "Not really. You're here and you brought me food. I talk to other family members all the time who let me interview them. My mother and father call me weekly each."

"Probably to make sure you're alive," she said.

"No, I get daily texts for that. I just need to send something back even if it's a meme or an emoji."

"That's funny."

"Grandpa visits often in the summer, but at least he calls first," Emma said.

"You could pick his brain for a lot of ideas," she said.

"I do. From a business standpoint. I get more from Roark and my father."

Roark was a defense attorney and Emma's father was a federal judge. She supposed her cousin had an all-access pass to more facts than fiction at times.

It also told her her cousin did talk to people often.

"What do you need from me?" she asked.

Emma grabbed her coffee and then a plate and some breakfast and started to eat while she pulled her laptop over.

"I've got a list of questions," Emma said. "I could have emailed these to you, but I asked you over instead. See, I talk to people in person."

"You wanted food," she said.

"That too," Emma said, grinning.

"You eat and give me your computer. I can type faster than you can one handed while you eat."

"Sure, if you think that is the case," Emma said. "I'm a pro."

But her cousin shifted her laptop over and Grace read the questions and answered them at the same time she was laughing.

What were the best knives to use for certain cuts of meat? Then which one would be best for murder? Slicing through flesh and bone. Poisonous foods that no one would detect. Best way to slip a food in that someone was deathly allergic to and have it show no trace.

When she was done, she said, "You're evil. I can't wait to read this."

"I haven't figured out how the murder is going to take

place yet. I want all my options. It's better to know the information so when I get to the murder it can lead me to the direction I want."

"Lead you?" she asked.

"Yep," Emma said. "I told you I talk to my characters all day long. Or more like they talk to me. They lead the story, not me guiding them."

"Interesting," she said. "I didn't realize that."

Grace did read her cousin's books, the same with her aunt's books, but she didn't have a lot of time to read and always felt she fell behind.

"So what is going on in your life?" Emma asked. "People think I'm lost in the outside world."

"You normally are, but maybe I'll tell you something that hasn't made it's way back to you and then you can prove that isn't the case."

"Do you have fresh gossip for me?" Emma asked, rubbing her hands together.

Maybe this wasn't a good idea.

She'd told Kayla to keep it to herself, but the fact she'd just shown up with breakfast for Lincoln and Egan meant it wasn't that quiet.

It wouldn't hurt and the more that knew the easier it might be for Lincoln to feel comfortable.

It's not like she wanted this to be a secret. After a lot of thought, if she did, he might think she was embarrassed or something and that was the furthest thing from the truth.

It's like Kayla had told her. Be patient.

Only that wasn't her so she had to nudge in her way.

Seeing Lincoln flush earlier and Egan pushing in her corner had helped.

When her phone went off, she pulled it out and saw a

text from Lincoln asking if she had plans Monday afternoon.

Oh yeah, it worked well. She replied and decided that there was no reason to not tell her other girl cousin what was going on.

She'd always been closer to Emma than Hailey. Hailey was older than them, but they all grew up in Boston close to each other.

"It's not gossip," she said. "I'm sort of seeing someone. It's going to make the rounds fast. I'm not keeping it a secret."

"Who is it?" Emma asked, eating.

"Lincoln."

"Oh, Egan's best friend? Damn, girl, fill me in. Have you seen him in one of his old Air Force uniforms?"

She started to laugh and realized how much she missed not having this in her life.

"Sadly, no," she said. "We've only had a handful of dates and it's been a lot of work. I'm not sure I've worked this hard in my life with a guy."

"Now I've got to know," Emma said.

She filled her cousin in up to this morning. "What are you doing?" she asked when Emma grabbed her laptop and started to type.

"Taking notes. Oh my. This is some good shit. I didn't even think about this. Using food to get to a guy. You know, the way to their heart, but this is more about attention."

Her shoulders dropped. "It started as a joke, but now I'm feeling bad about it. Do you think I'm playing him?"

"Absolutely not!" Emma shouted. "Sorry. Didn't mean to shout. I'm getting excited like I do when I'm writing something good."

"Why did you have that reaction?" she asked.

"Because this is no different than a man bringing a woman flowers on a date. Or chocolate. Men do it to women all the time. There is no reason you can't to a man."

"So I'm courting him?" she asked, frowning. She didn't like the sounds of that.

"Modern-day getting someone to like you," Emma said with her focus on the screen as she typed.

"That sounds childish."

"Nope," Emma said, still typing. She couldn't even make eye contact, but her cousin was following along at the same time. "This is awesome." Her cousin stopped typing and looked at her. "Grace. It's sweet. Cooking is your love language."

"Huh?" she asked. "I'm not some wuss."

"Of course you're not," Emma said. "Well, you don't want people to see that, but we all know you're not as tough as you portray."

She wasn't going to argue that point. No reason to.

"What's your point?"

"My point is, you like him. Enough that you want him to see that. You're working harder because he has doubts and insecurities and you want to help him through that. You're using the one thing that you know the best to relax him."

"Food?" she asked.

She wasn't going to address the doubts and insecurities that Lincoln might have since she'd had her mother point out that was one of her faults in life.

She'd have to keep that in the back of her mind.

"And family," Emma said. "You're putting it out there to those closest to you and him. You're letting him know that you're good with this. And if you are, there is no reason he can't be."

"I am trying to do that," she said. "With the family. I

could see Egan was busting his ass but the same way he always did. And the fact he just texted me to say he had Monday afternoon off tells me either he asked for it—"

"Or Egan forced it on him. Showing family support."

"Yeah," she said. "That is most likely what it is. I hope Lincoln isn't put off by that though."

"If he was, I'm sure he would have fought it and won," Emma said. "I don't know him that well. I've never ridden in a helicopter."

"Because you don't leave the island," she said.

"And when I have to, I take the ferry because my schedule is my own. I don't need to worry about squeezing things in."

"That's true," she said. "Anyway, this is where we are at. My parents know. I've been talking to my mom about it. I talked to Kayla on Wednesday."

"Kayla would understand the best," Emma said.

"Exactly. She gave me some good advice to be patient."

Emma started to laugh. "That's not you."

"Nope. Which is why I brought him breakfast this morning. It's working though. We both have to work this weekend. I won't see him and might not even talk to him much. Once I'm in the kitchen tonight and this weekend, I've got no time to even check my phone."

"I'm sure he understands that since he's not exactly texting and chatting while he's flying."

"That's right. I don't like clingy guys so this works even better."

"You don't think you came off as clingy this morning?" Emma asked, lifting her eyebrow.

She waited for a beat before she answered. "No. That was a push. He made the next step and now we won't do much more than text for a few days and figure out our plans."

"Good for you," Emma said. "I asked that to see if you'd doubt yourself. You rarely doubt yourself in anything and I'm glad to know you aren't now."

Guess she did a good job hiding that bad trait from everyone but her mother.

"No," she said. "I'm not doubting myself as much as just trying to navigate this. I don't want to be the person putting in all the effort either."

She'd given herself some timelines and a pep talk for the past few days.

There was only so much fighting for someone she'd do to just get to know them. She wasn't going to beg anyone.

"The fact he texted you to get together less than thirty minutes after you left him should give you your answer."

She smiled. "I guess you're right. Points for me."

"I'm glad to know one of us is getting some action," Emma said.

"I'm not getting much and you won't ever unless you leave your house."

"I'm good," Emma said.

"Then why make that comment?" she asked.

"No clue," Emma said, shrugging.

But Grace didn't believe that.

It wasn't the time to argue though. They were all adults and made their own choices in life.

Pursuing Lincoln was hers and she just hoped it didn't bite her in the ass.

14

WATCH AND LEARN

Lincoln felt like a fool standing on the doorstep of Grace's house on Monday afternoon.

Not even noon. It was a few minutes before.

He'd flown Rex and Hailey to Boston first thing this morning, then had a few hours to kill before Egan could bring him back to the island.

He could have gotten on the ferry and then taken an Uber back to the hangar, but the time to wait for the next ferry and the ride over, then an Uber... It might have saved him forty minutes today.

It wasn't worth the hassle and gave him time to take Egan's Range Rover and pick up a few things in Boston.

One of those things was a gift for Grace.

"Hi," Grace said, opening the door.

"I'm not too early, am I?" he asked. He got sick of waiting around his house.

He was back by eleven and had an hour to kill for a ten-minute drive. He never thought he was that impatient in his life but realized he was.

"No," she said. "Just in time."

"It smells good in here," he said.

"Just lunch," she said.

"It's your day off. You don't have to cook for me all the time. I can take you out."

"I enjoy doing it," she said. "And I've got to eat too. I'm not one to always throw a sandwich together. Well, I am and that is what I'm doing but not like a sandwich you get at a deli. What's in the box?"

"It's your dish from Friday," he said. "And something I picked up for you in Boston this morning."

"You worked?" she asked.

"I just had to fly Rex, Hailey and the baby back."

"J.B. sure is a cutie," she said. "I can't believe he's six months old already. Hailey is talking about having another soon."

"Really?" he asked.

"She's older. Men have it easy. They can have babies much later in life. They don't have to carry them."

"Good point," he said. He wondered if Grace thought that and then wasn't sure why he was thinking it.

"Lots of babies being born in the family now," she said. "Almost as many as marriages. I guess that is what happens when you wait so long to find someone."

He wasn't going to take her words to heart. He knew it was just conversation and facts.

"I can't keep track anymore," he said.

"Let's see if I can. J.B. was the last of last year. So far this year, we've got Penelope and Griffin's son, Micah, in February."

"I've seen him a few times. He looks just like Griffin."

He'd been hearing all about it too since Griffin was to Eli as he was to Egan.

"Bode and Sam's daughter, Gemma, was born in March

right after Kaden was born. Next month Hudson's twins will be born. Then we will be hit with three weddings almost back to back and Carson's twins in the fall."

"A busy summer for you too," he said.

"It seems it with the weddings," she said. She pulled her dish out of the box and laughed. "You got me herbs?"

"I did," he said. "I thought you might appreciate them more than flowers."

"Most definitely," she said, lifting the potted plant out. There were a few mixed in together. Like a starter garden. "I always wanted to grow my own herbs, but I don't have time to do it outside and keep track of it. Plus with the winter and all, they wouldn't last."

"You need them in the house on the walls. That is what my mother does."

"She does?" she asked. "I've seen them on home shows too."

"It'd look good on this wall," he said, moving to the wall by the glass doors going outside. "You could have floating shelves with them outside and then bring them in as the weather changes. Even have them in decorative pots."

She was grinning at him and he felt his manhood starting to shrivel up with this conversation.

"That's a great idea. I'll have to see if I can find someone to build the shelves for me. I know my cousins are more than busy. It's not my father's thing. Not Hunter and Roark. I'm sure Skyler could do it, but I can't keep track of him half the time."

He knew Skyler was Grace's brother, but he rarely saw him.

"I can do it for you," he said. "Tomorrow, if I can get the wood at the hardware store on the island."

"I can't ask you to do that," she said.

"You're not asking. I'm offering. Again, you're feeding me all the time. It's the least I can do."

"Only if you let me make some food for you to take home tomorrow."

He laughed and reached for her, pulled her in for a hug and landed his mouth on hers.

Her arms went around his neck, their tongues were dancing together and he knew she was feeling the same as him.

"I'll accept that."

She stepped back and put her hand to her face to fan it. "Why did you kiss me before you said you'd accept food."

"Just wanted to make sure there was more heat here than the kitchen getting used."

"I'm surprised you have asked that after I joked about a ride in front of Egan."

There went the blush again on his face. "He's never going to let me live that down."

"I'm sure you two talk like that all the time," she said.

He shrugged. "Not about family or never about Blake."

Egan drew the line there and that was when Lincoln knew how serious it was. Maybe Egan was testing him with Grace, but in his mind, they hadn't gotten that far.

It's not something he wanted to talk about with Egan either.

She nodded her head. "I'm sure you're hungry. I told you to bring an appetite."

The fact she didn't bring up anything about going to her room or "rides" told him she was probably just joking and he wouldn't push the issue.

"I'm always hungry," he said.

"Good," she said. "Come in the kitchen. I'm making fried chicken sandwiches. Tell me what you don't like."

"I like pretty much anything," he said. "I said that before."

He saw the chicken pounded out in a bowl, what looked to be flour or other things to bread it. He wasn't sure, as he didn't do much cooking.

There was an avocado along with some shredded cabbage in a bowl and a sauce he couldn't figure out. But it was creamy.

"Do you like heat?" she asked.

She was picking up the chicken, running it through flour, then eggs, then held it over two bowls while she waited for his answer.

"I do," he said.

She ran it through a coating of something that had flakes of red in it.

"Good," she said. "Me too. It won't burn your mouth and I'll make sure I counter it, but heat is nice."

When she had two large pieces of chicken covered, she put them in a pot of oil, then turned and started to toss the cabbage with what looked to be some vinegar and sugar and a few other things he wasn't sure of.

The avocado was sliced, and she glanced in another pan on the stove with oil, then started to pull out what appeared to be homemade potato chips.

"You went all out," he said.

"It's only lunch," she said. "We make a sandwich like this at The Retreat, but I'm using my own spices and sauce. I like the heat."

He was guessing there was some heat to the sauce too and maybe the other items would cool it off. He wasn't sure and didn't care.

Especially when she laid big thick butter rolls on a grill pan to get some color on them.

While she was cooking and moving around the kitchen, he asked. "Did you have plans for tomorrow?"

"Only if they are with you," she said.

"It seems Egan is giving me two days off a week now. Not saying we need to spend them together."

"It's fine if it works out," she said. "To me this is no different than a Saturday and Sunday for normal people."

He laughed. "I've never had a normal Monday through Friday job."

"Me neither," she said. "That doesn't exist in the restaurant industry."

Within another five minutes, he had a plate in front of him filled to the brim and looking like something he would have gotten out to eat at a fancy restaurant and not in a home kitchen.

Then he had to remind himself that Grace ran one of those fancy kitchens.

"Can I ask you something?"

"Of course," she said. "Eat up."

"I will. With your training why are you making meals like this for me?"

He picked his sandwich up and took a bite. The heat of the spices dancing on his tongue, the slaw and creamy avocado cooling it off.

"I don't always eat fancy food if that is what you're talking about. I enjoy it, but I'm just as happy having something like that."

She bit into hers. He tried not to laugh. "Most would look at you and think you don't eat much at all."

"I'm a pig on my days off," she said. "Because when I'm working I get maybe one meal a day. The rest of the time is spent tasting my food and that isn't much. Not to mention I sweat a lot and burn it off."

"I've got a really good metabolism," he said. "And I don't eat three meals a day."

"I think most people don't," she said. "I can see where you don't have time so you eat at least one big meal."

"I've done that for years. When I go home to visit and get three meals a day I almost always put a few pounds on and have to come back and work them off."

Her eyes lifted to his and then over his arms and chest. "What do you do to work out?"

"I lift weights mainly," he said. "I got all my running out of my system in the service. I like to swim, but there aren't a lot of places to do that. I wouldn't mind kayaking if I had one or being out on the water doing anything else."

"Me too," she said. "I've got a paddle board and kayak, but I'm on the wrong side of the water for that. Skyler faces Plymouth and the water is calmer. I tend to drive over to his place. I keep my stuff stored there too. He's not around much."

"Maybe we can try that sometime," he said. He didn't want her to think every time they were together it was only going to be her cooking for him.

"I'd like that," she said. "In a few months. Or at least kayaking next month. Though if you aren't getting in the water it's not a big deal."

"As long as it's not raining, I'm good at any point," he said.

"It's going to rain tomorrow," she said, frowning.

Which told him she wasn't keeping their dates from anyone.

"So I saw. I tend to watch the weather some the day before."

"Do you have to reschedule a lot?" she asked.

He had five bites into his sandwich. Massive bites that left only half so he put it down and went for some chips.

"Damn, is there Parmesan cheese on these?"

"There is," she said.

"If you bagged these up I'd never buy anything else."

He ate four more and, while she was chewing, she walked away from him and then came back with two more large potatoes and set them down. She took a bite of her sandwich after she turned the burner back on.

"I'll make you some more to take with you."

"You don't need to do that," he said. "I didn't say it for you to cook more."

"I know. But I might as well before I clean up. It doesn't take long."

She was eating and peeling the potatoes after she'd set up a bowl with water and ice in it.

"What are you doing?" he asked.

"Watch and learn," she said.

He couldn't help but do that for the next ten minutes while they both ate and she cooked at the same time.

The potatoes were peeled, then sliced thin on some machine that had him holding his breath she didn't cut her fingers while she moved it quickly over the blade.

The slices were put in ice water to soak, then patted dry before they were dropped in the oil.

By the time the first batch came out, his plate was cleared and he was stuffed.

When that batch was done, she had them in a bowl with salt and Parmesan cheese. Then she repeated another batch.

"It doesn't look like a lot of work, but I know it is," he said. "You just make it look effortless."

"Thanks," she said.

Family Bonds- Grace & Lincoln

She set them aside when they were done, her lunch plate empty too.

"Let me help you clean up," he said. "Or are you going to slap my hand if I come to the other side of the island?"

"Nope," she said. "I'm all for equal opportunity helpers."

He stood up and took both their plates, then went to the sink on the other wall. She had one on the island, but he was positive she didn't use that to wash her dishes.

He rinsed and wiped everything she brought to him before he loaded it in the dishwasher and within twenty minutes her kitchen was back in order.

"Thanks for lunch," he said.

"Thanks for coming to lunch," she said. "We've got all afternoon. The question is, what are we going to do with that time?"

"Play a game?" he asked.

She laughed. "Is that what we are calling it now?"

"We can call it anything you want," he said.

She moved over into his arms and pulled his head down for a kiss.

15

IT WAS WORKING

When Grace opened the door the next morning, she was stunned to see Lincoln backing his truck up to her garage and shouting out the open window, "Open the door so I can bring this wood in without getting it wet."

She didn't expect that he'd actually build her the shelves. She'd thought it was a joke. Or at the very least he wouldn't do it the next day.

But here he was with wood in the back of his truck and what looked to be a saw next to it.

Since she knew it was going to start raining soon, she ran back in and hit the button for the garage door to open and he backed the end of it in.

"Let me help you unload it," she said.

"Nope," he said. "I've got it. You just make sure you know where you want this. I've got enough wood to put outdoor ones up for you too but not today."

"You don't need to do this today," she said.

"Yep," he said. "I've got the saw, so I'm going to at least

measure and make the cuts. I rented that when I got the wood."

She wanted to argue with him, but it wouldn't do much good with him at this point.

He hopped out and she watched his muscles flexing as he moved the wood around and found her body heating up.

She finally snapped out of it.

She'd found it hilarious that he'd actually wanted to play a game yesterday afternoon.

It wasn't the game she *thought* they'd play, but she had a deck of cards and the next thing she knew they were playing poker.

She'd never laughed so hard getting her butt beat at anything before.

But they'd talked about his time in the service and how this was what they did to pass the lonely hours while they waited for calls from home.

He only talked about his parents calling him, but she often wondered if there was a girl. One that he wanted and never got?

He'd mentioned being burned so it had to be when he was in the service, she was sure.

She walked back to her living room and started to remove the art from the wall so that he could measure for her shelves.

When he came in a few minutes later, a tool belt on over his faded jeans, she thought she was going to dissolve into a puddle of mud.

Was this some kind of joke to get her so worked up that she'd be stripping for him in order for him to look her way?

It felt as if she was doing all the work to get this relationship going and wasn't sure why.

Though he was here and had no problem coming back so it was working.

By the way he was kissing her yesterday, she knew he was turned on. Was he just trying to be a gentleman? Or was it because of her relation to his boss?

She was guessing that was more of it than anything else.

Though he did clean her kitchen with her. He talked so openly about his parents and helping them out.

She'd been attracted to him before without even knowing him as a person.

Now that she knew more about him, she realized what a great caring person he was.

Not just one that served his country but one that had respect for his parents and women in general.

Her mother would be eating this up.

"This is the wall," she said.

"How big do you want it?"

"How big can you go?" she asked seductively.

There went the blush to his face again. Now this was a game she could get on board with.

"I can cover the whole wall if you want," he said.

"Damn, talk about impressive," she said, her eyes dropping to his crotch.

"You're killing me, Grace," he said.

"Good," she said. "The feeling is mutual. Just answer me this, what are you waiting for?"

"You," he said.

"How much clearer do I have to be?" she asked.

"Clear enough to ask and not joke, assume, or make innuendos," he said. "A guy can't take any chances and I don't want to mess up."

She stopped for a second and realized everything she'd done had been hints and jokes. Innuendos.

He was right.

She wondered if this went back to him talking about being burned.

She wished she knew more.

She'd never been one to shy away from anything before and wouldn't now.

She moved closer to him and grabbed his hand. "Before you get all sweaty building my shelves I want to get you all sweaty in my room."

She pulled him across the living room and toward the stairs without saying another word.

All he did was laugh and she took that as an answer enough.

When they got to her room, he asked, "Are you sure?"

"Very. I think you wore the tool belt as the final tease."

He slowly started to unbuckle it, his eyes never leaving hers. "I'd swing it around in a dance for you, but then if a tool came out and broke something I'd have to fix it."

She burst out laughing.

This was the Lincoln she'd been waiting for. The one she'd seen joking with Egan for years. Or heard he was like.

"It's about damn time. It took you long enough."

"No comment," he said.

"That's right," she said. "No more talking. At least not right now."

His tool belt was removed and laid down, then his shirt came up and over his head. "Oh my. You've got a tattoo."

If she'd known that she might have creamed her panties. She was close to doing it now.

"One of those things I did in the service."

"I'd ask if it was a drunken dare, but it's huge."

It was some kind of tribal symbol or lines or pattern that went over his left chest, his shoulder and down his arm a few inches that his shirt covered up. When he turned she saw more on his back but not as much as his chest.

"Not a dare," he said. "More a memorial for my family."

It wasn't the time to ask what that was about, but she'd do it another time.

When she could think and not drool.

When he was reaching for his jeans, he stopped and looked at her. "Keep going," she said.

"Are you going to catch up? Maybe you've got something to shock me too."

She grinned. "Not like that," she said.

Her shirt came up and off. Might as well remove her bra too and his eyes were landing right on her tiny boobs.

Nothing on her was big. She was used to it and didn't care. If men didn't like that she didn't have much more than barely size B boobs, they could shove it. She'd had some tell her with all her money she should enhance them.

Nope, not for her.

The minute his hands went for the button of his jeans, she did the same.

They both dropped everything at once. Yep, he was impressive there too.

There was a lot of muscle on him, but she was only looking at one.

"Shit," he said. "I didn't expect that." His eyes went to her lady parts.

She was bare as could be. "It's easier," she said. "Like shaving my legs. Do it daily."

He picked her up before she could say another word and had her on her back on the comforter.

She thought he might at least kiss her, but he went right for another set of lips to taste.

She wasn't complaining in the least.

Actually, she was screaming because he didn't hold back his attack and went right for her swollen bud, pulling it in and sucking hard.

Two fingers followed and the orgasm hit her so hard in the chest that she was gasping for air.

He kept up the assault until the muscles in her abs actually burned and she realized she'd been lifting her hips up and clenching to get closer to him.

When her hips went back on the bed, she let out a breath she'd been holding and it felt as if her whole body relaxed with a sigh.

"Don't go to sleep," he said. "I had to get that over with because something told me you were going to be done the minute I slid in."

"Oh yeah," she said. "I would have been." She opened her eyes and saw him covering his cock with a condom. "I still might."

"I'll get you there again," he said.

Rather than enter her, his mouth went back to her heat. Her eyes crossed when he started to suck again. Had to be his go-to move and she was completely fine with that!

Her hands went into his hair and held his head in place.

"Lincoln," she said. "I could let you do this all night, but I want something else."

"You'll get it when I'm ready," he said.

She loved this take-charge guy that was finally showing himself.

She was pretty sure a gush of fluid came out of her on those words too. She'd never been one that liked to be told what to do or controlled, but this sure the hell felt different.

When she was squirming on the bed, he moved back and she thought, finally, he's going to give me what I want.

He didn't though. He just moved his mouth up her stomach, her ribs and then latched onto a nipple.

"This is a new form of torture."

"Good," he said. "Because I need to taste these as well. They are perfect."

"Small," she said.

"More sensitive this way," he argued, then pinched her other nipple while he sucked on the one he'd found first.

She was squirming some more and letting out a few mortifying squeals at the same time.

It was as if he knew she was pretty much all but done and then he slanted his mouth across hers and entered her at the same time.

Now that was what it felt like to have your body sigh over something.

Her hips lifted once and then twice, but she couldn't keep up with him and it was as if he didn't want her to.

"You wanted a ride," he said. "You're going to hang on and get it."

Her and her big mouth.

But it was so worth it.

His hands went to her ass, cupping her cheeks while he kept her in place and all but slammed into her at the speed of the helicopter battling through a storm.

Her squeal turned to more shouts, he had a bunch of grunts mixed in, and then everything in her just lit up and burst into flames, tensing, squeezing, clenching him as she spun in circles and crashed to the ground in a glorious landing.

It wasn't two seconds later that he was lying on top of her, their bodies unmoving of everything other than throbbing between her legs where she felt him coming too.

His breathing was as labored as hers. Her hands went up to his back and came in contact with sweat.

She started to laugh and he leaned up to look at her.

"Sorry. You really worked up a sweat."

"You said you wanted me to," he said. "Only doing everything you asked for."

She frowned and then started to laugh. "Aren't you just so special and funny at the same time?"

"I've been called worse," he said, rolling off of her. He was standing next to the bed. "Is that your bathroom through there?"

"Yes," she said. She was still trying to process if he was joking or not with his last comment about being called something worse.

When he came back out, she was partially dressed in her bra and underwear.

He was reaching for his jeans and underwear on the floor. "Are you okay?"

"Yes," she said. "How about you? You did most of the work."

"You did all the yelling though."

That boyish grin was on his face. The one he always had before they started to date.

"Are you good now?" she asked.

"Sure," he said. "Why?"

"Because when I said it took you long enough, I meant I finally am seeing the guy I was drawn to before. Not that I don't enjoy the one I've been getting to know, but I'd been hoping you weren't holding something back."

"No," he said. "Or yes. I don't know. Probably a combination of trying to wrap my head around all of this."

They continued to get dressed. "Because you never thought you could get where you are?"

"Probably," he said. "I never let myself think it. Then next thing I know you're pushing me along with Egan."

Not what she wanted to hear. "I don't want you to feel pushed."

He moved closer to her and pulled her into his arms. "In a good way," he said. "It truly is. If you hadn't done it, I'd be admiring you from afar."

"And wishing you could get all these yummy treats I'm giving you."

"The food is a bonus," he said. "What I got now is what I've been thinking of for longer than I care to remember." She laughed. "I don't mean that in a bad way."

"I know what you mean," she said. "Attraction can be a powerful thing. I've been holding onto this for years." Her hand went to her mouth. "Oops. That slipped out."

He leaned back and looked into her eyes but didn't say a word.

It was probably for the best.

16

COMFORT OF HOME

Lincoln was in the garage cutting the wood for the shelves that he'd build inside and the ones for the outside he'd leave here for another day.

Even though her patio was covered, it was better to wait for a nicer day than to do it today with the wind and rain coming down in buckets.

He had a lot of thinking to do as it was.

Grace had no problem calling him out over loosening up.

He was almost embarrassed over it until she let it slip that she'd been thinking of him for years.

He supposed that helped somewhat.

When the last piece of wood was cut, he went in to see if Grace wanted these stained or painted. It hadn't occurred to him before to ask that.

She was baking in the kitchen and his mind started to wander like never before.

He'd always prided himself on being able to focus in any situation.

Put him in the kitchen with the scents of chocolate chip

cookies and he was transported back in time to a kid with his mother baking all those homey things and a feeling of comfort covered him like a warm Sherpa blanket on a snowy day.

"Hey," she said, turning. "Did you need something?"

"How about one of those?"

"They are for you, so take as many as you want. I'll be sending them home with you too."

He moved closer and pulled one off the sheet pan she'd taken out. He popped it from one side to the next before it went in his mouth, the chocolate pulling away.

"I taste peanut butter too," he said, shutting his eyes.

"I always add peanut butter to my chocolate chip cookies. Like a double dose of yumminess."

"Shit yeah," he said.

He finished off the first one and reached for another, then caught the smile on her face.

"You've got chocolate on your lip. Let me get it."

She reached up with her hand and caught it, then wiped it off. His hand caught hers. "You're not who I thought you'd be."

She lifted an eyebrow at him. "Good or bad?"

"Both," he said. He didn't expect her to be almost nurturing and didn't want to insult her by saying that.

Most of his life he was looking for this.

He wasn't being sexist. He just wanted the comfort of home.

He'd left for a better career and life than his parents had. He just never thought he'd be the type to go to college.

He wasn't a fan of sitting in a classroom and never saw himself working in an office.

The service called to him and his parents supported it.

It wasn't good enough for Lara's parents. It wasn't the life a lot of women would want.

It's not that he wanted a woman at home waiting on him. He just wanted someone who wanted a *home*.

A place that was theirs. Where they could relax together and make memories.

He hadn't realized it was going to be so hard to find that though and Grace was the last person he expected to see parts of it from.

Then he had to tell himself that was stupid.

She came from a family where the bond was tight.

"You might need to explain that to me," she said. "But I can see you don't want to and I won't push you now. Was there another reason you came in or was it the smell of the cookies?"

The fact that she even knew that about him was something too.

"The shelves," he said. "Do you want them stained or painted? I can install them today and we'll be able to take them down to finish them. I guess I should have asked that before."

"Hmm," she said. "I didn't think of that, but I know you have to at least put something on them, even if it's a clear stain. What do you think?"

He looked around her house. The trim was white, which wasn't common in a house this old, but she'd said she'd had work done and his guess was that was changed throughout the house.

"You could go white like the rest of the house, but I think keeping it to its natural color will add some warmth. Not that you don't have warmth here."

She laughed. "I know what you are saying and I agree.

So a clear stain is good enough. I'm sure I can handle that myself."

"I can do it," he said.

"I'm trying to figure out if you want to do the work for food or you are doing the work because I'm feeding you. As if you need to even things out."

His head went side to side and he snagged a third cookie. "Does it matter?"

"It does," she said. "If you're doing it to be nice, that's great. That is the reason I'm cooking. I enjoy cooking and it does feed my ego well to see people enjoy what I put in front of them."

"Maybe it does the same for me to help out," he said.

"If that is the case then I'll take it. But for no other reason. We both know I can call someone up and hire them to do these things."

"And wait months for it to get done," he pointed out.

"How about I help do the stain," she said. "I'd like to be able to put my stamp on it."

He liked the sounds of that better. Like his parents used to do things together.

He knew he was getting way ahead of himself and had to pull back on the throttle.

"We can tackle that next week," he said. "I'll pick some up."

She sighed. "I'll order it," she said. "And have it delivered. I'm going to look for pots to put on the shelves too."

He nodded his head. No reason to argue with her.

He grabbed a fourth cookie and went back to the garage. Her timer went off anyway so she was turning her back to deal with that.

An hour later, the last shelf was in place on the wall inside and he stood back to look it over. The wall was ten feet in length as it was just a side wall that was bumped out from the kitchen. There were three shelves centered, eight feet in length starting from four feet, six feet and then eight feet. She had ten-foot ceilings so it was perfect.

She was standing back and looking at it finished. "I think I'm going to order a little table to put against it too. I could place plants on the table. This could be my greenery wall. I'm not sure why I never thought of it before."

"It will look great," he said. "It won't take me long to get the shelves up outside the next time the weather is nice."

"I'm going to have so many herbs I can't wait."

"As long as I get to taste some of them," he said, smirking.

"Of course," she said. "How about that beer now?"

"I'd love it," he said, "but I want to return the saw since the rain stopped for the moment."

"You'll come back for dinner?" she asked.

"I will," he said.

He gave her a quick kiss and left to bring the saw back.

When he returned about thirty minutes later, there was a beer poured waiting for him and she had a glass of wine in her hand.

"Come sit and relax now," she said. "If you're going to do any more work it's going to be in my bedroom."

He laughed. "Gladly.

"I'll feed you first and then you can thank me there."

He took the beer out of her hand and followed her to the living room and took a seat on the couch. She went to the end and turned to tuck her feet under her after kicking off her sandals. Birkenstock like Egan wore. He held the laugh in.

She was in navy leggings and a green and navy T-shirt. There wasn't a speck of food on her for all the cooking she'd done for him today and she hadn't been wearing an apron either.

"Are you always so clean when you cook or bake?"

"Not usually," she said. "At home I'm not as rushed as I am working. I know you and others have said I should take a day off, but cooking for pleasure in my kitchen at my leisure is like having a day off."

He never thought of it that way. "Makes sense," he said. "When I'm flying for work, we have a schedule to keep. I can push the speed when the weather is nice. When we are doing tours we don't do that."

"Hard to admire from above if you're whizzing past it."

"Working for Egan is the first I've gotten to fly at a speed that wasn't in a hurry. Now, it's nice. Not that I take the helicopters out and just fly around for the hell of it. That would be wasteful."

"But I'm sure you could if you wanted to."

Egan only did it a handful of times without him and had a woman with him on a date. Blake was the last time it was done.

"It's not the same," he said. "I don't own it. I wouldn't ask Eli to borrow his Lamborghini which costs only a fraction of one of the helicopters, so I'm not going to ask Egan to take a helicopter on a date or for a joy ride."

"But you two must have done it together," she said.

"Sure," he said. "That's different."

That was when Egan was showing him around or they were planning out the routes of the tours and testing them.

"Tell me about your tattoo," she said suddenly.

"That was a big shift."

"Could be I was just warming you up," she said, her foot extending out and landing on his lap.

He ran his hand over her toes and had her yanking it back.

"Are you ticklish?"

"Isn't everyone?" she asked.

He shrugged. He didn't think he was, but it'd never been put to the test either.

"My tattoo isn't anything special. Not like a huge hidden meaning."

"You said family memories," she said.

"That's right. When I went into the service I got it as a reminder of what is important in life. I like the design and I didn't get it for people to look at it and know what it meant. It's for me."

And it was over his heart where his family and love belonged to those who cared for him.

For those who put him first in their life and didn't use him.

Being used was worse than anything, and in the end, he realized that was all he'd been to Lara.

It was an embarrassment for him to admit that to himself half the time, let alone to anyone else.

Maybe it was a copout or an excuse for him to keep it hidden away, but it was hard for him to accept he was nothing more than an escape from her parents, when in his eyes they weren't that bad as much as she just wanted to do what she wanted and when.

Who the hell didn't as a teen? But he was respectful enough to know rules had to be followed in life.

Lara never felt the rules applied to her.

"As it should be," she said. "There is one thing about you that no one could dispute."

"What's that?" he asked.

"You're far from obvious or ordinary."

He laughed. "I'd say the same applies to you."

No way did he expect to find what he had about Grace when he agreed to their date.

That she was everything he was looking for...only she came with the baggage of being out of his league and he wasn't sure he'd be able to move past that fully.

17

MEET ALL THE QUALIFICATIONS

"How come you're here alone?"

Grace fully expected that question almost two weeks later when she walked into Duke's for her cousin's wedding. She didn't expect it from her brother though, as it was the first time she'd seen him since she started to date Lincoln.

She wasn't surprised Duke shut his restaurant down to the public and had it transformed for his ceremony and reception afterward.

There were all sorts of places in the family the wedding could be held, but there were times in life when you had to do what felt right to you.

This was in Duke's heart and Hadley understood that.

Wasn't that what everyone wanted to find? Someone who understood them.

"Because it's not as if I've been dating Lincoln long. He has to work. He's covering for Egan who is here today. And how did you find out?"

"A lot of people know," Skyler said. "But Mom told me a few weeks ago. How come you didn't?"

"Do you tell me everyone you're dating?" she asked.

"No," Skyler said, grinning. "But I haven't dated anyone seriously in a long time."

"Which breaks your mother's heart," her father said. "Both of you are more focused on your careers."

She knew Skyler was just out trying to make his mark in the world too.

If any of them might have felt slighted over not getting part of The Retreat, she was sure it was Skyler.

Roark and Emma went their own route, with the law and being an author. Roark followed in his father's footsteps, Emma in her mother's.

Hailey went into law, Hunter had The Retreat, and Grace was passionate about food.

Skyler owned a few bed and breakfasts on the island, had multiple rental properties all over the island, Cape Cod and Boston and even bought her grandfather out of his half of a hotel in Cape Cod that Duke's father, Kyle Raymond, co-owned.

As close as she was with her grandfather, Skyler was equally because he had that love of tourism that their grandfather had.

And speaking of her grandfather, he moved over and joined them at the table. She wondered who the fifth person was as they were at a smaller table.

"There is my girl," her grandfather said. "What is this I hear from your mother that you've got a boyfriend and he's not here?"

She coughed on the water she was drinking. She wasn't sure she'd call Lincoln her boyfriend.

Though he did meet all the qualifications of it in her eyes.

They'd spent both Monday and Tuesday together again

this week. Both sets of shelves were stained and installed, there were pots and herbs inside for the moment. She'd put some outside when the weather got a bit nicer. She'd grow her collection in time.

"As I was just telling my brother, Lincoln is working. You'd have to take it up with his boss."

She said it loud enough and turned her head to catch Egan laughing at her. He was two tables over and stood up to join them.

That was what she got for opening her mouth.

"I wasn't aware Lincoln wanted to come," Egan said.

"He told me he had to work and I didn't bother to ask him to rearrange things, knowing you'd be here."

She'd let Lincoln and Egan work that out on their end.

There was no reason to ask and make him feel bad. But maybe by not asking he thought she didn't want him here.

She wasn't sure when life got to be so complicated about these things.

"Sounds like a communication issue," her father said.

She squinted one eye at her father.

"We communicate just fine," she said. "It's only been a few weeks. You all know him anyway. It's not like he's a stranger."

"We don't know him as your boyfriend," Skyler said.

She wanted to growl at her brother but didn't. That would just put more attention on the situation.

Though many knew her to be that way when she was annoyed so she might be able to get away with it.

"Can we put the attention on the couple getting married today?" she asked.

"Sure," Egan said. "Do I get cookies if I let Lincoln have the next family wedding off?"

Since she'd like Lincoln to be with her for Carter's

wedding in a few weeks, she figured it wouldn't hurt. "I'll even let you put a request in."

"More than cookies it is," Egan said. "That waffle breakfast sandwich. I still have dreams about that."

"You're too easy," she said.

"My future wife thinks so too."

She turned her head to see Blake at the table with Egan's parents, brothers and Bella. No kids here today since it was a night wedding. They probably needed all day to get the restaurant in shape and she was guessing it'd be closed tomorrow to put it back to its normal condition.

"You might need to go back to your future wife," her mother said. "If you want her to make it to the altar after saying that."

"She loves me like this," Egan said. Egan leaned down and whispered in her ear. "You are the best thing to happen to Lincoln. Don't blow it."

Great, just what she needed on her shoulders and she wished she knew why on top of it.

"What did he just say to you?" her mother asked.

"Nothing. He's being funny like Egan always is," she said.

No reason to let her family know what was said.

They'd want to know more and she didn't have much to offer them other than the past two weeks they'd spent their two days off together and planned on it again this coming Monday and Tuesday.

She enjoyed their quiet days at her house. She was going to see if he wanted to stay the night Monday.

It'd be nice to go to bed with him next to her, wake up and she could cook him breakfast.

He'd mentioned doing something too, but they hadn't figured out what yet. Something on the island.

"Egan can be serious too," her father said. "He just says it in his joking manner."

Which was too close to the truth.

"Skyler, I might stop over Monday or Tuesday with Lincoln to go kayaking. Can we borrow yours so he can go out?"

"Sure," he said. "I might just have to be around when you come over."

She let out a sigh. There was no reason to argue with him about this.

"You do what you have to do. Nothing is set in stone."

She was saved by the fact that it looked as if the wedding was going to start and everyone stopped talking about her new relationship with Lincoln.

Maybe if she was lucky, it'd be out of the way so she could convince him to go with her to Carter's wedding in a few weeks and they'd be left alone.

When dinner was being served, Duke's twin sister, Kelsey, came over. "How come you're by yourself?"

"It was kind of last minute," she said.

"Yeah, but I need more eyes on you and less on me," Kelsey said. "Today has not been fun for me."

Kelsey was laughing and Grace understood that statement. "Been there and done that with my cousins before me. At some point, eyes are going to shift your way with those questions."

"And I'm going to keep dodging them like Superwoman," Kelsey said, her arms moving as if she had gold bands on her wrists.

The two of them laughed while Kelsey moved away.

And by the end of the night, when more than five people made their way over asking if it was true about her dating Lincoln, she was positive she got her wish to get this out of the way before the next wedding.

18

FOOLISH MISTAKES

"It's going to be a nice day," Lincoln said when he climbed out of his truck around one.

They'd just come from Grace's house. She'd had lunch ready for him when he showed up, they ate, cleaned up together and now were going to spend some time kayaking in the bay.

"It is," she said. "I've been looking forward to doing this since we talked about it weeks ago."

They both had shorts on. Grace had a long-sleeved shirt and he had a T-shirt. It would probably be cooler on the water, but they'd be moving.

"Is your brother here?" he asked. Lincoln didn't see a car in the driveway, but that didn't mean it wasn't in the garage.

"I don't think so," she said. "He's probably in his office."

"I didn't know he had an office," he said. Not that he paid much attention to things. He knew Skyler had a ton of rental properties and was part owner of a hotel on the Cape. Things that he'd heard recently more than anything.

"Just a small one," she said. "He's got two staff there, the rest all work on the properties he owns. He has an assistant who deals with calls and any issues with the properties and someone who does payroll and pays bills. He's always out and about more than anything checking on properties or talking to the guests at the B&Bs, trying to run them. Sometimes he's there working them if he's short staffed."

"Like cleaning rooms?" he asked.

"No. He has a company he hires for that. I think he had staff at one point, but it was hard to keep them. I've gone and cooked for him before at the B&B's when he was in a bind."

"I'd come back again and again if I knew you were cooking there."

"It doesn't happen often," she said. "Not in a few years. He's got people on backup or if his cooks are out, he orders from Duke's or other places for them. Family-style meals. He makes it work."

Just like he was finding most in the Bond family did.

They had more money than Lara's family ever would and no one in the Bond family was afraid of hard work or getting dirty.

"Just like most people do," he said. "Where are the kayaks? I'll get them for you."

"I can handle it," she said. "I might be small, but I'm tough." She was flexing her muscles with a grin. "At least that is the reputation I've got in the kitchen."

"Which surprises me since you don't seem that way at home."

"Leisure cooking is different," she said. "I'm not striving for perfection at home. At The Retreat, I expect nothing less."

He frowned and followed her to a shed in the back. She had a key and opened it.

"Mine is the yellow one. Skyler's is red and you can use his."

He grabbed the yellow one out for her and handed it off, then returned to get the red one and set it down. The paddles came out next.

He wasn't going to argue with her about carrying it to the water. She'd only fight with him, he was sure.

"Do you feel the pressure to have to do so well to show that you earned the job and it wasn't handed to you for being a family member?"

"I do," she said. "I can say in life that nothing is free or nothing is handed to me, but very few believe it."

"Have you had guys you've dated in the past feel otherwise?" he asked.

"If I talk about my past, you have to talk about yours," she said in a singsong voice. "Are you willing to do that?"

"To a point," he said.

"Then the answer is yes," she said.

She walked to the end of the dock and put her kayak in. She'd had her vest on already and he'd grabbed one when he was in the shed. He was a strong swimmer, but he wasn't going to be stupid either. Anything could happen on the water just like it could happen in the sky.

"Tell me," he said.

She easily got into her kayak and he did the same into the one he was using, adjusted the paddle to his arm length and the two of them were off. He'd follow her to where she wanted to go, but she was staying close to the shore.

"It started in school. Girls only wanted to be friends with me once they realized who I was related to. I never felt I could trust them and their reasons. They always wanted to come over and do things that I had. Maybe go places with me. Vacations or concerts. Skyler and I were always allowed to bring friends places if none of our cousins were there."

"I could understand that," he said. "Trust has to be earned."

"It does. I don't give it easily. But because I always doubted people's intentions that might have driven some true friends away too."

He'd never thought of it that way. "We all think we know what is right until it doesn't work out the way we thought it would," he said.

"And I'm sure you're not going to elaborate on that."

"Not much more than foolish mistakes of the youth," he said.

"I don't buy that," she said, "but I'll let it go for now."

He laughed and adjusted his sunglasses some. She had a pair on her face too. The sun was bright, but he loved the feeling of the heat on his body.

"Go on," he said.

"From friends to boyfriends. Boys thought the same thing when I was younger. As I got older it was more about what I could bring or give them."

"They thought you'd buy them things, like a sugar mama or something?"

She burst out laughing and almost lost her paddle. "God, no. That is a funny thought. I mean, I think some of them thought we'd go on trips and stuff and maybe I'd pay for it all, but I wasn't doing that. I paid for an equal amount of things. I don't keep score, but I'm not going to be the one doing it all either."

"No one should," he said.

"Yet you've been paying for everything," she argued.

She was still annoyed he'd paid for all the supplies for her shelves. He didn't need her money and told her that.

"You pay for all the food you cook me," he said. "And we know you buy good ingredients."

She let out a sigh. "I won't argue there. See. I can be reasonable despite what many think."

He hadn't seen any part of her that wasn't, but he didn't work with her either.

He supposed in her position, not just being a family member trying to prove herself, but just a woman in her field, she had to climb more walls than men.

"You seem it to me," he said.

"What I meant about bringing this to the table was exposure or job opportunities. Those in culinary school with me looked at it as an open invitation to a job."

"Which you wouldn't do," he said.

"No. Even if they were worthy of it or good, they could find their own job like I was."

"Not to be mean, but I'm sure many didn't think you found your own job."

"You're not being mean but truthful and it was said. But I didn't hit the ground running with my job at The Retreat. I spent several years working my way up. Hunter and my Uncle Charlie aren't stupid. Family or not, you don't put an inexperienced person in a five-star hotel and resort."

Which went back to her family not taking the easy way out of anything.

"Not to mention all those celebrity weddings held there."

"It's not only celebrities but wealthy people who carry a lot of clout and can get our name out there more. The food is just as important as the atmosphere. I wasn't letting my family down there."

"But those you dated didn't see that?" he asked.

"No. As I got older, even before I was running things, I

still had responsibilities. I worked a lot and mainly nights. Always weekends."

"Those not in the field wouldn't understand that," he said. "I do. It's part of my job."

"That's right. So that was one obstacle. But many were willing to overlook it because of my name."

"How nice of them," he said drily of the strange faces of men who dated his girlfriend.

Then he wondered when he started to think of Grace as more than someone he was dating.

It didn't seem to matter other than he was going home next weekend for a visit with his parents.

He wouldn't ask her to join him. He knew she had to work and couldn't get time off easily on the weekends any more than him.

He wasn't put off she didn't ask him to go to the wedding a few days ago. She'd brought it up in passing, he said he had to work and then it was dropped.

He appreciated that she didn't put pressure on him to say no, but then Egan mentioned it and he knew damn well things could have been switched around for him to attend. It was one flight since it was a night wedding.

It was better this way in his eyes though. She'd told him how their relationship was the talk of the wedding and he knew how things went in their family.

The fact he wasn't there might have gotten it out of everyone's system for him to attend Carter's wedding. Egan already told him yesterday he was going before Grace could ask him.

He figured Grace would bring it up today or tomorrow since Egan told him how the conversation went down.

No reason to be annoyed over it either.

"Your sarcasm is creating waves in the water," she said.

"But I felt the same way. So that was another thing to get past. Then let's add on the fact that I live on an island that many don't want to move to. Puts a wrinkle in relationships."

"It does," he said. "I could move to Boston and still work the same as I am easily. I like it here. I don't want to leave it."

"Good," she said. "I'm glad to hear that. Not that I'm thinking of anything more than I'm glad to hear you like it here."

He smiled. "I know what you're saying," he said.

"The last big thing I dealt with was men I dated wanting to know why I was working for someone else. That if I owned my own business I could come and go and do what I wanted. Hire who I wanted to work for me."

"Owning your own business is more responsibility if you ask me," he said. "I see it with Egan. As laid back as he is, he still has to deal with things that I wouldn't want. I like showing up and filling the schedule and going home at night with no stress of payroll or getting customers."

"Exactly!" she said. "I leave that to Hunter. Nothing is easy, but this allows me to focus on what I enjoy. And when I'm not cooking, then I can relax with a sexy pilot that I can't wait to see naked soon. I don't have to have my brain filled with things to improve a business because I don't own one."

"But you'll have businesses come to you at some point," he said. Might as well get it out in the open.

"Sure, I will, but I won't do much with them. I think it will fall on Skyler when it gets there. Or there are six of us grandkids. My mother is one of three kids. All those businesses that my grandfather has, some are in his kids' names with him already. I'm not worried about those things. To me, there are plenty of others to worry about it. Hailey, Hunter, Roark and Skyler are at the top of the lists. Emma and I, we are doing our thing."

"Good for you," he said. "Everyone should be able to do that."

"They should," she said. "Oh crap. And there is my big brother over there on the dock."

They'd paddled some and then turned to head back. "Should we stop and say hi or keep paddling past him and make him wait until we are ready to be done?"

"I say make him wait," she said, laughing. "It's not like I don't have something for him."

She'd brought food that was in his truck that she was going to leave for her brother. He could appreciate that she thought to do that before they left.

They paddled back toward Skyler's house, moving along the dock where Skyler stood with his hands in his pocket.

"I'm just following your sister," he said, smirking. "She calls the shots."

Skyler laughed. "She might make you pay for that later even though she'll be happy you're letting her do it."

He looked over at Grace and saw the frown on her face. If she didn't have sunglasses on, he'd bet she was squinting on top of it.

He was only joking and being himself and he'd take his licks for that if it came to it.

But twenty minutes later when they returned, Skyler was sitting in a chair on the dock waiting still.

Lincoln got out of the kayak first and pulled it onto the dock, then turned to help get Grace's out of the water.

"I brought you food," Grace said to her brother.

"Sweet," Skyler said. "You two having a nice day off?"

There was no need for introductions. He and Skyler knew each other.

"We are," he said.

"I heard you built my sister some shelves," Skyler said.

"After I had to twist her arm," he said.

"I fed him," she said. "It's all he'd take."

"My sister doesn't accept help from many. Almost no one outside the family," Skyler said.

He wasn't shocked to hear that. "I'll count myself as lucky."

"You should," Skyler said, then turned to Grace. "What did you make me?"

"Asshole," she said, giving her brother a shove and sending him off the dock.

When Skyler surfaced, Lincoln wasn't sure which one of them was more shocked over that move.

He held his hand out and helped Grace's brother up. "Do I want to know what that was about?"

Skyler laughed. "My sister showing she doesn't like my interference. Good thing I left my phone on the chair."

"Maybe you should keep your opinions to yourself too," she said. "I don't need you scaring anyone else away."

This was news to him.

Grace stepped away carrying her kayak and he turned to Skyler. "You're not easily scared are you?"

"No," he said.

"Good. Don't let her push you away."

Maybe Skyler had actually done all of that for his benefit?

Was it possible this family was all that accepting?

19

STATING A FACT

"I'm so happy you're home," Lincoln's mother said to him on Saturday morning as she slid a plate of pancakes in front of him and topped his coffee off.

No one-cup coffeemaker here. His parents drank it out of the pot and had several cups each morning.

He was guilty of the same. He hadn't noticed at Grace's that she ground her own beans until he'd gotten out of the shower on Tuesday after spending the night, and he'd smelled that over the food.

"Me too," he said. Though he knew he might miss Grace he had to tell himself that was nuts.

He didn't see her on the weekends. She was probably at work already and would be home after ten tonight. She worked until after ten last night too.

"It was nice of Egan to force you to take a few days off. Wish you didn't have to leave on Monday though."

His mother knew he had Tuesdays off, but by staying this long he couldn't bring the helicopter and had to drive.

"I need to get Egan his car back."

"Why did you drive that over your truck?" his father asked. "Is there something wrong with it?"

"No," he said. "Egan was just saving me from putting my truck on the ferry and being locked to that schedule coming and going. His Range Rover sits in the parking garage most times anyway. He said it wasn't a big deal. I had to leave my helicopter in Boston anyway so when my last flight was done, I just drove here."

He saved an hour by leaving from Boston. The five-and-a-half-hour drive was bad enough, but once he got out of the city he was cruising pretty fast.

He'd arrived at his parents' at midnight and it worked in his favor to not have much traffic.

"That was nice he let you do that too," his mother said. "He seems like a great boss."

"He is," Lincoln said. "An even better friend. I'll get back Monday afternoon and since I'm off Tuesday, my helicopter will stay in Boston so I'll just fly over when he returns to the island. I've got to get there around one or I'll be stuck until after seven when he's done for the day."

He'd like to get back home early afternoon so he could spend some time and the night with Grace.

It's not like he could have asked her to come with him even if he wanted to. His mother would love it.

First he had to tell his mother about his girlfriend and get her up to speed.

"How has work been?" his father asked. "Sounds like you're keeping busy. Busy enough it's been hard for you to come home."

"I am," he said. "When it was just the two of us if I wanted to come home I could take a helicopter for a quick trip. Now that there are other pilots, someone is using my aircraft when I'm off."

"I'm sure it's nice to just have a set day off a week now," his mother said.

"Two days," he said. "Every Monday and Tuesday. I'm on call those nights but most times don't get a call."

"Oh," his mother said. She was still cooking more pancakes and he hadn't even gotten halfway through the stack in front of him. He loved it. "You didn't say you had two days off. I hope you didn't get cut or anything."

His parents were always worried about those things. Maybe because they were hourly employees and every hour they didn't work was a dime they weren't paid.

"I'm salary," he said. "No worries. I still put more than my time in."

No reason to tell them that there were days he'd be in the air at six in the morning and not back home until ten at night. Sure, he'd have some hour blocks of time in between, but that never meant anything. He could easily fit a trip in there to the island or back if someone called and someone almost always did in the Bond family.

"We are so proud of you and your hard work," his mother said.

"We had so many worries when you took this job," his father said. "That it might not be stable. You could have found a job in law enforcement. There is a need for your skills."

He finished chewing. "I know," he said. "I like this better. I had a lot of years where it was life or death. Where I saw or saved lives." Even took them, but he didn't talk about those things with his parents. With anyone.

"I told your father that," his mother said. "You needed to find a career that was fun."

He laughed. "I'm not sure many people think their jobs are fun."

"But you do," his mother said. "Now you just have to find a woman to accept that."

Which was the opening he needed. "Actually," he said, "I've been dating someone."

"You have?" his mother asked. She finished with the last pancake and set the plate in front of him to help himself. She'd grabbed one to eat and continued to drink her coffee.

She never ate until her men did. He'd always felt bad about that, but there was no arguing with her about it.

"I have," he said.

"Tell us about her," his father said.

"Her name is Grace Stone. She's the head chef at The Retreat."

"You've got to love the chef part," his mother said. "You do look as if you've been eating well."

He coughed on his bite of food. "Are you saying I look like I'm getting fat?"

He was working out a bit more than normal, but his clothes all fit the same.

It's not like he ate Grace's cooking all the time.

Monday and Tuesday and she'd send him home with leftovers. Then one day during the week, normally Friday when she went in later, she'd drop off some breakfast for him and Egan in the morning. Or something they could have for lunch.

He loved it when Egan wasn't there to get any and he'd bust his boss's ass with a picture of it and then a picture when it was all gone.

"No," his mother said. "You look great. Just that you look healthy."

"Huh?" he asked.

"You know I hate all that fast food and processed stuff you eat. It shows on you when you put that crap in your body. I've got a bunch of food to send you home with, but maybe you don't need it."

It was the sadness in his mother's voice. "I always need my mother's cooking," he said. "You better send it with me."

"Because of Grace's job, she couldn't come with you?"

"No," he said. "Maybe once you're out of work we can see if we can fly here one day when you're both around. She gets Monday and Tuesday off too." He saw his parents look at each other but did not say a word. "And since I'm not working it might be hard to take a helicopter for the day too. It'd take some planning, but we'll see."

He was sure maybe Grace could switch a day off but then he'd be working and if he took it off, someone would need his helicopter, so again, no. Not happening.

The days of flying home might be out the window at this point unless it was at night and they flew back first thing in the morning before work started.

That could work. He'd have to think about that one and his parents would be home too. Possibilities were always there.

Then he had to ask himself when the last time was that he planned *this* much in his life.

"You'll make it work," his father said. "You always do."

"Isn't The Retreat owned by the Bond family?" his mother asked. He'd talked about the island for years. His mother always loved the story about love at first sight and fate between Malcolm Bond and Elizabeth Rummer.

"It is," he said.

"That's a pretty prestigious job. Is she older than you?" his father asked.

"No," he said. "She's three years younger than me or thereabouts." He wasn't one to count months to be exact.

"Is she a relation to the Bonds?" his mother asked.

"She is," he said. "Direct from the line that owns The Retreat. Her grandfather is Steven Bond. So her first cousin is Hunter who runs The Retreat now."

"Ahhh," his father said. "And how do you feel about that?"

"What is there to feel?" he asked. "It's a fact and not something to change."

"Who approached who?" his mother asked.

He looked up from his plate where his head was down stabbing the last bite of pancake, then put a few more in its place.

"She did me," he said.

"You're okay with that? With everything?"

He expected all of this. "Since we are dating, I'd say yes."

"Don't get snippy with your mother," his father said.

"I'm not," he said. "Again, just stating a fact."

"What does she know about you?" his mother asked.

"A lot. I've lived on the island for years. I'm best friends with her cousin. Most of the family knows me and has met me."

His parents knew that Mitchell and Janet Bond all but took him in like another son. They accepted him for who he was and his mother loved them for it.

His parents had visited the island three times since he'd lived there. Always over the summer, taking a week off and staying with him. While he worked, they explored the place he called home.

The first time Janet found out his parents were on the island she drove over and introduced herself, told his mother what a wonderful son she raised and then invited them to a cookout at their mansion.

He'd thought for sure his parents would feel out of place, but they acted as if they were comfortable as could be.

Janet was good at making people feel that way.

Most of the family was, he reminded himself.

Which was how he was slipping from dating to a relationship in his mind.

Based on what Skyler said on Monday and Grace's reaction, she was feeling it too.

But they were going to take it at their pace.

She'd said a lot about her past with dating, but he never got the opportunity to give his side and was happy about that.

He was pretty sure she wouldn't let it slide too long though.

"That isn't what I meant," his mother asked. "Does she know about Lara?"

"No," he said. "It's in the past. I don't tell everyone my dating history. Least of all someone from high school."

He was so used to giving himself that line of bullcrap that he almost believed it himself.

"This is different and you know it," his father said. Guess his parents didn't believe it though.

"I ran into her mother the other day in the store," his mother said.

He let out a sigh. "I hope she at least walked the other way rather than saying something nasty to you."

"I can handle myself," his mother asked. "I asked about Lara."

"Why?" he asked.

"Because she all but cornered me and it was the right thing to do. At one point you two planned on getting married."

He snorted. "I doubt it would have ever happened."

He'd learned that fast enough.

All he'd been was an outlet for Lara to escape what she

considered controlling parents. But he was positive Lara would have caved and gone to college, probably met another guy that fit her image. Or gave her a way out of town that she wanted so badly.

He was her ticket out and when it didn't work the way she wanted then he was the enemy.

In his mind, the fool.

Not many want to admit they'd been a sucker to the current woman they were with.

"You don't know that," his father said.

"I do," he said. "She didn't love me, only the idea of what I represented. A way out."

There was no way Lara could have handled his life in the service. It wouldn't be posh enough for her.

Not that he wanted things to happen the way they had, but sometimes fate just stepped in and gave you a punch to the gut.

"What was that look for?" his mother asked.

"What look?"

"You just had a half smile on your face. Why?"

"I did?" he asked. He hadn't realized it.

"You did. Are you thinking of Grace? Do you have a picture of her you can share at least?"

He pulled his phone out of his pocket, found a picture he'd taken of her in the kitchen on Tuesday while she was cooking. She was laughing when he said he needed it because he planned on telling his parents about her.

He thought for sure she might be worried it was moving too fast, but she only joked that it was about time since her entire family knew and was questioning her at the wedding.

Then she joked he'd be by her side for Carter's.

That was her way of asking. It was just assumed and he'd go with it. No reason not to.

He wanted to see her all dressed up anyway.

"Here," he said, handing it over.

"She looks small," his father said, moving out.

"Very pretty," his mother said.

"Yes to both," he said. "She's funny. Most times. She has a bit of a temper on her."

That he'd finally witnessed on her brother's dock.

Well, not really the first time. Their first date at her house he'd seen a bit of it too, but she'd reined it in.

He didn't mind it one bit. He didn't want to be with a woman that had no backbone.

"I thought most chefs did," his mother said, handing his phone back.

"Could be," he said. "But she's had to prove herself a lot. She doesn't want anyone to think her job was just handed to her."

"Sounds like someone else we know that has had to prove a lot of his life," his mother said.

"Yeah," he said. "We understand each other...for now. It's early yet."

"Don't talk yourself out of being enough," his father said. "You've done that too much in your life."

"Not much I can do about that fault then is there?" he said, grinning.

"Sure, there is," his mother said. "Just stop being a stubborn fool."

His mother had a temper on her too and turned her back to go to the kitchen after that.

20

GET THE JOB DONE

"How are things going, Tracy?" Grace asked on Saturday morning.

She came in early. There was no reason not to. There was a wedding this afternoon she had to get ready for and make sure everything was exactly right. The wedding was later tonight and they had time, but she wanted to check in on Tracy who was still working on room service in the mornings. But she was actually plating the cooked food to bring up now.

"It's going great," Tracy said as she put the finishing touches on the Eggs Benedict, then wiped the plate clean fast and efficiently.

"And school is good?" she asked.

"It is," Tracy said. "I made a friend. I think you know though."

She grinned. "Ashley?"

"Yes," Tracy said. "She's nice." Tracy was talking quietly like she always did. Her head was down and she was still shy but a hard worker. "I know you asked her to come over and introduce herself to me."

"I did," she said. "She's family."

"She told me," Tracy said. "Family of sorts."

"Family," she said again. Chelsea French had custody of her younger sister and Roark took the teen in as if it was his younger sister and treated her as such from day one. "She's spent some time here too."

"She told me. And that she's going to culinary school. Just two years."

"That's right," she said. "I was happy to convince her to do that. She doesn't work here during the school year. Her sister and my cousin have said no working other than babysitting."

Ashley did babysit Ben and Jack a lot and several of the other cousins who had young children at times.

"That's nice," Tracy said. She wondered if she shouldn't have said that.

"Once she graduates, she'll be in the kitchen with you," she said.

"Oh," Tracy said. "She didn't say that."

"She probably assumed you knew. And you're doing a great job. I'll be here tomorrow and I'd like to put you on one of the stations in the morning to prepare some of the orders."

"Really?" Tracy asked, lifting her head, a bit of hope for a change in her eyes.

"Yes. You're doing a great job in the few weeks you've been here."

She'd been told Tracy was faster than most of those in the kitchen, eager to learn and to work hard.

"Thank you," Tracy said.

Grace walked away after nodding her head and went to check on the preparations for the wedding. She'd be working in the kitchen soon enough, but most of her time would be spent on the wedding rather than for the restaurant.

"How are we doing?" she asked Matt. He was one of her executive chefs and he'd be working with her all night. She trusted him more than she did most.

"It's all in line so far," Matt said. "Other than some snootiness."

She let out a sigh. Matt could be worse than a woman at times. "Who?"

"It's nothing," Matt said.

"If it was nothing you wouldn't have brought it up," she said firmly. Matt could cause drama and she was going to nip it fast. She wished he'd just get to the point rather than play this game. But this way he could go back and say he was asked rather than him being the one who brought it up.

"Beth is annoyed that she's not working the wedding today. She's made more than one comment about it."

Matt's voice was low even though the two of them were off to the side. Matt was butchering the steaks for the dinner tonight. There was chicken marinating and fish that would be fileted next.

Everything was fresh in her kitchen even if that meant it came over on the ferry this morning. Which most of it did.

"Then she can take it up with me," she said.

Beth wasn't working right now. She'd come in later and work the restaurant when the rest of them were dealing with the wedding.

Though Beth was a good chef, she couldn't keep up the speed needed for some events. She might even get behind in the kitchen for the dinner service tonight, but Grace would be there to keep them on pace while working the wedding also.

That was when the drill sergeant part of her personality came out that many didn't like.

It wasn't that she yelled at people, but she had to raise her voice in general to be heard over the noise and keep people on track.

She liked to think of herself more as a coach with a whistle getting them to hustle. She used encouragement too, but many didn't see or remember that part.

In the end, she just told herself she had to get the job done.

"You know she won't," Matt said.

"Then that is her problem and not mine or yours," she said. "I'll be back soon to help. I've got a few things to take care of."

She needed to go back over the menu for the wedding, the staffing she had on, then meet with the servers when they came in for their shifts to make sure everything was done according to plan and the bride's specifications.

When she walked back through where Tracy was returning from doing a room service delivery, she heard Vivian scolding.

"Get over here and finish this, Tracy. Just because Grace has taken you on like a pet doesn't give you a license to take forever to deliver something. I don't want it cold."

"Sorry," Tracy said, her head down and quickly plating the breakfast, then looking at the ticket before she left. Grace stayed off to the side to see if Tracy did anything before she intervened if needed. She didn't want to make it worse for Tracy but wouldn't tolerate that treatment either. "There should be home fries with the pancakes."

"What?" Vivian snapped.

"I was looking at the ticket as I plated. They wanted a side of home fries."

Vivian marched over to the computer, punched it in and saw it. "They must have added that last minute."

Which wasn't possible, but she wouldn't say that. "I'll make them if you want," Tracy offered. "I can do it quickly if you're in the middle of that order."

"I don't care," Vivian said, whipping her head and stalking back to her station. "And if you mess them up and they are returned, it's on you. Maybe you'll learn to do your job better then."

Grace rolled her eyes but watched as Tracy quickly got a pan out, found the prepared potatoes, dropped them in the fryer to crisp them and got a nice par-cook, then put them in a pan to finish them off with seasonings.

Exactly how she'd been teaching the line cooks to do it.

She knew that no one had trained Tracy so that meant her new employee was observing and taking notes.

When Tracy finished with the breakfast, she left to deliver it.

Grace walked closer. "Tracy did a good job with the home fries just now. I didn't realize you had taught her how to make them."

She wanted to see what Vivian said. "Yeah, she catches on fast."

Not lying but not offering the truth either. "Good," Grace said. "Tomorrow I'm going to spend some time with her in the morning and then next weekend for her shifts, she's going to be preparing several of the breakfast items. Not all, but several."

Vivian just nodded her head. "Heard."

"And since she's new, I'd appreciate a little bit of patience with her the same as anyone else that is new."

"Always," Vivian said. "I'm not sure what you might have heard that made you think it doesn't happen."

"It's not always what I hear but what I see," she said. "I'm *always* watching and you'd do well to remember that."

She said it firmly, her eyes never leaving Vivian. "Got it."

"Do you though? Just because it's not always easy to find staff on the island doesn't mean people aren't banging down my door to get in here. People should remember and respect that. If one rotten apple is going to make the rest turn bad, that one's going no matter how sweet they think they are."

She could see Vivian's face turn red. She got her point across.

Nor did she miss the swear word under Vivian's breath when Grace walked away.

She'd been called worse before and would be again.

Sometimes you just had to be strict with staff because being nice didn't cut it.

When she got back to her office, she noticed her phone had a message on it. She'd left it on the desk.

She picked it up to see a text and a picture from Lincoln. He was showing her his mother's herb garden.

Home garden goals, she typed.

My mother was happy to hear about you. She's sending me home with cuttings of her herbs for you to grow from. Hope you know how because I don't.

The smile filled her face. Talk about super sweet.

She typed that she had it covered and told him to say thanks for her.

"What has you grinning like that?"

Grace looked over to see Hunter standing in her doorway. He hardly ever came into the kitchen unless he was looking for her or he wanted food.

Which normally meant searching her out if she was working.

"Just a text from Lincoln."

Hunter snorted. "Don't let anyone else see you smile like that. All your staff will realize you aren't a hard ass."

"I doubt that," she said, thinking of the encounter with Vivian. "What can I do for you?"

"The bride is nervous. She's driving everyone crazy and Marissa came to get me. She couldn't find you. The bride wants to ensure the food is set and the fresh fish arrived."

"Sure," she said. "I'll come out and calm her. I'll even put a smile on my face."

"Put one on like you just got a text from your boyfriend," Hunter said. "That will work."

"Jerk," she said.

She almost called him an asshole like she had Skyler on Monday, but while she was working, that was a no-no in her book. Hunter was still her boss.

Her brother though, the last thing she needed was him making Lincoln think that he might not be good enough. That he should be *lucky* to be with her.

She still was annoyed over that and vented to her mother.

Her mother had laughed and said that Skyler didn't do anything different than he has with anyone else she's dated and that if Skyler treated Lincoln differently, she'd be ticked about that too.

Her mother was right. There was no winning.

At least Lincoln didn't seem upset over it when they'd gotten back to her place.

She followed Hunter out of the kitchen and into the wedding planner's office. The bride was there with big rollers in her hair and not a lick of makeup on. She wanted to laugh but wouldn't.

"I'm Grace Stone. I'm the head chef here and I can

assure you the fish arrived this morning. We are getting ready to break it down for the dinner."

"Can I see them?" the bride asked. She couldn't remember her name and it didn't matter.

She looked at Hunter who shrugged. "I can't let you in the kitchen, but if you want to follow me toward it, I'll bring one of them out for you to look over."

"Yes, please," the bride said, letting out a sigh. "My mother-in-law wanted the fish and she's never going to let me live this down if it's not here or fresh. Can I take a picture in case she complains? She always finds something to complain about, but I don't want my mother to get wind of this after all the work and money they've put into my wedding."

She wanted to be annoyed thinking this woman was a bridezilla but realized that she was just protecting her parents.

"We can do a selfie together if you'd like. Then she'd know the timing of it."

"Perfect," the bride said smiling. "Thank you."

"No problem," she said, then turned to Hunter. "See, nice."

Hunter snorted. "Because you were thinking of Lincoln."

She wouldn't laugh. She couldn't. Because there was part of her that knew Lincoln might be that protective of his mother too. So, yes, she was thinking of him.

21

MEANT EVERYTHING

Over a month later, Lincoln asked Egan, "Are you ready for this?"

"I've been ready for a year," Egan said, adjusting his tie. "I hate these fuckers, but Blake said I had to wear one. At least it's not a bow tie."

Lincoln had never been in a tux before. A suit, sure. Dress whites, yes. But a tux...nope.

He'd joke about Egan owning his, but his best buddy was probably the only one in his family who didn't own more than four ties and two suits so a tux was out of the question.

He looked down at Egan's feet. At least he had shoes on, even if they looked a bit more like sneakers with the white soles. That worked for him because he was sporting the same thing. Those rental shoes weren't touching his feet.

"I'm surprised she wanted the tie more than no sandals on your feet."

Egan finished with his tie. "My mother bought these shoes and told me I'm not allowed to put sandals on my feet until the reception is done. I don't get it. We know I get pedicures all the time. My feet are prettier than Blake's."

Lincoln snorted. He had no choice. He always found it hilarious that Egan wore Birkenstocks half the time when flying the helicopter. He'd said he'd go barefoot if he could but knew the passengers might not appreciate it.

"Got to love your mother," he said.

"She kept me in line. It was good for Blake too. It's going to be a hard day for her."

He knew Blake's mother had passed away less than two years ago. Blake moved here to work for her father and brother, who she hadn't had a good relationship with.

A lot of those fences had been mended from what he'd heard and he was happy to hear that.

Family had always meant everything to him, but he knew not everyone felt the same way.

The one thing he was glad about was weeks ago he'd gone to Carter and Avery's wedding with Grace.

By then in his mind it was old news about their relationship, but there were plenty that had to come up to chat and get the scoop.

It was over with and out of the way, so today should be smooth sailing.

At least on that front. His duties as best man though, yeah, he had to give a speech. No problem. He had this.

He didn't even feel bad that he was the best man and Egan's brothers, Eli and Ethan weren't in the wedding.

Blake wanted it small, but she should know by now that nothing is that small in the Bond family.

Most of the guests today were family and coworkers. Blake's family consisted of her father, brother and her brother's family.

Even the wedding party was Lincoln as the best man,

and Blake's sister-in-law Carissa, as the matron of honor. Kaden was a ring bearer. One of the grandparents would be holding the baby during the ceremony.

"Blake will get through it with your family," he said.

They were at the casino right now and getting ready in Griffin's old penthouse suite. Blake and Carissa were next door with Janet in Eli's penthouse getting ready there.

He couldn't wait to see Grace though and looked at his watch knowing there was an hour left before guests would be arriving.

When the door opened connecting the two penthouses, he saw Janet come through carrying Kaden in his little tux. The baby was awake but at three months old probably not even aware of what was going on and not liking the outfit he was wearing.

"Someone wanted to see his Daddy. The photographer would like to come over and get a few pictures of you two together."

"They were just here taking pictures of me dressing," Egan complained. "I know that was your idea. I told him to get lost."

Lincoln had found that funny, but what did he know about weddings?

Janet sighed. "So we were told. You said you'd cooperate today, Egan."

"I will and I am," Egan said. "But I don't need someone taking pictures of me tying this stupid tie. But it's on. See?" Egan was moving his hands in front of it as if framing it so his mother could examine it properly.

"It is and you look very handsome. Both of you do," Janet said. Janet moved over and adjusted Egan's tie a bit.

"Thanks," Lincoln said.

"You and Grace are going to look stunning today," Janet said.

"All eyes should be on the bride and groom."

"They will be," Janet said. "However, the new couple is you."

"We were the new couple at the last wedding. Someone else can get the spotlight now."

"There are still plenty of single cousins here but no one that I've heard that is seeing someone, so sorry," Janet said.

He rolled his eyes and moved back when the photographer came through the same door Janet had.

Pictures were being snapped between father and son, Egan being silly in half of them and holding Kaden over his head. "Hope he didn't have a bottle recently and spits it up on you."

The minute he said that Kaden came back down into Egan's arms. "It'd be a nice decoration on my tux, but by the look on my mother's face, she wouldn't appreciate it in the pictures."

"Anything can be edited," the photographer said.

"Sweet," Egan said, lifting his son again and jiggling him to get a smile.

He had to give Egan credit for being bold.

"Both of you now with Kaden," Janet said. "Maybe Grace wouldn't mind seeing some shots of Lincoln holding a baby."

"Not subtle at all, Mom," Egan said.

"I wasn't trying to be. You both should know that by now."

Lincoln took Kaden out of Egan's hands and held the baby, Egan putting his arm around Lincoln's shoulder and them smiling.

An hour later, he found himself down in the big ballroom, standing at the altar next to Egan while they waited for the wedding to start.

Eli and Ethan both walked their mother down together.

The music changed and Carissa came down next in a light blue dress, followed by the bride on her father's arm.

When he heard sniffling he leaned forward and Egan turned to look at him. Yep, his best friend was starting to get teary-eyed and caught one tear before it escaped.

He was looking around and saw Grace, her eyes on his. He smiled and turned his attention back to the wedding party.

Conrad, Blake's father, was carrying Kaden in his right arm while Blake had her arm through her father's left.

When they got to the end, Kaden was handed to Carissa and Blake presented to Egan. "There's my girl," Egan said with a smile almost filling the room.

Everyone laughed, Blake included.

"Soon to be wife," Blake said.

"Thank God," Egan said, wiping a hand over his brow.

The officiant marrying them cleared his throat and the ceremony started.

It was short and to the point, everyone walking back down after. The wedding party and parents went off to take more pictures, some down on the beach while the guests would go to another room for food and drink so this room could be transformed for the reception.

After an hour of pictures, and Egan even taking his shoes off and arguing they were on the beach and it'd be expected, they found themselves getting ready to be announced into the reception.

Lincoln walked in with Carissa, Egan and Blake all but strutting in when they were called. Well, Egan was and, again, to be expected.

The first dance was done and everyone was seated.

When it came time for his toast, Lincoln grabbed the mic and said, "I'm not going to make this long. We are all hungry." Kaden let out a shout. "See what I mean." There was laughter there, and Janet quickly put a bottle in Kaden's mouth. "Years ago, I came to Boston with a friend. We got lost on the docks looking for a pub. I walked into Bond Charter to ask for directions. That's right, I wasn't afraid to do that."

"Best decision of his life," Egan said, laughing.

"It was," he said. "And two years ago, Blake missed the ferry and was cursing and swearing over it. Out walked Egan to save the day once again, giving his new wife a lift to the island."

"Best day of my life missing that ferry," Blake said.

There was a roar of clapping to that statement and cheers when Egan kissed Blake.

"It amazes me how those docks and this island can change so many people's lives for the better. And I know, the lore and legend and all. We get it. But the truth is, it's the newly married couple that is getting it. Their happy ever after." He raised his glass. "To many more memories."

"And babies," Egan said.

Blake rolled her eyes.

"I could finish this faster if everyone stopped interrupting me." He paused and grinned at the married couple. "Everyone raise your glass and toast the happy couple. As I said, to many more beautiful memories. When two people are meant for each other, they know it the minute they lock eyes." Blake and Egan were looking at each other and kissed almost on cue. He didn't even have to say anything else as there were cheers and clapping and he could sip his champagne and sit his ass down.

"Dude," Egan said with his eyes all glossy again. "That was perfect."

"Blake, he's getting emotional again. Did you know you signed up for this?"

Egan laughed and Blake leaned forward. "The good with the bad. One of us has to be the emotional one. It's his turn."

He felt a tingling on the back of his neck and turned his head to see Grace's eyes on his. She smiled and he winked at her.

"Looks like someone else is locking eyes too," Egan said.

"Ass," he said, but he kept his grin in place.

22

MY BLOOD PUMPING

"That was a great speech," Grace said to Lincoln forty minutes later.

The minute Lincoln was done talking, the head table got their first course and everyone else's was brought out within minutes.

Every single employee must have been working, in her mind, with how fast the food was being delivered.

Even the main course came out faster than she'd been able to do and wanted to find out how that was possible.

If it was the fact that it was staffing, she didn't see how Hunter would ever approve that many working at once, but if the price was right for a higher-end wedding, she might be able to convince him.

She'd make some mental notes to bring to her cousin next week and let him talk to Eli about it. Or let her reach out to the restaurant here at the casino to verify what she believed was the case.

Eli's reception had moved quickly too but not as fast as this. Of course Eli had a much bigger wedding so that stood to reason.

"Thanks," Lincoln said.

He'd walked over to her table when he was done with his meal. Most were done eating here too. It was her and her family, her Aunt Melissa, Uncle Noah, Roark, Chelsea and Emma. Ashley was babysitting multiple kids in Eli's penthouse with the help of two of her friends.

"I have to say you look very nice." She ran her hand over his arm.

"The same," he said.

"Look at you two dancing around each other," Emma said. "Are you going to at least dance together?"

"I'm not into dancing," he said.

"A slow song," Grace said. "We did that at Carter's wedding and we can do it again."

"We can," he said. "I'll be back."

He left when she noticed Egan waving him over by Eli, Ethan and Griffin. Janet was standing by the photographer so she was guessing that was a picture they wanted of the men Janet considered all of her boys.

"You two are getting pretty cozy," Aunt Melissa said. "Are you taking notes, Emma?"

Grace shrugged. "We are."

"Mom," Roark said, "Emma has to leave the house for more than just a family event to find a man."

"Thanks, Roark," Emma said, picking her drink up. "I don't need you to come to bat for me but appreciate it. Maybe everyone can pick on Skyler. He's older and still single."

Grace laughed over her brother getting the shade thrown at him.

Though she wasn't mad at her brother anymore in regards to his comment to Lincoln on the docks, she was still annoyed.

The two of them didn't talk about it anymore and it was for the best.

"Yeah," she said. "Pick on Skyler."

Her brother squinted one eye at her but kept his mouth closed.

Thirty minutes later, the DJ had the music playing and people were on the dance floor. She excused herself to track down her boyfriend and saw him talking to some woman at another table that she didn't know.

"Hey, Grace. I was just going to come get you. This is Roxy and Rob. Both are the pilots I work with now that live in Boston."

"It's nice to meet you," she said, shaking Rob's hand and then Roxy's. She hadn't been expecting someone so young and attractive.

Rob was with a date, Roxy not.

"Lincoln did a great job with that speech," Roxy said. "He's always been a talker."

Grace lifted her eyebrows. "Do you two know each other aside from work?"

"Oh," Roxy said. "We served together in the Air Force. He reached out to me when they were looking for a full-time pilot to see if I was interested. I'd left the service a year before him."

She'd had no clue. It had never come up.

"That's great," she said, forcing a smile. "Glad it's working out for you."

When a slow song started to play, Lincoln tugged her onto the floor. "What was that about?" he asked.

She put her arms around his neck. She was reaching up for it but didn't care. He had his hands on her waist.

"What are you talking about?"

"Your look and tone when you found out I knew Roxy," he said.

She turned and looked at him. "You never said anything."

"I didn't know I needed to."

She had to play this in her head. "How close of friends were you two?"

He laughed and leaned down to whisper in her ear. "Are you jealous?"

"No," she said. But those stupid doubts and pushing people away in her past were popping into her head.

"Could have fooled me," he said.

"You didn't answer my question."

"If you're asking me if Roxy and I dated, the answer is no. She was engaged at the time."

"But not married now?" she asked. She figured it was a good guess considering Roxy was alone and Grace hadn't noticed a wedding ring on the pilot's left hand.

"No," he said. "They called the wedding off last year."

"So you've kept in touch since you've been out of the service," she said. Lincoln had been here for a few years now.

"Not like you think," he said. "I had her number and reached out when Egan was struggling to find someone. That is when she told me they never got married. She was looking for a change and said it came at the right time. You know, like one of those fate things."

"Yeah," she said drily. "Fate."

He laughed. "Stop," he said. "We are friends and nothing more. She's never gotten my blood pumping like you. That should mean something."

"It does," she said. That statement helped somewhat.

She'd never thought she was a jealous person before and didn't know where this was even coming from.

"Good," he said, kissing her on the lips. "What do you have on under this dress?"

"You have to wait to find out," she said.

"I don't even get a hint?"

"There isn't much at all," she said and moved out of his arms when the song ended, going back to her table for her drink.

"How come you left Lincoln alone?" her mother asked.

"I didn't. I mean I just came for my drink. I thought he was behind me."

She turned and didn't see Lincoln, then located him at the bar with Griffin.

"It looked to me like you were frowning while you were dancing," her mother said.

"Melanie, leave Grace alone," his father said.

"It's nothing," she said. "I'm not sure what you saw."

She'd have to do better with her facial expressions too.

When she was younger she'd had that problem. People just annoyed her too easily. Probably years of not knowing who was being truthful and who wasn't.

She shouldn't and wouldn't lump Lincoln into that.

He hadn't lied to her once. She had no reason to doubt anything with him.

Just because she found something out she hadn't known didn't mean anything.

"We'd like to have Lincoln over for dinner sometime," her mother said.

"That isn't going to be easy," she said. "We work weekends when you're off. You live in Boston and us on the island."

"I don't like to invite myself to your house and have you cook," her mother said.

"But I like to do it. If you and Dad can come on a Monday or Tuesday, that will work. Otherwise, it's going to take some flexing of schedules. The summer is both of our busy times."

Her mother sighed. "Aren't you taking a week off this summer?"

"I plan on it," she said. "I haven't figured out when yet."

Maybe she could see if Lincoln could take some time off with her. A conversation for another night.

"Then your father and I can look at our schedules for a Monday or Tuesday. I'll cook at our house. You don't need to cook."

Her parents had a house on the island. They spent more time there in the summer than winter and normally came over on the weekends.

"That works," she said.

And what worked even better was hours later when she was leaving and caught Lincoln's attention. As part of the wedding party, she expected he had to stay until the end.

"Are you going?" he asked. "Sorry I've been moving around so much. It seems like Egan is high maintenance today."

"It's his wedding day," she said. "He's entitled. And yes, everything is winding down."

"Then I'm leaving too," he said.

"Can you?"

"Yep. The wedding is ending in ten minutes. There is no reason for me to stick around."

She'd stayed as long as she had because she was hoping they could leave together. A lot of people went from the wedding to the casino to try their luck there. She should have thought of getting a room, but it didn't make sense to do that when she didn't live that far away. Thirty minutes didn't seem like a big deal to her.

"Ready?" she asked when he came back.

"Yep. How about going to my place?" he asked. "It's closer and I need to get you out of that dress."

They'd been to his place a few times but for nothing more than running there to get something when they were together.

"I don't have anything to stay the night," she said.

"You don't need to sleep in anything," he said. "Or I'll give you a shirt."

"Sure," she said. There was no way she was going to tell him no with the boyish grin on his face.

She'd been thinking about getting him out of that tux for hours and did it matter whose house they were at?

The two of them left together. She followed him to his house and parked behind him in the driveway.

The minute they were in the front door, she kicked her heels off. She'd had them off most of the time under the table at the wedding. She wasn't meant to dress like this.

The off-the-shoulder black dress that fell to the floor and was loose from her hips down was at least comfortable enough.

"Can I tell you how beautiful you looked today?" he asked.

"You've said it a few times," she said, smiling.

"I want you to know I mean it."

"Now I'm worried you think I've got a problem with Roxy."

Stupid on her part.

"Nope," he said. "Not worried in the least because there

is nothing to be worried about. Just wanted to tell you what I'm thinking."

Guess he put her in her place.

"Then I'll return the favor and say I've been thinking about getting you out of this tux all night."

"Not as much as I've wanted to get out of it," he said, picking her up so her feet were hanging above the floor, his mouth landing on hers.

It took her a few seconds to realize that he was bunching her dress up in his hands as he held her and now there was cool air on her ass.

She pulled her mouth away from his. "What do you think?"

"I can't see what color it is, but I can appreciate that it's a thong. You said not much."

"It's the only thing on besides this dress."

No bra would look good in her mind and it's not as if she had much on top. The dress was lined and fit her tight enough that everything stayed in place.

"Shit," he said. He nudged her more and her legs went around his waist.

"Easy movements in this dress too."

"Did you buy it for that reason?" he asked.

"Nope. Just wanted something comfortable. I'll be more comfortable when it comes off."

He carried her to his room and all but dropped her on the bed while he stood back and started to unbutton his shirt.

His tie had come off a while ago along with his jacket.

She rolled on her stomach and pointed to the zipper and he stopped what he was doing to address that for her. She kicked her dress off at the same time he was yanking his pants and underwear down.

"It's black," he said of her lace thong.

"It is," she said. "Everything matching."

His dick was already firm and ready for action. She felt she didn't get enough of him. They only spent time together two days a week. Not even another night. Though she was normally home early enough on Wednesday, he didn't tend to be.

"The question of the night is if it stays on or comes off?" he asked.

"Off," she said, wiggling out of it. "I can't give you a ride as well as I want if it's on."

"You're going to give me one?" he asked. He pulled a condom out of a drawer in his dresser and brought it to the bed.

"Yep. Lie down," she said. "It's my turn."

He got on the bed and lay on his back, his hands behind his head.

She opened the condom and covered him, then spread her knees around his hips, guided his dick to her opening and slid down easily.

"Didn't even need to work you up," he said.

"I'm almost always warmed up around you," she said. Her hands landed on his chest, one palm over his heart and tattoo. She felt his heart racing under it. "Time for us to make those memories too."

Her eyes were locked on his. Just like when he was giving his speech earlier.

She wasn't sure she could say she ever loved anyone before. Not like what she felt when she was with Lincoln.

It was too soon to even say it, maybe think it, so she'd keep it locked up tight.

She started to ride him, using his chest as leverage. His

hands went to her hips holding her for feel alone. She didn't need the help, but she liked his hands on her body.

She was slowly moving up and down, his hands now shifting up her ribs and covering her breasts, his thumbs pinching and flicking at her nipples.

"We've made more than you realize," he said.

She nodded. She couldn't form any more words let alone thoughts when he was touching her like this.

When she was feeling him inside her body.

Her eyes shut as she continued to move up and down. When she felt his hands in her hair, she opened her eyes to look at him just in time for him to pull her down and crush his mouth to hers.

His hips were moving up and down with hers. Together with the perfect timing.

"Don't stop," she said, breaking the kiss.

"You're the only one I ever think about, Grace. Just remember that when you have doubts. That's what I tell myself."

She wanted to ask what doubts he had but didn't get a chance when he started to kiss her again.

Their tongues were dancing as fast as their bodies were moving.

She felt the sweat gathering at the base of her neck and then dribbling down her back. There was some on her chest and must be his too because the noises coming between their bodies were both exotic and erotic.

Everything seemed to just tighten at once inside of her and she wanted him deeper.

To do that she had to sit up.

She pushed away from him, arched back and put her hands on his thighs behind her.

He steadied her by her hips and just pounded up into her as she kept sitting down on him.

They were both moaning and groaning and then she was chanting his name at the time everything exploded inside of her.

He didn't stop what he was doing and it was only dragging her orgasm out even longer.

When she thought her body couldn't take a minute more of the pleasure, he was pulling her back against his chest but this time rubbing her back in a caress.

She let out a big sigh. "I'm going to be thinking of this for a long time."

"Like one of those memories we just created together."

"Yeah," she said softly and shut her eyes, then let her body just drift off to sleep.

23

HOW TO HANDLE A LADY

The next morning, Lincoln was up before Grace and that surprised him.

But he'd never been someone that required a lot of sleep. Now with Kaden born, he'd taken most of the on call after hours so Egan didn't have to leave in the middle of the night.

He was in the kitchen getting the coffee started when he heard the bathroom door shut.

When Grace came out a minute later in his T-shirt, he grinned and handed her the cup. "I don't have creamer, sorry."

"It's fine," she said. "Do you have milk and sugar?"

"Milk, yes. Sugar, not sure. It's not like I bake or anything."

He was opening up cabinets and drawers and found some little bags from a takeout order or something he must have tossed in there.

She burst out laughing and moved him out of the way to check his drawer. "There is everything imaginable in here in tiny servings."

"I do a lot of takeout," he said.

"You must like Chinese. I've never seen so many sauces in one drawer before."

"It's easy and they give you a lot. Then I've got leftovers."

"I guess I'm going to have to make you some real stir fry food next time."

She moved over and started to look through his fridge for food while she sipped her coffee.

"I don't have much to offer," he said.

"Eggs and bread," she said. "I can do something fast with that. What time do you need to get to the airstrip?"

He looked at his watch. It was seven thirty. "I've got about forty-five minutes before I have to leave. I'm sure I'm going to beat Egan there. We've got a bunch of people to fly back to Boston from the wedding. Egan is flying Blake's family over and anyone else in his family he can fit in his new helicopter."

"How many does he fit in that?"

"Twelve," he said. "I'll be using it this week and doing tours on the island while he's gone. No days off, sorry."

"Don't be sorry," she said. "I understand."

"I'm flying a bunch over too, then leaving my helicopter there and taking his back here to get the next set of people to bring back after I drop them at Logan. It won't be a long day or anything. It's mainly family. The first group going over at nine, then again at eleven and the last at one. Then I'm done for the day."

"I'll be in the restaurant so no biggie. It was nice having the day off with you yesterday." She started to crack eggs and whisk them in a bowl that she'd found. He grabbed a pan from the tray under the oven and handed it over.

"The night was better," he said.

She walked over and gave him a quick kiss. "It was."

He was glad to see the smile on her face. Her jealousy over Roxy had come out of left field.

He'd dealt with that with Lara and hated it.

Sure, they were young and had friends and parties with groups, but if any other girl talked to him and she wasn't around, she'd freak out and accuse him of cheating.

It was hard work to convince her otherwise and he often wondered if maybe she said those things to her parents and that was why they didn't like him.

No, it was where he came from that caused the dislike from her parents. None of that was ever going to change and he knew it. He just didn't understand why he put up with it.

Stupid young love and it bit him in the ass and left a lot of scars with it.

He was realizing those mental scars were a lot worse than his physical ones ever would be.

The world saw him as this hero and in his mind he was an idiot.

Breakfast was on his small table quickly, the two of them eating the scrambled eggs and toast.

"I don't know how it's possible that everything you make or touch tastes so freaking good."

He was trying not to shovel the food in but couldn't help himself.

"Years of practice," she said, winking at him.

They finished breakfast, him cleaning up the kitchen. "Sorry you've got to leave," he said.

"I've got to get home and shower and get to work," she said.

She came out of his bedroom a few minutes later in her dress from last night. It was more wrinkled than it should be, still fitted to her upper body, off one shoulder and falling to the ground. She had her heels in her hand.

"You look like you're ready to do the walk of shame," he said, laughing.

Her face was scrubbed clean, her dark hair a little messy. It's not like he had anything for her to tie it up and only a comb that he used on his hair. He heard her yelping trying to pull it through hers last night. Must be the curls and product in it from yesterday that made it not a pleasant experience.

"The fact I'm walking a little funny only adds to it," she said, moving closer and hugging him. "Your neighbors are going to love this sight. Unless they are used to it."

She said it as a joke when she stepped back and he smiled, but it brought back her comments about Roxy last night too.

Rather than address that and maybe start something, he slapped her ass and yanked her in for one final kiss.

"I'll talk to you later or tomorrow," he said.

"Bye, Lincoln."

He watched her walk out and then finished getting ready and left early for the airstrip. It wasn't all that much earlier than he'd planned, maybe fifteen minutes, but there was no reason to sit around the house either.

His rented two-bedroom cottage never felt like home to him.

He wasn't one for decorating, but he kept it clean and as comfortable as possible.

When Egan lived with him, they were like two single bachelors. He'd have to say that Egan's condo in Boston was more stylish, but having two pilots flying out of Boston now meant there wasn't much of a need for him to stay there anymore.

He was fine with that. Soon, he was sure his room would be turned into a nursery. They had a crib in Egan's room right now. He'd have that talk with his best friend at some point. He didn't want Egan to think he had any bad feelings over it. It made sense and it was Egan's place.

With Blake based out of Boston for her job, there were times they were staying there anyway. Blake would be back to work full time when they returned from the honeymoon. He knew full well she'd been doing some work while she was out, but not full time by any means.

He was pulling his helicopter out of the hangar and getting it set when he saw Egan driving in with Blake.

"You're early," he said to his boss.

"Thought I'd get set up and knew you'd be here. We can go over a few things before I leave."

"We've got it covered," Lincoln said. "It's not the first time you've taken a vacation. I can handle it."

He'd told himself he wasn't going to call his boss for anything. He tried never to reach out to him when Egan was on vacation. Most times Egan was checking in with him more than anything.

Since Mitchell owned twenty-five percent of the Charter company, it wasn't like there wasn't someone else to go to if he needed him.

"I know you can," Egan said. "Maybe I'm just thrilled to get a start on my honeymoon." Egan was wiggling his eyebrows. "Got to try for baby number two."

Lincoln looked for Blake, but she must have gone to Egan's office. He helped his buddy pull out his helicopter to get it ready too.

"Have fun with that," he said, grinning.

"Oh, I plan on it. You're going to take care of my baby this week, right?"

"Kaden is going to love every minute of my attention," he said.

"Asshole," Egan said, smirking. "I meant this baby." Egan was slapping his hand on the helicopter.

"Dude, this one is going to love me more than you too when you get back. I know how to handle a lady."

Egan started to laugh. They'd always joked the new bird was a chick that needed to be handled with care.

"So I saw yesterday with my cousin," Egan said.

He didn't want to talk about his relationship with Grace so let it drop.

An hour later, he was landing in Boston with some of the extended Bond family that lived there.

When everyone was off and on their way, he went into the office to wait for Egan, then he'd take Egan and Blake to Logan International and drop them off there to catch their flight to Aruba. He'd pick them up when they returned on Saturday.

"That was a great wedding yesterday."

He turned his head when Roxy walked in. Rob did a lot of cargo deliveries now. Mostly at night when Roxy was done and they shared her helicopter. But with summer in full swing, there were more tours and Roxy was helping out with them on Lincoln's day off rather than her flying clients in and out of the Northeast. When the fall and winter rolled around, they wouldn't have to worry about leaving his helicopter in Boston for Rob on his days off but for now he did what needed to be done.

"It was," he said. "How many tours do you have today?"

"Two," she said. "I think Rob said he'll be here around two to get a cargo to fly out. He'll be gone for about five hours. You get the boss's big boy for the week. Lucky you."

"It's the only time I've got it," he said.

Egan took one full day off a week and his helicopter didn't normally fly on those days. He knew Egan tried to give himself a light schedule other days, but during their busy season it wasn't always possible, which was why Lincoln was taking all the night calls if they came in.

"You'll get spoiled having it," Roxy said.

"Not a big deal," he said. "I'm pretty basic."

"I know that," Roxy said, grinning. "It's what I've always loved about you."

He turned and looked at her. He wasn't sure why those words surprised him, but they did.

"I don't think I could be any different," he said. "Here comes Egan. See you at some point, I'm sure."

He left to meet Egan and when everyone was off, climbed in while Egan brought them to Logan. He helped them get their luggage down, wished them well and took off for Amore Island for his next group to bring back to Boston.

Before he was ready to fly back to the island for the night, Rob came in.

"That was crazy yesterday," Rob said.

"It was," he said. "I expected it with Egan and the casino going all out."

"They spared no expense," Rob said.

He wasn't sure why Rob would think they would. "Nope. Egan's mother pretty much did it all. Blake was more laid back about it and Conrad said anything that Blake wanted she was getting."

"Must be nice to come from a family like that," Rob said. "Meredith was just in awe of it all. She told me if I have a chance to come on here full time I should take it."

He knew Rob flew for one of the hospitals. He was full time, but it was only three days a week and long shifts."

"That would be up to Egan," he said.

"Roxy seemed surprised about your girlfriend," Rob said.

"What?" he asked. "Why?"

"She didn't know you had a girlfriend. I guess I thought you two might have had something at some point and were working back toward it."

"No," he said. What was he missing? "Why would you think that?"

"She talks about you all the time. Just comments she's said about the one that got away. I thought it was you."

"We are friends," he said. "I knew her in the Air Force. I hadn't talked to her or seen her for years prior."

"I know," Rob said. "But it's the things she says. I don't know. Ignore me. I could be getting a different vibe. I just figured she moved here and all..."

"Not sure what to say," he said, shrugging. "We've never been anything other than friends and now colleagues."

"And now that you're dating Egan's cousin, she might be a bit bummed. Just giving you a heads up."

"Thanks," he said and left for home.

When did he become so clueless about women liking him before?

24

ABOUT FAMILY

Two and a half weeks later, Grace walked into her office on Wednesday morning surprised to see Hunter there.

"Hey," she said. "What brings you down here? We didn't have a meeting, did we?"

"No," Hunter said. "But I got a call yesterday afternoon that I need to talk to you about."

"Everything okay?" she asked.

The last thing she wanted to do was start her day dealing with complaints or personnel issues, but that happened more than necessary.

She could honestly say that her two days off a week were so peaceful spending them with Lincoln, but she knew that might be coming to an end. At least two full days. The Charter company was crazy busy and so was The Retreat. Already Lincoln had worked some of Monday last week to do a tour scheduled last minute. She'd been told a lot of the cargo shipments were being done later in the afternoon or at night so that tours could be added for the summer.

She was fine with it. She knew how it worked on the island.

There would be plenty of months when they could be slower.

"Yep. I want you to hear me out before you say no."

She let out a sigh. She hated it when he started like this. It meant he knew she was going to protest, but when it came down to it, it wasn't going to be her decision anyway.

"Go on," she said.

He shut the door to her office. "I got a call from Bravo. They are taping a show in California. It's a competition of West versus East wedding destination hot spots. It's about the food and the chefs initially but exposure on the locations."

"Shit," she said. "That is huge."

"It is," he said. "I'm glad you feel that way. They had a last minute cancellation and want you."

"Me?" she asked.

"Yes," he said. "Filming starts in two weeks. It's only for a week. The show will air over eight weeks but filming is done all at once."

"I know how that works," she said. She'd been asked before to be part of cooking competitions. She never wanted to. Hunter knew that.

But this was different. This wasn't just about her as a chef. This was about The Retreat. This was about family.

"Two weeks," she said. It's like that just hit her. "That's our busiest time. I never take a week off in the summer."

"You're not taking a week off. This is work," he said.

Which meant she didn't have as much of a say as she thought. "You already talked to Grandpa about this, didn't you? And Uncle Charlie?" They'd have to approve something like this. Uncle Charlie was more low-key and didn't always like all the TV stuff.

"Yes," Hunter said. "They are all for it. It's big for the island. You know my father was hesitant about everything that was done at the casino and the competitions. The magician was a big hit. So was the musician."

She knew those things too. It brought a lot of business to the island in the slower months.

"They were," she said. "It got a lot of acts booked full time now."

"You also know that Bella and Hailey had been shopping things out for reality shows on the island."

Her eyes got a little big. "Yeah," she said. "But your father hasn't been on board with that."

"He's softened," Hunter said. "There are talks now. You being in this competition will give us the push we need. Or them to see what the island has to offer and viewers' reaction."

Her jaw dropped. "Why am I just hearing this now? What's it about?"

"Because it's not public knowledge," Hunter said, smirking. "That's why you aren't being told."

"Do I get to find out what the show is about?" she asked.

"Nope," Hunter said. "Because I don't know. It's through Bravo and there are a few different ideas on the board. Just know that getting you and The Retreat out there will get more eyes on the island."

"Which benefits everyone," she said, sighing. "I get it. Guess I don't have a choice in the matter."

"Not really. Sorry about that. I know you'll do great."

"I'm going to crush it," she said. "Just wish I had more time to prepare. Do they let me know anything in advance?"

"You'll find out more. I'm going to call them back and

then Hailey will reach out right after and get all the legal documents and go from there. You'll be talking to her about it."

Hailey handled all the Bond business.

"Hopefully I'll have some answers by the end of the day."

"It might not even be a full week," Hunter said. "Depends on how long you last."

"I'm going to last long," she said, pretending shock over his comment. "Have some faith."

"I've got all the faith in the world," Hunter said. Hunter put his hands in his pockets. Her cousin always was dressed to show his name and title. "But don't put that kind of pressure on yourself either. Maybe see if Lincoln can go with you. You won't be filming the whole time. Mix it in with a vacation." Hunter would understand the pressure part of the family too. His offer was kind, she had to admit.

"I highly doubt Lincoln can take a week off on short notice like that," she said. Though she'd love nothing more if he could go too.

"Filming starts on Monday and goes through Friday. It's not a full week since he gets a few days off," Hunter said. "But that is between you two."

"Yeah," she said. "And Egan. He's got a business to run too."

"Lincoln on set with you in a Bond Charter shirt...more publicity," Hunter said, laughing.

She threw her hands up. "I'm going to assume Mitchell is aware of this?"

"He is," Hunter said.

"Which means it's already been talked about in terms of Lincoln."

She wasn't sure how she felt about that. That maybe she

and Lincoln were being manipulated for the island. For her, she got it. It was her family. But not Lincoln's.

"I know what is going through your mind," Hunter said. "It's business, but it's more. Why can't it be combined together and family is giving you both a little nudge?"

"I didn't know we needed a nudge," she said with her hands on her hips. "I thought things were going just fine. What have you heard?"

"I haven't heard anything to say otherwise," Hunter said, putting his hands up now. It was the cool-down sign he gave her. "I'm following orders like you. Sometimes things happen beyond our control and we go with them. This is a good thing. An adventure. I'm giving you a heads up about Lincoln, that's all."

She narrowed her eyes. "Whose idea was it for him to go too?"

Hunter looked around as if he might be worried he would get caught telling secrets. "Grandpa's. I think he might be concerned you'll be stressed or lose your patience during this because of the stress."

Her shoulders dropped. "And that won't look good for The Retreat. Grandpa thinks having Lincoln with me will keep me in check?"

She felt herself getting worked up over their lack of faith in her and that she needed a babysitter.

"You have been known to be on the cool side in the kitchen. We don't want negative publicity either. You're also very competitive, and shows like this, they do try to create drama. Maybe Grandpa is looking to show another side..."

She wanted to grind her teeth. "Having me there with my boyfriend who happens to work for another family business and was in the Air Force. He has medals for his service.

He's good-looking. They will see the rich girl and the hero. The reverse Cinderella story?"

Oh my God. The last thing she wanted was for Lincoln to feel like he was being used for her family's benefit. She'd never expected this of them.

"Yes and no," Hunter said. "You're making a bigger deal out of this. It benefits everyone, including Lincoln's job."

"Good luck trying to get him to feel that way," she said. This might be worse than what Skyler said to him.

"I don't think he's going to have an issue with it," Hunter said. "Don't think that. I think he might want to be there with you anyway."

"To watch out for me?" she asked, getting agitated. "Like I need security of some kind."

"No," Hunter said. "But I think I'd struggle to let Kayla go somewhere alone where she knows no one. It's nothing more than that. You're not sheltered."

"Sheltered enough," she said. "I get it. I've got a big name behind me and all. There will be a lot of eyes on me." Eyes that she always hated. "They are going to do a history on the contestants, aren't they?"

"They will be here filming next week and interviewing you first in your domain. They will want to know your personal life too. It will come up. It always does for these things. That is how it will start. I think Hailey is going to make sure that when they talk about your life and background and ties to this island, they are going to have you in a helicopter with the crews and flying over the island and the casino."

"Are the contestants going to know my ties to the island?" she asked. "My personal history?"

"I don't believe so. They won't see the filming of the

personal sides of the contestants until it's live. What people decide to share is up to them."

"This is really huge for the island, isn't it?"

"Major," Hunter said. "I'm sure Egan will be flying during that in his new baby. It won't be Lincoln."

She nodded. "I'll do what I need to do. Can I at least let Lincoln know ahead of time?"

"Give me to the end of the day to get back to Bravo and get Hailey what she needs. You know there are contracts you're going to have to sign about what you can and can't say."

"I do know that, but if you're wanting him there with me, he'll be part of it," she said.

Hunter's head went back and forth. "Again, give me to the end of the day. I think it might have to come from Egan or Mitchell for him. We'll keep you posted."

She wanted to swear but didn't. "Thanks for messing up my day."

"It's going to be fun," Hunter said.

"Says the guy that wouldn't do this if it was him."

"I can't cook worth shit," Hunter said, grinning. "It'd never be me."

"You know what I mean. I always liked not having your last name."

"I know," Hunter said softly. "I get it. But it's still who you are. Embrace it. It's not a bad thing at this point in your life, is it?"

"No," she said. Because she got the guy she wanted. She just hoped this didn't mess things up with him.

25

NOTHING TO HIDE

"What's going on?" Lincoln asked when he walked into Bond Charter at the end of the day. He hadn't expected to see Egan still here let alone Mitchell. "Am I getting fired?"

"Hardly that," Egan said, snorting. "You might be getting a raise if not a big bonus."

Mitchell shot his son a look. The one that said cut out the joking. "I'm all for that but not sure what I did to get it."

"Don't do that to yourself," Egan said. "You know you're a great pilot and an asset to this business."

Egan didn't often get serious and he was now. "Again, what's going on?"

"Come into my office," Egan said. "We'll talk there."

"You need your father with you. That's not good."

Lincoln was grinning but only because he wasn't sure what was going on and didn't want to show any weaknesses by appearing nervous.

He'd done that enough in his life and was damned if he was going to let anyone see it again.

"I'll start," Mitchell said. "If we let Egan tell this we'll be here all night."

He frowned. "Go on."

"What I'm going to say is confidential. It goes no further than the three of us in this room. When I'm done you'll know more people will be aware, but we all have to sign off on nondisclosure paperwork. Hailey is drawing everything up and we'll get it signed and sent off tomorrow."

"Hand delivered," Egan said. "I'll do it tomorrow via the jet."

That was news to him. Egan hardly ever flew the family jet, but he was a backup pilot if needed. Since it was the jet and not a helicopter it had to be far enough away.

"Hunter received a call Tuesday afternoon from an executive at Bravo. As you know, Hailey and Bella have been pitching reality shows for the island through them."

He'd known that for years. Ever since the first magician competition and then a musician one too.

"Oh boy," he said. "This sounds promising."

"It is," Mitchell said. "And what is going to happen soon will hopefully lead into that reality show. Right now, something else is going on, but it's giving us hope they are feeling the island out. They are filming a cooking competition of West Coast versus East Coast wedding destinations. It's all about the food but is going to focus on the resorts too. Good publicity."

And since Hunter was contacted that meant The Retreat.

It was then the cooking competitions hit him.

"Grace?" he asked. He wasn't aware she was interested in anything like that.

"Yes," Mitchell said. "She has no say in the matter."

"So she wasn't happy about it?" he asked, frowning again. He didn't like where this was going.

"It's not that," Egan said. "Grace has always liked that her last name was Stone and she could do her own thing. This show is going to focus on her tie to the family when it's aired."

"Oh," he said. Yeah, he knew his girlfriend wouldn't be happy over that. "Did she fight back over it?"

"No," Mitchell said. "She wouldn't. She is competitive so I don't think the show is the problem. Now that she's wrapped her head around things, I think she's on board."

He'd find out later tonight. "I'm assuming film crews are going to be here at some point to get a background on her?" he asked. Being Grace's boyfriend, he understood why he'd have to sign legal documents.

"Yes," Egan said. "Next week."

"Wow," he said. "That's fast."

"This show was already set up and it was a last minute cancellation. They called to get Grace in their place," Mitchell said.

"Wouldn't she have to have applied or something?" he asked.

"You'd think, but she didn't. We are pretty sure this is tied to Bella and Hailey and their proposals."

"Which is why this is a good thing," he said. "Got it."

"I don't think you do," Egan said. "Not yet."

"What am I missing?" All he had going through his head was the fact that his girlfriend was going to be gone for a bit. He'd get those facts from her.

Egan sat forward. "They are going to focus on her life here on the island. That is part of it. Though it's a food competition they will show The Retreat. They are also going to ask personal questions. If she's single, married, et cetera.

It will come up during the taping. We'll be flying people around, so they are going to know our family businesses have a far reach."

"So I might be on TV?" he asked, grimacing. Not what he wanted, but he'd do it for Grace and his best friend. For his job too.

"Oh, you're going to be seen," Egan said, laughing. "You're going to California with her."

"What?" he asked, his mouth opening and then closing.

"It was discussed that these shows like to draw up drama. Grace can have a bit of a temper. If you're there, maybe you can calm her," Mitchell said.

"No one is using you," Egan said quickly. "It's not that. Think of it as us giving you a week to spend time and support your girlfriend. I don't think I'd like Blake traveling alone without me. You know what happened to Laine not that long ago."

Egan was putting the guilt there and he knew it by the grin on his buddy's face.

Laine was engaged to Carson Mills, and in the fall she'd been in Chicago at a gallery showing and got into some trouble and ended up in jail. Carson woke Egan up to get him flown there and get it all sorted.

So yeah, that was popping into his head too.

"No, I wouldn't want her there alone. But...if I'm on TV, then people will start looking into me, right? Or not. I'm not anyone."

Mitchell and Egan started to laugh. "Sorry, dude," Egan said. "They already know about you. Decorated fighter pilot. Not that I lean this way, but you're also pretty good on the eyes. The viewers are going to eat you up. The producers will too. And that is why I'm telling you, we aren't using you, so don't think it."

"We kind of are," Mitchell said, shrugging, "but not in a bad way. It makes for good TV, but we aren't making anything up. Everything we are saying is a fact."

He knew that. But his past... "Egan. Someone could look into me and find out about my past."

He was looking at Mitchell while he said it. "You've got nothing in your past that is going to come back to you," Mitchell said, grinning. "You do realize that Griffin would have discovered anything that was there to find before we even hired you."

Lincoln sighed. "I know that. It's something else."

"My father knows about Lara," Egan said. "Griffin found that too. You were a seventeen-year-old kid as a passenger in a car accident. No drugs or alcohol were involved. You've got nothing to hide."

He hadn't realized that Egan and his family knew about that before he'd confessed it in one night of drinking to Egan when they'd been living together.

He supposed he should have since it was all over the local news back then. A deep enough internet search would find it in thirty minutes or less.

"Nothing illegal," he argued.

"Nothing at all," Egan said firmly.

"It doesn't mean someone might not start trouble once everything is aired."

"They don't have Hailey Bond as their lawyer," Mitchell said, smirking. "If we aren't worried, you've got no reason to be worried either. Trust me."

If there was anyone he trusted more than his parents, it was the two men in this room.

But speaking of his parents. "Am I allowed to let my family know? I hate to have them find out when they start watching this on TV."

"You can," Mitchell said. "They will have to sign the nondisclosure forms too. Right now, the main players that are going to show up on TV have to get them there first. We'll look at the schedule and get you home in the next day or so to get your parents' signature."

"Maybe bring Grace with you," Egan said. "Let them meet the girl that could make you a star."

"Asshole," he said when Egan was wiggling his eyebrows. "I'm far from a star. Don't be jealous that I might become the face of Bond Charter."

Egan grinned. "I get to pilot the crew around, not you. But I'm positive they are going to film you up in the air at some point. Maybe even with Grace. That would make for good TV."

He let out a sigh. He wanted to say none of this was what he signed up for but not much he could do about it.

"Are we done now?" he asked. "I'd like to get back to the island and talk to Grace. Does she know about me going with her?" He wasn't so sure she'd be happy that it was being forced on her.

On the other hand, it was probably a good thing since he wouldn't have to convince her to let him go or worry about rearranging the schedule.

That was going to all fall on Egan since it seemed the decision wasn't his to make.

"She was informed of everything this morning. Hunter asked her to hold off contacting you until you were done for the night as we were getting everything set. As far as I know, Hailey has all the paperwork now and is reviewing it. We'll get our copies to look over in the morning and sign, then Egan will take off for Santa Monica."

"California," he said. Across the country and not a place he ever saw himself going.

"Yep," Egan said. "Where you will enjoy a week away with your girlfriend. It might be less. They are going to film the whole competition in that week but spread it out over several weeks for viewing. If she's eliminated early, you'll be back."

"She won't be," he said. "Not if this is for family."

"She said the same thing," Mitchell said.

"Another benefit to our family," Egan said. "You get to take the family jet there and back. Making flight arrangements this short of notice is going to be a pain in the ass and more time traveling than needed."

"Grace isn't going to like having that advantage," he said.

"She didn't fight it when she was told due to the last minute addition it was a good fourteen hours of travel time going coach."

He shivered. "Yeah, not fun. The flight time has to be half that."

"About six hours," Egan said. "I'm heading over and staying the night. With the time change, we'll get there with a few hours to spare for Hailey, Hunter and Charlie to meet and hand the papers over. We couldn't get our pilot last minute for this."

Which explained why Egan was flying the jet there.

"I'll sign whatever I need to," Lincoln said. "Do you need anything else from me?"

"No," Mitchell said.

The three of them walked out together, he and Egan going to their helicopters to fly back to the island. "Sorry about dropping this on you."

"Not a problem. I'd want to be with her anyway and this avoids the fight."

"There is that," Egan said. "Race you back?"

"Like I've got a chance against your baby," he said but took off running for his helicopter before Egan.

"No fair. I can't run in these."

"Then don't wear Birks," he shouted and was lifting up before Egan could even get his helicopter started. It wouldn't matter, Egan would pass him soon enough, but he appreciated his buddy lightening the mood.

When he landed he'd shoot a text off to Grace and see how she felt about all of this and then ask if she'd be willing to meet his parents before they could form an opinion about her based on editing of the producers.

He could only hope the two of them could weather the next few weeks because he wasn't as confident as everyone else that his being with Grace was a good thing.

26

FAMILY ACCEPTANCE

Four days later, Grace found herself climbing into Lincoln's helicopter. "How are you feeling about everything?" she asked.

She was still trying to wrap her mind around everything that had been happening.

All the legal documents were signed and delivered on Thursday. Lincoln had given his parents a heads-up. They were excited for him and thrilled *they* wouldn't be on TV.

Her parents said the same thing. Her mother was happy for the exposure to the island but wanted no part of being filmed.

The fact if she won this, people would be looking into her family more would give her mother's business a bit of a lift, but it wasn't enough for Melanie Stone to step out into the limelight any more than it would be for some of her other family.

It would help her brother's businesses along with many more.

It all came down to her family and that was why she was going with Lincoln to meet his.

In the few months that they'd been dating, she started to realize that she was falling in love with him. She wasn't sure of his thoughts on the matter, but maybe this was the push they needed.

"It's fine," he said.

He'd called her the night she found out everything that was happening. Lincoln had been blindsided as much as her, but he seemed to be going with the flow better than she was.

"You're not annoyed this is being forced on you?"

He lifted the helicopter and took off. "Nothing is being forced. As Mitchell has pointed out, it's about the island and the business. It's my job."

She snorted. "It's not your job to babysit me."

He grinned and turned his head to look at her. "I don't know if babysitting is the right word."

"Sure, it is," she said. "They want you to keep me calm. So I don't come off in a negative light to give The Retreat a bad name."

"I'd like to think no one was going to come off in a negative light," he said. "It could ruin a whole business if someone in the kitchen was a jerk."

She laughed. "There are a lot of jerks in the kitchen. They aren't the face of the destinations. If their food is great, that is all the guests care about."

She knew that better than most. She never cared to get her name or face on The Retreat. She just wanted to do her best to make sure the business grew.

"I guess we'll find out," he said. "The truth is, Grace. I'd want to be there with you anyway. I would have never asked for the time off. It was too short notice."

"So it's working out in your favor," she said. "You should be happy."

He held his smile in place. "Not that happy, but I'm not going to complain about having a week away with you. You said the filming was long days, but we'll have the nights to relax."

"We will," she said. "Probably the one good thing about this."

She wanted to spend more time with him and she couldn't be upset over that.

"And you get to meet my parents. My mother is thrilled. She's been wanting to meet you."

"I'm happy to meet them," she said. "You know my parents want dinner with you too, but I'm not sure when that is going to happen now."

Her mother understood that life was just too crazy. It's not like they didn't know Lincoln.

Even her parents were thrilled that Lincoln was going with her.

Guess everyone was happy and she hoped that Lincoln understood the family acceptance of this move.

She'd wanted to bring up whether he felt used over this whole thing, but when he'd called her on Wednesday he brushed it all off as if this was exciting and he was thrilled for her and she was going to kick some butt.

Maybe that was exactly what she needed to hear without knowing. It at least relieved some of the concerns in her mind about this.

"We'll try to work it out," he said. "Egan told me we are part of the filming starting tomorrow."

"Yeah," she said. "I hate they are doing that. Like putting my personal life on show, but I get it. They said everyone will have these things filmed in case they need to use them."

"So it's not a guarantee?" he asked.

"No. They are filming all sorts of things and will piece it

together as they go. My guess is Egan flying them over The Retreat and talking about the island as a destination will be an opening for me. But the shots of you flying me might not come out at all."

She knew the longer she lasted in the competition the better chance there was of that. The only thing she was happy about was that the other contestants weren't going to know about this or her connection to The Retreat until it was aired.

She had no plans on talking about it. To her she was just another chef in the competition and nothing more.

An employee who got a weekly check.

Which she did. End of story. No one needed to know the rest during the competition.

Once it aired though, then it'd come out, but she'd be back home in her comfort place.

"Whatever happens does," he said.

"Your biggest job is to keep me calm," she said, grinning. "Think you can do that?"

"I'm going to give it my best. Tell me what works the best."

"Sex," she said. "Give me lots of that to keep my mind off the rest."

"Sweet," he said. "This is absolutely turning out in my favor."

The two of them joked the rest of the ninety-minute flight until he was landing on his parents' farm.

The house was quaint in her eyes. She saw the barn, nothing big but well-maintained.

The gardens were larger than she expected too.

"Wow," she said. "Those have to take a lot of work."

"They do," he said. "My mother loves it. Before we go in, she's worried about cooking for you."

"What?" she asked. "Why?"

"Because you're this big chef and she's a home cook."

"Please," she said. "It's your mother. And I'm not a snob."

"I told her not to make tuna noodle casserole," he said.

She started to laugh. "That was mean."

"I saw your face when I told you about Egan's reaction to it in the microwave."

"Listen," she said. "No fish smells good in the microwave."

"It does if you like to eat it," he argued.

She rolled her eyes and they got out together. They'd be flying back later today. Just a day trip.

She was never one that liked traveling for the whole day, but flying in the helicopter wasn't the same as being in the car and worrying about traffic or delays.

This was relaxing. She could understand where a job like Lincoln's would be more relaxing than stressful.

His parents were waiting outside on the deck for them as they walked closer.

"Hi," she said, moving forward. "I'm so happy to meet you."

Lincoln's mother's face lit right up and she walked closer. "Not as thrilled as we are to meet you. I had lost hope that Lincoln would find anyone that he could have a serious relationship with."

She saw Lincoln frown and didn't know the reason for that, but she bumped her hip with his. "My mother felt the same way. I'm glad I finally told myself to just pursue him. He's kind of blind when it comes to women."

"I never thought I was," he said. It was the look on his face that made her wonder what more was going on.

"You're not anymore," his father said.

"Mom, Dad, this is Grace Stone. Grace, my mother, Katy, and my father, Brice."

She moved forward and shook hands with them both. "Your gardens from above are spectacular. I told Lincoln I wished I had the space and the time to have a garden."

"Lincoln told me that," Katy said. "If you two have time, we can walk through them. I always have too much and freeze a ton to cook for later. I'd love if you would take what you want. It will do my heart well to know you are feeding my son food from my garden."

That just made her heart swell like never before. "I'd love to," she said.

They went in the house and Lincoln handed the papers to his parents and explained everything to them. She jumped in a few times when they had questions and assured them they wouldn't be on TV but since there was a chance Lincoln would be they had to cover their bases.

"They've got to make sure that if I tell you the outcome, you don't tell anyone else," Lincoln said.

"You wouldn't tell us," Katy said. "Lincoln locks things in tight and there is no way to get them out unless he wants to tell you. And if he signed something saying he won't, it won't happen. Lincoln takes those things seriously. He's loyal that way."

"Thanks for making me sound like a dog," he said to his mother.

"I think it's nice and I know those traits myself," Grace said. "But it's hard to keep things like this to yourself. Especially when you're excited. I'll admit I wasn't thrilled when I found out Lincoln was going but was happy after. I'll need someone to vent to."

"Grace is hard on herself," he said. "I've been told more than once that someone will have to talk her down."

"Who told you that?" she asked to turn to him.

He put his fingers to his lips. "No comment."

She squinted her eyes at him and when his parents laughed, she knew that there was probably no chance she was going to get an answer out of him.

It couldn't be her mother or father. They would have told her they said something.

So that left two people.

Hunter. And she didn't see her cousin saying that.

Or her grandfather. Since her grandfather flew back and forth from Boston to the island, there was a good chance Lincoln might have seen him.

She'd figure it out on her own.

When the paperwork was cleared up, she and Lincoln visited for a few hours and then flew back home with a huge crate of vegetables that she'd picked out of the garden. She loved that she was off for the next two days. She knew the film crews were coming to the island today and tomorrow would start filming. Most of tomorrow would be spent running around, but she'd cook some tonight and then more on Monday and a lot on Tuesday.

"I'll make up for you not getting food from your mother today," she said.

"She gave me a lot," he said.

"Not like she normally does," she argued. "She didn't have enough time to stock you up."

"I don't think she feels the need to do it as much since I've got you."

"Yeah," she said. "You've got me. Remember that."

She said it firmly and his smile dropped. "I know it," he said. "Why so serious?"

"Just wanted you to know it's not always about fun and games. Didn't want you to get any ideas in your head is all."

It seemed to be the time to say it, without getting too deep of a conversation.

"I could say the same to you," he said.

She nodded. "Then we understand each other well."

"We do," he said.

Though something told her that might not be the case. She'd just have to play it all by ear.

27

A HOT GUY

"I need this," Grace said at the end of the day on Monday. She and Lincoln were sitting on her beach and she was in shorts, a tank top, barefoot and had a large glass of wine in her hand. This was what dreams were made of in her mind. A hot guy and a glass of wine.

Lincoln stretched his long legs out in front of him. They were sitting in Adirondack chairs around a little fire she had by the beach. She didn't have a lot of beach space but more than enough for her.

Being on the Atlantic Ocean side, her house was sitting higher up and she had to walk down. Better for flooding during storms.

"Tell me how it went for you," he said. "Then I can fill you in on what Egan told me when he got back to the airstrip."

"It was just a long day," she said. "It's all happening so fast. I spent most of the time this weekend making sure the kitchen was in its best shape all the while cooking in it."

"I'm sure it always is," he said.

"For the most part," she said. "But this means more.

They filmed me making some dishes and talking to my staff. I had to present one of my favorite dishes to them when it was done."

He laughed. "Did they film you making the whole thing and what did you make?"

"Yes," she said. "I had to keep a smile on my face and that isn't easy. I was focusing on what I was doing since it was being filmed and in the back of my head I was hoping no one swore in the background."

She was more concerned it wasn't her that swore as she was known to do under her breath.

"I'm sure they can edit that stuff out," he said.

"No one did," she said. "And I made a duck dish. This is silly, but I used some of the vegetables from your mother's garden for them. I doubt she'll know that, but it felt good to do. And they were just so big and vibrant looking. The best I had in my kitchen."

"She'll know because I'll tell her and she'll eat that up. That was very kind of you to do."

She wasn't sure what made her bring them with her today, but she'd felt so comfortable on Lincoln's parents' farm yesterday and she wanted some of that to remind her of the joy she found in what she did. Maybe she wanted to think of the sexy pilot who cared as much for his family as she did hers. The one that tattooed a symbol of family memories on his body to remind her that she was doing this for her family.

"Now I'm embarrassed," she said.

"Don't be." He was grinning at her and she just shrugged. Nothing more she could do. "I've never had duck before," he said.

"We make it a lot. It's not often requested at weddings, but you'd be surprised what some people want. It's been known to happen."

She wanted to make sure that the dish she presented showed her skill and plating finesse. All the while she was answering questions during the lunch rush going on around them.

She'd asked to see what was filmed and they said they couldn't. That was the most frustrating part for her.

She liked to have things under her control and nothing that was going to happen would be.

"What else did they film?" he asked.

"Hunter, Hailey and Uncle Charlie were on site the whole time watching everything. Hailey is going to be a hawk. I think if she didn't have the baby, she'd want to go to California instead of you."

She loved her cousin for her fierce protection of the family legacy, but she had this and told them that. She just wished she felt more confident that they believed her.

"Your cousins can be intimidating," he said.

Grace took another sip of her wine and smirked. "It runs in our family. It's in the blood."

"It is."

"Just like you are intimidating too," she said. Her eyes were roaming over his body. Lots of lean muscles to go with his height. Though he often had a smile on his face, she'd seen the more serious side and looks too. Along with the tender ones. In her mind, the tender was intimidating to her peace of mind. "I had to answer a lot of questions. Like personal ones. My favorite foods or dislikes. Stories about when I decided this was the field for me."

"Did you tell them your dislikes?" he asked. "I'd be afraid they were doing that so they could set you up with it during the competition."

"That was my thought too. I wasn't going to be completely honest. I told them seafood."

"You live on the coast," he said, laughing. "I know you get fresh lobster and crabs daily as long as it's in season."

"That's right," she said. "I cook it well, but it's not my favorite to do. I don't hate it or anything, but I had to give them something."

"And they didn't question you? I'd think that would be a flag."

She turned her head and winked at him. "They did question me. I gave a story about hating how it sounds as if the lobster screams when you put them in the water. It *is* the truth."

The first time she'd heard it, it'd freaked her out. The lobster wasn't in pain. It didn't have a voice. It was most likely the sound of the water through the shells, but it still made her think of screaming.

She knew it was part of her job. She had to butcher all sorts of animals, but dropping live ones into boiling water just tugged at her inside.

As much as she hated showing any weakness in the kitchen—because bosses and employees were like hawks circling to find and feed off of it—that was one thing she couldn't control.

She knew if they had to cook them for the competition she was going to screech like she always did. It'd probably make for good TV on top of it.

"Trust me, I'm sure they'll do it. I'll just prepare myself for it. If that is the worst thing then I'll be fine."

Though she hated all the personal questions about who inspired her to want to be a chef. Childhood memories she had to guard too. It was hard because she didn't want her memories to be about her growing up in The Retreat, but they kept asking her questions geared toward it. She'd finally looked at Hailey and Hunter and gotten their nod to answer rather than avoid.

The worst thing to her was the fact when this was done, everyone would know she was a member of the Bond family. Not embarrassed over that. But that The Retreat won't come to her because of that stupid clause and she wondered if that would cause issues for the family. In this day and age it was sexist and they could be judged.

Hailey told her it wouldn't be an issue. That some will find it wonderful that Hailey had already found loopholes in it and if they had the reality show, that would be brought up. The changing of the tides if Hunter had a daughter or granddaughter.

In her mind, she felt some of the questions were them trying to get information not for the current competition but maybe one in the future.

Which was good for the family and the business.

"Are you nervous?" he asked.

"Not right now. I'm sure I will be. I'm not working myself up too much before we get there. That is a waste of time and energy. I was asked some questions about you," she said angling her head. She was mortified her voice had gotten a little like a teenage girl with a crush.

He lifted his eyebrows at her. "We figured that would happen. Why the look?"

"What look?"

"The one that says you didn't want to answer them or didn't know if it might be the right thing to say at the same time blushing?"

"They asked me about your time in the service. I was honest and said I didn't have much to offer. We'd been dating a few months and you've lived here for years. After you left the service."

"What did they say?" he asked.

"They pressed on some more about what you did in the Air Force. I said you were a fighter pilot. Or did search and rescue? I don't know much more."

"That's the right answer," he said, nodding his head and going back to his beer. He never talked to her about it no matter how many times it came up.

"Why don't you talk about it more?" she asked like she'd done more than once.

He closed one eye at her. "Do you want to talk about this now?"

"We are relaxing. Tomorrow is going to be another day of filming, then I'm working and we won't have much time together until we leave on Sunday. I should know more, don't you think? What if it comes up?"

She knew she was only using that as an excuse.

"There isn't much more to say, Grace. You know what I did. You can imagine the things I saw."

She sighed and reached her hand over to his. No reason to push when he took stubbornness to a whole new level. "I don't want to think of you in the line of fire. You could have been hurt or gotten killed."

"That's right," he said. "It's in the past though. It's what we signed up for and knew."

"I've seen the scars on you. You've never been shot, right?"

"No," he said. "No scars from that, but I've got a lot of cuts and bruises from training and recon and fighting."

"Some scars aren't seen on the flesh," she said.

"No," he said softly. "They aren't. And it's not something

that we need to talk about now. There are other things. Do you want to know what Egan said?"

"Sure," she said. She didn't want to change the subject, but he was right and it wasn't what she should be focused on. Maybe it was better to not know anything he went through. At least right now.

"Egan said they asked a lot of questions about the island in general. They wanted shots not just of The Retreat but also Bond Casino, the Main Street. They wanted a partial tour that we'd give. They got the whole coastline from The Retreat to the casino."

"Oh," she said. "This all sounds like I'm a contestant as a way to give them more information to decide on whatever Hailey and Bella are proposing. The whole coastline shows a lot of family-owned businesses."

"That is Egan's feeling on it. He knows more of what was proposed because Eli has mentioned it."

Though she doubted Egan knew it all. He only owned a small portion of the casino along with Ethan. Mitchell had a bigger portion.

"It's beautiful out here tonight," she said, finishing off her glass of wine and setting it down.

"It is," he said. "You need the distraction, right?"

"I do," she said. "Why don't we go back in the house and you can distract me another way."

He stood up and put his hand out for hers. "Food," he said. "I'm always hungry."

She laughed. "I can do that too," she said.

She picked up her empty glass and they made their way to the kitchen. She was trying to think of what to make. She'd use some of Katy's vegetables with dinner too.

When they got in the kitchen, she opened the fridge, but

Lincoln turned her around and pulled her in his arms. "I'm hungry for you."

"That's good," she said. "Because I feel the same way."

He moved past her to the door of her pantry, pulled out an apron and handed it over. Her confusion must have shown on her face.

"I want you to wear this."

"I don't need to wear one," she said, letting out a snort.

"But I want you to. With nothing on under it."

She started to laugh. "Now that is a way to get my mind off of what is going on."

"You're okay with it?" he asked.

"I am," she said. "And I'm going to cook that way for you too. Might as well wind you up."

She'd never done this before, but it'd be fun.

She grabbed the apron and went into the half bath off the living room, undressed down to her birthday suit and put the red apron on over it.

The cool air on her ass reminded her that she wasn't covered by anything there.

That was what he wanted though and she'd give him that. They'd see who had more control now.

When she was walking back to the kitchen, his jaw dropped as if he didn't think she'd do it.

"Damn," he said. "You're covered, but I know you're not."

She turned and gave him a shake of her ass. "Nope."

"Shit," he said. "You're not going to cook for me, are you?"

"I am," she said. "What's the matter? Didn't you think I'd do it?"

"I kind of thought you'd call my bluff," he said.

"Nope," she said. He'd learn that she was up for the challenge.

She pulled a chicken out of the fridge, bent over just right, knowing he was watching, then set that on the counter and started to look over the vegetables she'd brought home from Katy's garden.

"Fuck the food," he said, walking to her briskly. He had her trapped against the island facing away from him. "I'm going to take you just like this."

"What are you waiting for?" she asked, rubbing up against him, the feel of his shorts rough on her bare ass cheeks.

"Nothing," he said. She could tell he was lowering his shorts and then she heard the wrapper opening.

The next thing she knew, he was pulling her hips back so that she was bent over with her hands on the counter. She wasn't tall enough to actually lay her body over it comfortably and he must have realized that.

She felt his fingers go between her lower lips, find her already wet and spread it around.

"I'm waiting for you," she said, her breath catching. She'd never done this before. Never had sex in a kitchen and wasn't sure why when it'd always been the place that called to her the most.

She felt him close to her opening and then sliding in slowly. Teasing her like she'd been doing to him since he'd brought this up.

"Like this?" he asked.

"Always like that," she said, moaning.

He started to move in and out, hips going forward and back. Not big movements, not fast ones either. Just perfect.

Her eyes closed as he continued to work her up. Her mind was blank of everything other than what Lincoln was doing to her. Making her feel.

Helping her cope.

Yeah, that was what he was doing.

It was like he knew what she needed more than she did.

"I only want you to think of me," he said. His voice was deep and husky sounding. Sensual. If she wasn't bent over and getting it good right now, she'd be thinking about when that could happen just by listening to him talk in this tone.

"Always," she said. "It's all I ever do when we aren't together."

Even at work she noticed Lincoln slipping into her thoughts when she'd never let another man occupy that space in the past.

"Glad to know I'm not the only one," he said.

His hands moved from her hips, under the apron and covered one of her breasts, his finger and thumb pinching her nipple.

She let out a little screech like she always did when he applied a little bit of pain to her overly sensitive flesh.

"I love when you do that," she said.

"I love when you react to me doing it," he said.

His hips were moving faster now.

Her breath was catching.

Her body was building up to let go of all the tension of the past week. She hadn't realized how much she needed it until his moment.

"I'm so close," she said.

His hand went from her nipple to between her legs, found her swollen bud and treated it the same way as he'd done up above. Pinching and then flicking at it.

It was as if that little bit of pain down there was all she needed before she felt herself coming and moaning, her head down and her fists just gripping the counter.

Lincoln started to move as if he went full throttle in an air race to outrun enemy fire.

She was coming before him and he was trying to catch up.

The minute he slammed into her and held her still, she knew he was done. She felt it inside of her and was always thrilled she could bring that out of him.

When he stepped back, she stood up, her back a little sore.

"Now I'm really hungry," he said.

"God, I love you," she said, her hand flying to her mouth. Where had those words come from? Too late to take them back. "Sorry."

"Don't be sorry," he said, adjusting his shorts after he took care of the condom. "I've been waiting for you to catch up to me."

"Really?" she asked. She knew her voice sounded as if she was insecure. She was when it came to this stuff.

"Really," he said, kissing her on the forehead and pulling her in tight. It was a tender hug that was needed after what they'd just experienced.

She wanted to ask when he knew but then told herself it didn't matter. Because if he asked her the same question, she'd have no answer.

She didn't know when it happened, she just knew that she felt it and that was good enough.

28

SHE HAD HIM

"Are you ready for today?" Lincoln asked in the middle of the following week.

It was the third day of the competition. They'd arrived Sunday afternoon, had some time to check in and chill out. They explored the beach they were staying close by because Grace was relaxed by the sound of the water. He thought they could get some dinner and relax that night, but all the contestants had to gather and go over the rules and meet each other. He stayed in their room and watched TV.

Monday morning, all the contestants had to be at the studio by six a.m. Grace didn't return to their hotel room until seven that night, all but dragging through the door.

He'd been shocked to see her so beat and asked what happened.

Since he'd signed the same paperwork as her, she'd told him that there had been two people eliminated and right now she was in the middle. The competition had been stiff, but she was fine with it working out the way it was. No target on her back and she wanted it that way.

Tuesday ended up being two more eliminations, another long day.

He was bored out of his mind, but did his best to keep her mind off of what was going on and in a good frame when they were together.

Though there were two eliminations on each day, they were actually shot for four episodes.

He would have given anything to be home and flying around the island. But he had to be here for the woman he loved and support her.

So far he hadn't done much more than listen and give her some back rubs.

"At least it's a change of pace," she said. "I like that the competition is on the beach today. I think you can sneak down and watch it."

That had been his hope. He hadn't been able to get anywhere near her during production in the studio, but today he was going to try to be close by and see if he could catch what was going on.

Grace had said everyone had their own room, but only one other person had a spouse with them. Everyone else was by themselves.

"I planned on it," he said.

"Sorry you are just sitting here doing nothing while I'm gone," she said. "Go out and explore."

"I have been," he said. But he didn't want to use this as a vacation. What if she needed him? Or she got eliminated early on and came back looking for him and he wasn't around.

He wasn't sure why it bothered him when in the past he hated any woman that relied on him so heavily. Or at least since Lara did and he'd failed.

There was part of him that wasn't sure how he'd feel

knowing the Bond family put so much weight on him to be there for Grace. He didn't want to let another person down.

But was he really letting her down or was it that his mind couldn't separate his past teenage love from his current one?

When had he ever been so confused over something? But the fear of making the wrong decision again just weighed heavily on his shoulders.

He knew Grace felt the pressure to represent the family well and he matched that by doing his part to make sure she was in the right frame of mind.

"Just not enough," she said. "Sorry this is so boring for you. I guess I hoped you could see what was going on too."

"I'll see it all when it's aired on TV," he said.

Grace couldn't even tell her family the results each day. Nothing. He supposed it helped that she had him.

"You're more patient than I am," she said.

"I'd say you've got more patience than anyone gives you credit for. You did wait a few years to approach me."

She laughed. "You're not going to let me hear the end of that, are you?" she asked.

"Nope. Come kiss me and go kick some butt today. Do you know if two more people are being eliminated again?"

"No clue," she said. "We'll find out when we get there. After this morning though, if it's a double, then half of the people are gone. My guess is, yes, two more today, then tomorrow could be a longer day to get to the final two and then Friday is the finale. The time is going by fast at least."

"Regardless of what happens today or the outcome, I'm proud of you."

"I'm proud of me too," she said. "I never thought I'd enjoy something like this, but I do."

"Then maybe you can end up doing more competitions," he said.

"Nah," she said. "It's fun, but I miss my island."

"Me too," he said. He kissed her and sent her on her way. She'd go to the studio first, they'd be clued in on what was going on and then be driven to the beach.

He was going to make his way there after breakfast and see if he could see the setup and get as close as possible. The contestants were all encouraged to eat together and were fed at the studio when they arrived.

He was getting ready to leave when his phone rang. He didn't recognize the number but saw it was from Massachusetts and answered, "Hello?"

"Lincoln. This is Melanie Stone."

"Hi," he said.

"I hope it was okay to call. I know it's early there."

It was almost seven and breakfast was opening up at the restaurant in the hotel. "We've been up for a while," he said.

"I'm not going to ask for details. I know she's still in it or you'd be on your way home."

"She is," he said. "She left about fifteen minutes ago. I can't give you details because I don't know much other than some of the foods she's prepared and where she's placed."

"I'll get all that from her when she comes home," Melanie said. "I'm more concerned about how well she is holding up."

"Like a champ," he said. "And she says she's going to be one too."

Grace's mother laughed on the other end. The grand prize was a hundred thousand dollars. Grace didn't need the money, but she'd said everyone else talked about what they were going to do with the winnings. She'd just kept it quiet.

It seemed no one knew that she was part of the Bond

family. Or if they did, it wasn't brought up around her. He wasn't sure how anyone would find out anyway. Grace had said some of the contestants were hanging out and getting drinks at the end of the day, but a few others went back to their room to prepare.

He wasn't sure what preparing meant, but she'd been on her computer and looking at recipes and ingredients and anything else that meant very little to him.

He wanted to say he didn't need to be here, but he knew he'd want to be to ensure she was safe and in a good state of mind. He just wished most of the time wasn't spent worrying and thinking of her because he had nothing else to do.

"I'm sure she is doing everyone proud."

"You know it," he said.

"We are very happy you are there with her," Melanie said. "And we don't want you to think ill of it."

"I don't," he said. "I'm glad to be here and help in any way I can. She has it covered though."

There had been a few moments where he thought he might be taken advantage of when he was approached and then squashed it. If Grace weren't a member of the Bond family and in this competition, he would have wanted to be here but knew he'd never get the time off of work.

It worked out the way it should have and he'd like to think maybe her family was pushing more on a personal level than business. He was fine with that too.

"She always thinks she has it covered," Melanie said. "She puts a front on for many and then at the worst time that curtain is lifted and all her insecurities are there for the world to see."

Since he'd been witness to some of them in the past, he

understood what was being said. "And you'd rather it not happen on TV?" he asked, grinning.

There was part of him that was upset that so much pressure was being put on Grace's shoulders over this.

He understood how much was a stake, but it bothered him no one asked her to do this but rather told her.

He knew the family cared. They all told her to do her best and, regardless of the outcome, it was a win for the island and the publicity.

But Grace was hard on herself and he didn't like seeing her that way.

Which was why he was here, he reminded himself. To get her to not do that and try to enjoy it for what it was rather than what could come out of it.

Maybe there was another motive behind this. Thinking back, he did think there was more going on in Steven's mind when they had their talk last week.

Though Grace was doing what she always wanted to do in her life, she also wouldn't risk a chance at her island and her family legacy to get a nice boost.

It went back to the Bonds not sitting on their wealth and hoping everything was handed to them in life.

But the island also could be putting some kind of life lesson in there too. It's not as if he hadn't seen that before. He'd never been one to think much of the lore and legend...but he could be right smack dab in the middle of it too.

He should have never held back for so long approaching Grace because he lumped her in the same category as Lara.

That was him being sucked into something that he didn't have a lot of control over. Letting someone else play mind games with him when he'd said he was better than that.

"I think she does have it covered though," he said. "Only a few more days. They are filming outside today. I'm going to see if I can get close by."

"Great," Melanie said. "I'll keep my fingers crossed for her today."

He hung up a minute later and then went to get some food. He ate quickly, got a coffee to go and started to walk the four blocks to the beachfront. No reason to take the car he'd rented. He wasn't sure he'd find a parking spot anyway.

It was easy enough to see where production was setting everything up. There were signs that said no phones allowed. Not that he'd take his out and snap any pictures, but he knew a lot of people did.

He moved closer to where things were being set up and just watched. He was good at watching. He'd done enough of that in the military.

"It's going to be a hot one today," one of the cameramen said off to the side. "Hey, I remember you."

Lincoln noticed they were looking at him. "Me?" he asked, looking around.

"Yeah. The helicopter pilot, right?"

He laughed. With his sunglasses on he supposed he might get mistaken for Egan and didn't think his boss would appreciate that. Though they joked about him wearing a Bond Charter shirt here, he wouldn't do that and draw attention to Grace.

"I am one but probably not the one you're thinking of."

"No, you are," another guy said who was a few feet away. "I'm with production and editing. You were flying one of the contestants when we did the shoots early on. Grace, right?"

He had been flying her Tuesday. They'd told him they wanted the two of them in the helicopter flying over the island. That they'd use some of the shots to introduce her and the island and resort she worked for.

In his mind though, the questions they were asking and the fact they wanted him flying and not Egan said that they were looking for more of the personal aspect of it. If this guy viewed that film, he'd know.

"That's me," he said.

"What do you think about the fact that there are only two East Coast chefs left and three West Coast?"

Lincoln shrugged. "Not much to think about. My guess is everyone is good or they wouldn't be here."

Someone snorted close by. "Some got invited for other reasons."

He looked over at the woman who said that. "Don't start in on it, Susan. You know how this works and she's still in it so she has every right to be here."

Since there were only two women left, there was a fifty-fifty shot that they were talking about Grace.

Deep down they all knew she was asked not because she applied but because of the proposals. Grace just didn't want anyone to know that while she was competing. Or even while it was airing.

If it came out after the fact, she wouldn't care.

He was starting to wonder if she won if people would think it was rigged or not.

The last thing he wanted to do was bring this up to Grace though.

She had enough on her mind.

The cameraman looked at him and rolled his eyes. "There is always bickering and opinions. Everyone has money riding on the winner."

"They do?" he asked.

"Those of us filming and watching it live. Susan is just jealous because who she picked got eliminated first."

The woman named Susan walked away and he continued to watch everything being set up and hoped that he was able to stay and see Grace in action today. If not, it at least gave him something to do to kill the time today.

29

PLAY NICE IN THE SANDBOX

Grace was sweating her butt off on the beach.

At first she'd been thrilled to find out they'd be competing here in what she thought was her calm spot.

It was where she went to go and relax at home, but it was far from relaxing now.

There were five of them left. Three guys and two girls. The only other person from the East Coast was Pierre. He was in his forties and sweating as if he'd been in a sauna for five hours.

Pierre's arm went across his forehead. "Are you okay?" she asked him. They were cooking side by side and his face was redder than the lobster she was going to drop in the boiling water.

They had grills and open flames they would be using for their heat sources. She was sharing her fire pit with Pierre and since it was just the two of them, had more room.

"Yes," Pierre said in a thick accent. "Even my kitchen in Florida isn't this bad."

"I know," she said. At least she had air conditioning she could escape to or that took the edge off at home.

She picked up her three lobsters. They were given several choices of seafood and fish to prepare an appetizer, main course and side dish. She'd taken crab for her appetizer and was going to do her version of an elevated crab cake. Scallops would be added to the lobster dish and she was going to do them last in the pan on the grill. She could have taken the easy way out and selected anything other than lobster, but she didn't take the easy way out of anything.

She moved closer to the large pot, held her lobsters at arm's length, dropped them in and let out a little screech of her own.

"Are you okay?" Pierre asked her quickly turning his head. "Did you burn yourself?"

"No," she said. She was mortified she'd made that sound but knew it was going to happen. "Just got a thing about dropping them in the water."

Pierre laughed at her and then wobbled a second, suddenly looking unsteady on his feet. She hurried over to get some of the water in buckets of ice and opened the top to bring him one quickly.

Yep, they were being timed and she didn't have a minute to spare that couldn't be on her food, but she wasn't going to let a competitor go down either.

"Thanks," he said, reaching for it.

"Finish it," she said. "We need it."

She stood there and watched him drink it the same as she would have her own staff. He nodded and thanked her again, then she went back to her meal.

The time was ticking, she pulled her lobsters out when they were ready and she broke them down and then put them back in the shell on ice.

The three chefs from the West Coast were bickering on the other side over space on the grills and the fire pit, but she and Pierre were working well together. She was glad this wasn't a team competition though because she didn't think she was always someone to play nice in the sandbox.

"Five minutes left," one of the judges called.

Her scallops were in the pan and she was plating the rest of her food as she wanted them. She couldn't wait until this was done and she could take a shower, but they'd been told already they'd go back to the studio for afternoon filming. Which meant two more people would leave today.

She moved away from her plates to get her scallops and two of them looked to be slightly burned on one side. Shit. She didn't have time to start new ones either. She should have been shifting the pan around on the grill.

She plated as fast as she could and hoped it was good enough because even her plates didn't look as pristine as she could have wished.

That minute while she got water and stood next to Pierre while he drank would have gone a long way, but it was done at this point and she'd just have to see where the chips fell.

"Bring your appetizers to the table," the second judge said.

Everyone brought their appetizers up and the only other woman in the competition, Destiny, beat the two guys on her team to the table while giving them dirty looks. There were some fiery looks over that, but Grace kept to herself as best as she could.

She wasn't here to make friends and she wasn't looking to be the next TV star like the others either.

In her mind, she just had to represent for her family and she felt she was doing a damn good job at it.

When all the appetizers were tasted, she got more positives on hers than anyone else. Not one negative comment either. That made her feel somewhat safe in her mind.

But when their main dishes were presented she got a few dings for the scallops and her plating. She hoped it wasn't enough to send her to the bottom two but with only five people left, it was anyone's guess.

The judges talked and then called the winner as Pierre. She was happy for him. She even congratulated him. He walked back in line after he'd been told all the reasons he'd won and tapped her on the shoulder, leaned down and thanked her for watching out for him.

And it was Grace on the bottom with Tony from the West Coast. The judges asked if they'd do anything differently.

Tony argued he would have gotten to the fire pit faster and played dirtier as some contestants were doing that.

The shot was taken at Destiny. She wouldn't do that. She wasn't going to even make a comment about needing more time or wishing she didn't use it to get water.

She shook her head and said, "I might have overextended myself, but I wouldn't change a thing other than take my scallops off twenty seconds sooner. I stand by my dish."

The three judges looked at each other and lifted the lid and Tony's name was there. She let out a breath. She felt she'd dodged a bullet and was surprised she was so nervous about being eliminated when she wasn't even positive she wanted to be here.

Tony took his leave and the four of them were shuttled back to the van to drive to the studio. She'd seen Lincoln on the walk out. She'd noticed him in a distance before the cooking started but then put it from her mind.

He wouldn't have been able to see what the results were,

but the fact she was still with the group gave him the answers.

"I need a shower," she said when they were all buckled in. "I'm sure I stink too."

"We all do," Sam said. He was pretty quiet from the West Coast, but she knew he'd been rolling his eyes over Destiny and Tony bickering.

"Speak for yourself," Destiny said. "I'm fine and am ready to take on the next challenge."

"As long as it's in air conditioning," Pierre said, "I don't care what it is."

"I bet you it's desserts," Destiny said. "That is big now at weddings. Having more than the cake. I've been looking forward to this."

Grace tried to keep the snarl from her face. Desserts weren't her thing. She could do it, but she didn't think she was strong at it. All she could hope for was that it wasn't desserts.

Five hours later, she was opening the door to the hotel room with her shoulders dragging.

"I need a shower," she said.

"You looked great out there," Lincoln said.

"Thanks." She was stripping where she stood and Lincoln moved past her to turn the water on for her in the bathroom.

"Here," he said. "Drink it."

It was a sports drink. Not her favorite thing, but she probably needed it too.

"Thanks," she said, downing half of it before she took a breath.

"Do you not want to talk about it?" he asked.

"Bottom two twice today. How I managed to stay in it is beyond me."

"Wow," he said. "Good for you."

"I'm beat," she said. "Mentally beat. I would have gone home if Sam's panna cotta had set. But it didn't and it's the only thing that saved me. I played it too safe making a berry tartlet and knew it. I didn't want to take a risk again and run out of time like I had this morning."

"That was the only critique?" he asked.

"Yes," she said. "And this far into it, that is enough. I just hope it doesn't come back to bite me when it's aired that I didn't do something more adventurous."

Lincoln laughed. She was naked at this point and pulling her hair out of her ponytail.

"You have pastry chefs and other people who specialize in that, right? Even I know that."

"Good point," she said. "I just can't think right now."

"Go shower. Did you eat?"

"Not much," she said.

"I'll order us food," he said.

She nodded and then shut the bathroom door, climbed under the hot spray and turned it down some so that it would cool her body off.

When she was done washing up, she just stood under the cool water and let her body try to feel somewhat normal. After five minutes of that, she shut the water off, climbed out and dried off.

She'd forgotten to grab clothes but noticed that the door was open and shorts, a T-shirt and underclothing were on the sink.

She smiled and got dressed. She'd never had someone take care of her like Lincoln was.

"I appreciate the clothes," she said, coming out. Her hair was still wet and hanging around her shoulders. She'd done nothing more than towel dry it.

"You're welcome. Dinner will be here in about ten minutes. I got us some steaks. You need the protein."

She shut one eye at him. "You waited to eat with me?"

"Yes," he said. "I explored the area a bit this afternoon and got some street food to hold me over."

"Fast food," she said. "Should have figured you'd get your fair share of it here."

"Not as much as you think," he said. "They have some nice food trucks. Not everything around here is fatty and greasy."

"No," she said. "California has a lighter healthier cuisine in general."

"Sit down," he said.

She sat on the end of the bed rather than a chair. He got behind her and started to rub her shoulders and her eyes shut. "I can't tell you how good that feels. It amazes me how exhausted I am."

"It's almost over with," he said. "Two more days."

"Or one," she said, letting out a little moan. "Right there in that spot."

He continued to rub her neck until there was a knock at the door. He moved to go get their food and she went to sit at the little table in the room.

He was almost serving her like a parent would a child and she wanted to laugh over it, but wouldn't. She'd found it sweet and considerate.

Loving too.

"Eat up," he said. "Then I'll finish the massage for you in bed."

She smiled. "I'm going to let you too."

They were eating for a good two minutes when he said, "It was a nice thing you did, stopping to give your competitor water and making sure he drank it. It almost cost you by the sounds of it."

"It was the right thing to do," she said. "Him going down would have distracted me and cost me time either way. Not to mention worry. I'd never let anyone in my kitchen get to that point."

"Not as tough as everyone says you are," he said.

"I think it's more about being human. I'm not here for the money or personal fame. I hope what I've done is enough."

"Your family will think so and you know it."

She believed that, but it didn't stop her from wondering how she was being portrayed to the world.

There were times she wanted to curse and swear. Like over her scallops today.

That wouldn't have looked good. She just had to shake it off and own it.

She didn't finish her whole dinner, but Lincoln cleaned her plate for her. She found herself yawning. As much as she worked back home, she wasn't often up at four in the morning. But she was spending as much time prepping as she could before the next competition.

"I'm tired," she said. "I'm sorry I'm not much company."

"I'm going to put this in the hall and then you're getting your massage. Close your eyes and try to get some sleep. Don't worry about me."

She took her shorts off. Lincoln was pulling her shirt over her head and she didn't protest. She lay face down on the cool sheets and closed her eyes.

The minute his hands touched her back, she was positive she was sleeping rather than being worked up.

She'd make it up to him when they got home.

30

PROUD OF MYSELF

"So, I got some interesting information last night," Destiny said to her and Pierre the next morning.

Grace could tell by the look on her competitor's face she wasn't going to like what was about to be said.

The last day before they got to the final two. It should be somewhat of a light day. A half a day they'd been told because the finale tomorrow was going to be huge, even though they'd been given no clue what it was.

Since this was the first time this competition had aired, there were no previous seasons for anyone to study up on.

"What's that?" Pierre asked. She wasn't going to be baited and even Pierre had looked at her before he asked.

"That there were only supposed to be eight contestants for the show, but at the last minute they added a ninth person."

Grace shrugged. At this point she didn't care. All she knew was that someone dropped out. That was what she'd been told.

Nope, she didn't apply and she'd never admit that to

anyone. Actually, it'd been part of the papers she'd signed to not disclose that information.

"I don't know anything about that," she said. "Not sure how you found out."

"My husband was at the beach when they were setting up yesterday. He overheard the crew talking that someone was invited and had every right to still be here because *she* was good enough to get this far. Since it wasn't me that was invited, it must be you."

She didn't know if Destiny was playing with her or not. "I'm here for the same reasons you are. The same as Pierre. Not sure what your husband overheard or from whom."

It wasn't a lie. She was here to get publicity for the resort she worked at. Sure, the chefs would win the money, but the object of this was exposure to the wedding destinations on the East and West Coast.

"Did your boss put you up to this?" Destiny asked her. "Mine were contacted and applied. I didn't know the competition existed. Just trying to see if everyone else got here the same way."

It didn't sound too far off from what happened to her. Hunter was contacted, but he hadn't applied.

She looked at Pierre. "That is how it went down for me," he said. "I didn't apply personally. The owners of my resort did. This is about them, but the prize goes to me if I win. They are winning right now by me making it this far."

"The same," she said. That wasn't a lie in the least and made her feel better.

Nope, she didn't apply personally.

"Is it true that you're related to the Bond family, Grace?" Destiny asked with a huge smile on her face. "You know, the ones that own The Retreat on Amore Island. The *Bond* Retreat."

Shit. She'd hoped this wouldn't come out until the competition was completed.

"Does it matter?" she asked. "I'm the head chef just like the two of you are. We both work at highly sought out wedding destinations."

"She's got a point," Pierre said.

"Yes," Destiny said, "but Grace has a bigger stake in it. My husband did a little research on you both last night. Since I'm going to the end with one of you, might as well know what I'm up against. Once he got into the rabbit hole of the internet he found out all sorts of things. You're not just related to the Bond family, your grandfather is Steven Bond. Your uncle and first cousin now run The Retreat. Correct?"

"You know what they say, everything you read on the internet is true."

Pierre laughed at her sarcastic comment.

"It's not like you need the money," Destiny said.

"As Pierre said, the money isn't what this is about," she said.

"Everyone, gather around," one of the producers said. "We are going to get started today and then you can enjoy the rest of the afternoon."

They listened to what the next challenge was going to be. Not a meal but seven bite-sized appetizers. Seven dishes to perfect. It wasn't going to be about individual plating this time, but what looked good to the guests on a platter and could be easily picked up and eaten while standing or talking.

The Retreat had weddings and other events like this before. They specialized in them. Grace knew how this worked and hoped it played in her favor.

"Three hours for this," Pierre said. "Not a lot of time for seven different dishes."

"No," Grace said. She was trying to figure this out in her head right now. They were given thirty minutes to plan their menu and she and Pierre were sitting at the table next to each other writing notes.

"When can we see what is available to use?" Destiny asked.

"Part of this challenge is to see if you can adapt," one of the judges said, walking over while they were making their menu. "You have an idea of what we provide. There may be more or less options or variety. As you know, in a kitchen, food could spoil or not be up to your standards at the last minute."

Grace held her grin in place. She knew that more than most, living on an island. Pierre winked at her, as he knew what she was thinking. He was in the same situation.

"That's ridiculous," Destiny said. "We just send people to the store."

She rolled her eyes and got back to her menu.

"Five more minutes of planning," another judge said. "Then the clock starts."

Pierre looked at her. "How many dishes did you come up with?"

"Fourteen," she said. "I don't know what they are giving me. I've got a few in the same categories. Some hot, some cold. Fish, chicken, beef, vegetarian. You?"

"The same," Pierre said. Destiny was further away and trying to see if she could hear what was being said behind the doors in hopes of knowing what food was available in the pantry. "How many do you think she has planned out?"

"Maybe eight," she said. "I think she's cocky enough to believe what she is going to do will be there. Maybe she's playing it safe. I'm not. Not at this point of the game. I'm hoping for some surprises back there."

"We think alike," Pierre said. "Let's hope it's the right way of thinking."

And six hours later, Grace was laughing as she let herself into the hotel room. Lincoln was nowhere to be found. Part of her was disappointed, the other part happy he wasn't sitting here waiting.

She grabbed a change of clothes and went into the bathroom to shower and change. It was just after two and she'd hoped they could relax and then get a nice dinner out tonight.

When she came out of the bathroom ten minutes later, she heard the TV on and looked around the corner to see Lincoln sitting in the chair.

"Hey," he said. "Sorry I wasn't here when you got back."

She noticed the package on the table next to him. "It's fine. What did you buy?"

"Eli asked me to pick up some kind of taffy or something for Griffin. I have no idea. You know Griffin and his sweet tooth. It's supposed to be a joke and Eli found out it wasn't that far."

"That's nice. That's a big bag."

She walked over and looked inside and saw all sorts of sweets and chocolates in it. "Some is for Egan and Blake. The rest for the pilots too for picking up the slack while I was out."

"Does Roxy like candy?" she asked.

He lifted an eyebrow at her. "Everyone does. I think it's the right thing to do."

"It is," she said. "Sorry. Didn't mean to ask that. I'm not even sure where it came from."

"It's fine," he said. "You're smiling. Did it go well today or are we calling for the jet to go home tomorrow?"

She burst out laughing, "It went awesome! Pierre and I are in the final. It's going to be an East Coast win either way."

He stood up and hugged her tight. "I'm so proud of you."

"I'm proud of myself. Destiny got cocky. I think she had so much jealousy in her head and nastiness it clouded her judgment and ruined her mojo."

"Her mojo?" he asked.

She let out a sigh and sat on his lap when he returned to his chair. She'd never done this before and wasn't sure why she did it now, but it felt right to be held by this big strong man.

"Yeah," she said. "She started the day out talking about what her husband overheard at the beach yesterday. About the way one of the women ended up here. Since it was just the two of us, it had to be her or me. I'm guessing it was talk about me."

"I heard some talk too," he said.

"Why didn't you say anything?"

"No reason to distract you. I had no idea her husband was there or who he was. It's not like I've seen anyone other than you and the other contestants from a distance."

"True," she said. "Fill me in on what you heard because then her husband went back to do a check on Pierre and me and she found out who my family is."

He kissed her on the neck and squeezed her. "I don't think it was meant to be a secret."

"No," she said. "I just hoped it wouldn't come out until after the filming. I guess not having that last name helped me until this point."

"It's not hard to find out who your family is," he said.

"No, but Bond is a common enough last name. Tell me what you heard."

"Not much other than one of the workers was a little snotty about saying someone didn't belong or that they only got invited for a certain reason. It's not like she said the reason."

"But you and I both know that reason was probably the proposal for a reality show on the island."

"You're guessing," he said. "Maybe Bravo had an idea no one knows about and this is the lead-in. Could be the winner or any of the contestants could inspire them to do a spin-off show."

Her head went back and forth. "You've got a point there too."

"That's right," he said. "So don't focus on it. You deserve to be here just as much as them."

"I know, but then I got thinking maybe I'm being given a pass to get to the end. For TV or something if they are trying to get media attention for another show."

"Don't do that to yourself," he said. "Where is that confident person I always knew you to be? It's too late for you to be playing mind games with yourself on this. Whatever the reasons are that you're here, they are. All you can do is go out and do your best. It's not like it's been easy sailing for you."

"No," she said. "I won one competition, was in the bottom for two. I almost went home on one and got lucky. The rest of them I was in the upper section of contestants, but still, not like a shining star."

"You're shining now," he said. "You'll always shine to me. I hope you aren't thinking you're getting a pass because of your name."

It had started to cross her mind and she hated that happened too.

Destiny did get into her brain and she had to shove those thoughts out with a big rig and just focus on her menu for the competition.

"I'm trying not to do that again, but it happens more than I care for."

"Then let me take your mind off of it. You've got the rest of the day and night. What do you want to do, or do you have to prep for tomorrow?"

"They told us what the competition is. We've got to prepare a three-course meal for fifty people. Two smaller dishes and a main."

"Fifty plates?" he asked. "You've got to do it all by yourself?"

"I do," she said. "So that takes planning. If I sit here and spend the whole time stressing it's not going to help me. I want to shut it off for a few hours and things will come to me. I have an idea but want to let it float around some." She picked the remote up to shut the TV off and saw some crime show playing, a helicopter flying in with a SWAT officer on the side getting ready to take aim. "Whoa, did you do those things?"

He looked at the TV. "What things?"

"Did you fly like that in the Air Force?"

He took the remote out of her hand. "You need to shut your brain off, not think of that."

The TV shut off. "It's sexy though," she said, laughing.

"Don't try to get me to talk about it."

"Why don't you ever talk about it?"

"I will tomorrow night when this is over. For now, this is about you relaxing. Tell me what you want to do."

"I want to walk along the beach and feel the sand in my

toes and the sun on my back. I'm putting my suit on. I feel at peace there and that will help."

"Then that is what we will do," he said, standing up with her still in his arms. He cradled her for a minute, kissed her, then set her down and slapped her ass.

She laughed and turned to wink at him, then found her suit and changed into it. She thought maybe with her standing there naked he'd want to do something else, but he only grinned.

It was probably for the best. She needed to have a clear head and the water was the best way for that to happen.

31

GUARDING YOUR WORDS

"When are you going to tell me if you won or not?" Lincoln asked when they were seated on the Bond jet the next night.

"I can't believe it's taken you this long to ask," Grace said, bumping her elbow into his.

"I'm used to not asking questions," he said. Too many years just being told to do his job. The less he knew the better at times too.

Maybe Grace asking him that question last night after seeing a SWAT rescue on TV brought back some of it.

He was also good about compartmentalizing a lot of his life too.

Could be he was too good at it because he'd missed the signs with Roxy. Which he'd been pushing from his brain too, but Grace's question yesterday brought that up again.

"I don't want to let people know when I get home," she said. "Not even my family. Do you think that is wrong of me?"

"No," he said. "It's your choice to celebrate or mourn. I

know you, you'd be beating yourself up over it. You're happy right now so I think I know what happened."

She laughed even harder. "Then I've got you fooled and will everyone else."

"You didn't win?" he asked, shocked if that was the case since she didn't seem upset or disappointed.

"Between us, because I know I can trust you—no, I didn't. And I'm glad about that."

He frowned. "Why?"

"One, I don't want anyone to think I won because of who I am. Or if they find out that maybe I was added on last minute. I have no idea if there were supposed to be eight or nine contestants."

"Producers have the right to change their minds at all times," he said.

"That is right. It did seem as if everyone was contacted like Hunter was and asked if they were interested and to apply. I didn't have to apply and we know that." She held her hand up when he went to speak. "Before you say anything about a cancellation. I'm sure they had hundreds of applicants they could have filled that slot with. We both know that. There is more to this, I just feel it."

He'd thought the same thing. "You're probably right but it's not something you can control. Don't tell me you threw it."

"I'd never do that," she said. "I can't in good conscience. I wouldn't be able to live with myself and I wouldn't do it to make The Retreat look bad. Not only did Pierre deserve to win because he had some better dishes than me, but he could use the money."

"It was never about the money for you," he said.

"No. But a lot of chefs don't make a lot and they work

long horrible hours. He's got three kids he rarely sees and his wife is pregnant with a fourth. She's a stay-at-home mother. That money would go a long way for them. For me, it'd get invested."

Lincoln couldn't imagine what he'd do with a large payout like that.

He had more money than he ever thought he'd have. When he got bonuses, he was still stunned by the amount and did the same thing. He invested wisely.

He'd lived too much of his life knowing that tomorrow might bring heartache and disaster.

"Your family is going to be proud of you regardless of winning or even making it to the finale," he said. "Which they know you did."

"They do. Employees won't. It was agreed that everyone would be told I'd be there the whole week regardless in case they bring people back to help out at the end. I'm glad that didn't come about. I didn't care for some of the contestants and wouldn't want them touching my food." She wiped her hand over her forehead. "Phew. It feels so good to say that and not worry about a camera being in my face. I don't know how people do it. Guarding your words nonstop is hard work."

He laughed at her. The jet was getting ready for takeoff and they buckled in and relaxed. It was only seven in the morning, but with the time change and the flight time, then Egan meeting them at Logan and getting back to the island, they'd be back around dinner.

"Not everyone likes all eyes on them," he said.

"Never me. Another reason I like not having the last name of Bond."

He knew that about her. He supposed what happened a

few days ago was just another example of what she'd have to live with.

Many would say that was a small price to pay for the wealth and privilege.

"But as you found out, it means nothing," he said.

"Exactly. Another reason to go back to my island and live my quiet life."

"Tell me about it," he said. "I know you've got to work tomorrow."

"You too," she said. "I feel bad you spent most of the week doing nothing. You're working all next week like me, right?"

"I've got Tuesday off," he said.

He knew she was going to work the whole week after being gone last minute. He'd told Egan to schedule him too, but Egan said he'd still get Tuesday off. He supposed he'd need it to get shit done around his house after being gone for a week.

"I'm going to just be working in the kitchen days Monday and Tuesday," she said. "Maybe you can stay Monday night if you're back early enough."

"I can do that," he said. "If I know Egan he kept it light for me. Or an early day."

"Good," she said. "So no more talk about this past week. I'm going to get enough questions when I return home. Let's talk about you."

"Me?" he asked.

"You said you'd talk about your time in the service when it was done. Did you think I'd forget?"

She was laughing when she said it. "I'd hoped," he said. "But I don't have much to hide. There are things I can't tell you. You know that, I'm sure."

"I do. Just answer the question I asked you yesterday."

"Yes," he said. "I've flown a helicopter for a sniper before. More times than I care to remember. Rescue missions too. I'm not sure what is worse."

She laid her head on his shoulder and reached for his hand. "Why? Sometimes I think you need to talk about your past and you don't want to. I don't know if that makes you who you are or not. You've talked about being burned before and there is a part of me that thinks it had to do with a woman you dated in the service that couldn't handle it."

He wasn't going to lie, but he wasn't going to tell her about Lara either. It didn't seem to be the place and unless she asked for specifics, he'd hold it back. Being a coward again, he knew. He wasn't going to be able to brush this off and wondered why he kept doing it.

"No," he said. "I didn't date anyone seriously in the service." She could read that any way she wanted. She could take it as the years after or before. "As for what is worse, snipers are killing. Killing enemies, but death is still death. It's hard to push that from your mind. That you played a part in the ending of someone's life."

"Even if that person had it coming to them?" she asked. "Not that I think I could ever do that, but the truth is, we never know what we are fully capable of until we are put into a situation like that."

"That's right," he said. "You don't. But when you enlist you know what you're signing up for. It's your job and you have to look at it as such. But rescue missions. Bringing home one of your own that is injured or dead or dying while you're flying. You see your own life flash at the same time. You think that it could have been you. That it still could be."

"I'm sorry, Lincoln. I guess I never thought of it that way. You probably lost a lot of friends."

"Enough," he said. "It wears you down little by little until you don't know what you feel about anything anymore."

"That has to be hard," she said. "I know what it's like to doubt myself but never like that."

"It's not the same, trust me," he said. He was doubting his actions in the service even though he knew they were right. He doubted everything he did prior to the service and if he'd ever be able to trust another woman in his life.

He could say he found someone he could trust. But that didn't mean he was ready to let all his demons out either.

"When you left, you could have tried to get a job with law enforcement or a hospital," she said. "There has to be a demand for helicopter pilots."

"I could have, but then I'd be right back to what I was doing in the service if I worked for the State Police or FBI. Both were an option. My parents thought I'd do that. I couldn't tell them why I didn't want to."

They'd been so proud of him and his decisions in life. But he didn't want to let them know and say that maybe it wasn't the best decision for him.

That if he'd never said he was going into the service, maybe Lara wouldn't have looked at him as a way out. She would have moved on to someone else to date and her life would have turned out differently.

"Your parents would have understood," she said. "You know that."

"They would have, but there were things I didn't want them to worry about. They worried enough when I was in the service. No reason to continue for another twenty years until I could retire."

"It's the parents' job to worry. Or so my parents remind me all the time."

"I know," he said. "Mine have said the same thing. As for a hospital...you know, that's like a rescue mission."

"Bringing back the injured and not sure if they will live or die," she said.

"Exactly. I still fly over for the hospital if needed on the island, but Egan knows I'd rather not. It's a job, so I'd never tell him no either."

"That is how I feel. I do what needs to be done with my job. It's not just for me, it's for my family. I don't have regular employers and neither do you. It's family for you too."

"It is," he said. Maybe sometimes he needed to hear those things too. "Landing at the docks that night. I think it saved me in more ways than one. It gave me a job. It gave me a life and it gave me a purpose."

"A purpose?" she asked.

"To be doing something to make people happy. Most times clients are on vacation. They are excited and thrilled and happy."

"Do you get lonely or bored when you're flying alone with cargo?" she asked.

"Nope," he said. "I use that time to just enjoy the nature around me. I don't think we as people get enough time in our lives to do that. Least of all in our jobs."

"That's why I love the island and where I live. I feel the same way. Just having the time to sit and look at the water. On a beautiful day or a rainy one, it calms me both the same. You get to enjoy it much more than me."

"I do," he said. "I wouldn't change anything about what I do."

"Neither would I," she said. "And you know what else this job brought you?"

"What?" he asked.

"Me. It brought me to you and you to me. I never thought much of the whole island legend and lore, but maybe it does work."

He turned to kiss her on the forehead. "Maybe it does."

32

DID WHAT YOU HAD TO

"This is crazy," Tracy said. "I've never flown before let alone in a helicopter."

Grace grinned and turned to the girl sitting next to her as they waited at the airstrip on the island. "I know. But you didn't want to miss a lot of work and this way, you won't. You're with me, you're going to meet with your case manager, then we are going to shop and get a few things you've wanted. I'm going to bring you to where I purchase knives."

"I doubt I can afford what you get," Tracy said.

"They've got a wide range of prices and quality. I'm going to teach you how to look for those things. I need to meet with my mother too. In two weeks I've got the clinic that I teach in Boston so I've got to get everything set up for that at the facility we are using."

She wouldn't stay in Boston for it. Being off for a week and leaving her cousin short staffed unplanned was too much. This time, since the clinic was only mornings, she was going to stay with Lincoln in Boston at Egan's condo Sunday night, teach her class Monday morning, stay that night, teach Tuesday morning, then fly back to the island. For the rest of the week, Lincoln would fly her to Boston before the clinic and after so she could still work Wednesday through Friday at The Retreat for the dinner crowd.

It'd be a lot and she'd be exhausted, but sometimes you just did what you had to.

In her mind, she was young and could handle it. She'd rather take time off later in the year when business was slower. She and Lincoln could enjoy each other more that way.

"I appreciate you letting me come over with you this early and not have to board the ferry. This way I can get to work on time."

She rolled her eyes. Tracy was a go-getter. "You're doing a great job. I'm impressed with the way you're handling the breakfast service. Everyone treating you okay?"

"Sure," Tracy said, looking away.

She wanted to find out more, but she knew the answers. She'd witnessed some of it in the past, but she hadn't heard anything recently. Not that she'd been around much either.

"No one is giving you a hard time?" she asked. "More than normal. Everyone is given a hard time in the kitchen at one point or another. I'm sorry about that. I try to keep it to a minimum, but I got it too when I started and I can't always be around."

"It's fine. You're right. It's nothing more than normal and not everyone."

"That is part of the life in a kitchen," she said. "I do run a tight ship as best as I can."

"Everyone respects you," Tracy said.

"I'm sure they said that," she said. "Not sure they like me though."

"Why are you laughing?" Tracy asked.

"Because it's the truth and I don't let it bother me. To move up in the industry you've got to have a thick skin. I believe what comes around goes around and if you treat people with respect they will do the same back. Work isn't about having friends but getting the job done."

"I know," Tracy said. "It helps working with Ashley. Not that we always work together or at the same stations, but it's nice having a friendly face in the kitchen."

"I'm glad," she said. Grace did the schedule and purposely tried to put them together for a few days.

Because Ashley was going to culinary school in a month, Grace made sure to put her cousin's stepsister-in-law by more experienced chefs in the kitchen. It was about teaching Ashley the basics to get her a leg up before schooling. Maybe even giving her some tricks that others wouldn't know.

With Tracy, it was about training her to have a job and that meant starting from the ground up. Stations that Ashley had spent time in last summer.

"I know we aren't supposed to talk about you being on TV soon," Tracy said quietly. Since there was no one in the airstrip but Egan's assistant at the front counter and they were seated off the side waiting on Lincoln's return from Boson, Tracy didn't need to whisper. "But I need to know, was it exciting for you or did you just look at it like another day's work?"

So many people had been asking her questions since her return to work on Sunday. Three days of questions that she had to ignore or joke about.

Even her family she'd given no answer to how it ended. Only Lincoln was aware she'd come in second. Her family, they'd told her how proud they were of her to get so far and that they were positive it would do the island well regardless of the outcome.

No one cared all that much if she won or lost. She had told them she'd been interviewed in confessionals several times each day, but she had no idea what would be shown and what wouldn't.

Her questions ranged from how she felt about the competition that day to if she missed home or what she missed the most.

She'd let Lincoln slip in there a time or two. It's not as if she had a choice when they asked questions like that. Then she told herself she would have done it anyway because he almost always popped into her head.

"It was both," she confessed. "It was exciting because it was something new. I'm a competitive person by nature. But I tried to look at it as another day of work. Maybe someday you can try for a cooking show."

"I doubt that," Tracy said. "I just want a job and a place of my own and to live a simple life. I want something stable. I know most people think that is boring, but for me, it's the dream."

Her heart broke for the girl who only wanted that out of life.

She put her hand on Tracy's. "I want to help you get that. Keep working hard and you'll be good."

"Thank you. So far, it's great. I'm putting all my money away. I really am. I know my rent won't be covered after the end of the year, but Marissa told me I could continue to stay there and they won't charge me much. I've been working with the case manager on budgets and what I could afford and I'll still be able to put money away if I have to pay what they are getting now."

"I'm glad for you," she said. She hoped Tracy wouldn't

be charged even that much since her mother had told her that the Weatherbys didn't want to change anything at all. "You're comfortable there? You have everything you need?"

"It's great," Tracy said. "It really is. Marissa is wonderful. She's been teaching me to drive and I've got an appointment for my driver's license in September. My caseworker told me that once I get it, they've got cars that are donated and I'd qualify. I can't thank you enough for everything you've done."

"Don't thank me," she said. "You're doing all the work."

Tracy sniffled a little. "I've done work my whole life, but it never made a difference."

"Don't think that," she said. "Never. It's working out for you now." She heard the helicopter coming in the distance. "And you're going to get your first flight in a second."

The two of them stood up. "Is it going to be with your boyfriend?"

"It is," she said.

"Everyone talks about him in the kitchen."

"They do?" she asked. This was news to her.

"Not bad. Just that he's really good-looking. I've never met him."

"You're about to. And yes, he's really good-looking. But he's funny too."

Grace wasn't surprised she was talked about but didn't think it would have to do with who she was dating.

When the helicopter landed, she walked over to Lincoln. "Morning," he said. "Looks like I've got two pretty passengers today."

"You do," she said, grinning. "Tracy Gingham, this is Lincoln Harrington. He's going to be flying us safely to Boston this morning."

"My most precious cargo of the day," he said. "Climb in and we'll get you to your destination."

"See," she said. "Funny."

Two hours later, the two girls had shopped for knives and a few other essentials that Tracy could use. She let Tracy use The Retreat discount, which was why she brought the teen here. Tracy had been shocked and thanked her a few more times.

To her it wasn't a big deal. Since she'd ordered a few things to go into the kitchen, there was no reason to not let Tracy get the same discount. As much as she wanted to pay for the teen's purchase, she knew that might be overkill.

Besides, Tracy had her pride.

"Thank you so much for the lift over and a great time," Tracy told her when they walked into her mother's office. "I appreciate it. It was almost like a girl's day. I've never had one."

Which hit her square in the chest with a medicine ball of sympathy. She wouldn't let it be shown. "Anytime. I want you to come to me whenever you need anything or have a question."

"I will," Tracy said. But she knew the teen wouldn't. The only time Tracy talked to her was when Grace sought her out. She wasn't sure if Tracy didn't feel right approaching the big boss or didn't want more eyes on her.

For now she'd continue to do things the way they were being done.

"I'll see you at work later," she said.

Tracy went on to meet her case manager and then would get a lift back to the docks and take the ferry and an Uber to The Retreat.

She walked to her mother's office, knocked on the door and opened it.

"Hi, Grace," her mother said. "You're early."

"Tracy and I got our shopping done quicker than I thought. She's fast that way. She is meeting with her case manager now and then will get a ride back to the ferry. She wants to get to work on time, but I told her to not worry about it."

"She is the type of client we love to help. Someone who wants to help herself and not rely on the system to do everything for her. I check in on her more."

"Because you know I want to know?" she asked.

"Yes, but I also like to know what could be good success stories. You're not the only one with a vested interest."

"I know," she said. "I get that all from my mother."

"You're a good duck," her mother said.

"Quack, quack." Her mother laughed like she always did when they exchanged those words when she was a kid. "If you're ready, can we go check out the facilities for the cooking clinic you'll be leading? Lincoln can fly me back at one; otherwise, I've got to wait until two thirty for Egan."

"Then let's go," her mother said, "so you can go see your man."

She giggled and was shocked that the sound came out of her mouth. "Yeah, my man."

And several hours later she was at the docks waiting for her man, who hadn't arrived back yet. She knew she was early, but she'd rather be early than late.

When she heard a helicopter coming, she thought for sure it was Lincoln, but when she stood up was told, "It's Roxy coming in. Lincoln is still fifteen minutes out."

"Oh," she said, sitting back down.

She picked her phone up to go through some emails and looked up when Roxy came over to her.

"Hi," Roxy said. "How are you doing?"

"Good," she said. "How are you liking Boston? I never found out where you were from, but just knew you moved here when Lincoln reached out."

"I'm from Ohio," Roxy said. "Rural farm country. Just like Lincoln. I think that is why he and I got along so well."

Grace smiled. "He's easy to get along with."

"He is," Roxy said. "Which is surprising considering what he went through before. He doesn't trust easily. Especially women. It was too bad that I was seeing someone when we met."

She lifted her eyebrows. "Meaning if you weren't you would have tried to be more than friends?"

Roxy shrugged. "Just saying. He's a great guy. Maybe someone to hold onto. Consider yourself lucky."

"Lincoln is coming in," Missy said from her desk not that far away. Grace wondered if Egan's assistant heard the conversation and was saving her or it was just good timing.

"Thanks," she said, standing up. "I'll go out and wait for him."

Just the thing she didn't want to hear from Roxy, but she wouldn't let Lincoln know either.

She had to hope that whatever was going on with Lincoln, or was in his past, he'd open up to her just like she had him. Until then, she had to accept that maybe they'd only be able to get so far.

33

STRUCK GOLD

"How busy are you today?" Roxy asked Lincoln on Saturday. "I've got a few cargo trips and then I'm done by three."

"Picking up a tour group in thirty minutes," he said. "I can hear Missy out there talking to some of them now. I've got two today and then tonight I'll be bringing over some whales to the casino that are staying the night."

He'd taken that last flight so that Egan could get home at a decent time. Blake didn't work much on the weekends, or she tried not to, so he'd take anything later so Egan could have family time.

Since Grace was working nights, it didn't matter to him if he started his day later and ended later on the weekends.

"That's right," Roxy said. "Grace isn't around anyway."

"No," he said. Though Rob told him that Roxy had hoped the two of them would get something going, he'd never really seen that. He'd been looking for signs of it too, but it wasn't materializing.

"I talked to Grace a few days ago when she was here," Roxy said.

"You did?" he asked.

Grace had never said a word to him. She was waiting for him when he landed, then just climbed in and they flew home.

"I did," Roxy said. "She was inside when I got there. She's nice and all. You struck gold with her, didn't you?"

He frowned over the choice of words. He and Roxy had a lot of talks over the years when they were stationed together.

She'd been from a similar background as him. Her parents were farmers though. Full-time farmers and she didn't want that life. She wanted something different and more exciting.

Her boyfriend, who ended up her fiancé, had worked on heavy machinery. He'd said he could get a job anywhere and would follow her.

Lincoln had been shocked they hadn't gotten married while she was in the service and wondered what was stopping it. At that time, she could have had him with her, but Roxy kept putting it off.

He was even more shocked to find out she never married. He'd only reached out to her as a shot in the dark because he remembered the man who should have been her spouse by now, could have worked anywhere.

Maybe Roxy was looking for someone to strike gold with. It'd been conversations they'd had too. That it'd be nice to have someone take care of her like he'd said he was going to do for Lara.

He wondered if Roxy commented to Grace about Lara. One of those drunken nights he'd said more than he should.

Roxy had latched on and then would ask him more questions. Though he'd always thought they were friends, maybe, looking back, Roxy was thinking or feeling more. It had just never been a thought in his head.

She was taken and you never poached on another man's woman.

When she was single and moved here, he didn't look at her that way. Guess it was true that when you slapped someone in the friends category that was where they stayed.

"I'm not looking for gold, silver, or even coal," he said, grinning.

They were in the break room. Roxy would be leaving soon.

"You know what I mean," Roxy said.

"No," he said. "I don't. If you mean she's a great person and we love each other, then sure. I'd say we both struck gold."

"You didn't say you were in love with her," Roxy said. She had a smile on her face, but it was a forced one. Her eyes were telling another story. A little bit of desperation and hurt in them. Thinking back, maybe that look was there before too and he never caught it.

"I didn't know it was something I had to say," he said. He went and got a bottle of water out of the fridge. He'd be talking during the tour. More than he normally did. Egan loved it. Lincoln enjoyed it, but wouldn't say he loved it.

Then he thought back to the flights he had in his past with passengers, and yeah, this was much better.

That was what he considered striking gold. His career and his job. Not the woman he loved. He'd never look at her that way and was pissed that Roxy used those words the more he thought of it.

It's like she was trying to remind him of his past. That Lara came from money and only wanted one thing. Someone to take care of her.

And didn't Roxy make a comment or two about Lincoln having to go with Grace away for a week? Roxy didn't know what that was all about, just that it was last minute and she'd made comments as if Grace couldn't be alone. That she couldn't handle it.

That was the farthest thing from the truth. Grace could have handled it well and didn't need him, but he was glad he was there for her. For him too.

He needed to be there for her more than she needed him for her.

It was scary as all fuck, but he couldn't change the way he felt.

"That's right," Roxy said. "Guys don't talk about those things like women do."

"No," he said. "They don't."

"I told Grace she was lucky to have you and that she should make sure she held onto you, that there'd be plenty to snatch you up. You're a good catch and all."

"Thanks," he said. "I'm sure she appreciated hearing that."

"Don't laugh," Roxy said, giving him a playful shove. "Really. It's the truth."

He didn't know what Roxy was doing or saying or if she had an end game. Maybe she was being truthful and stepping back but letting it also be known that he was a good catch.

Not that he ever thought he was. Probably the reason he held so much back in his life.

It made him wonder if he should tell Grace about Lara and then reminded himself more than once it was in the past.

It's not like it was holding him back now. If it was, he wouldn't have fallen in love with Grace.

He wouldn't be looking toward the future and waiting for them to have a few days in Boston together and then him flying her over for her clinic for three days.

He was thrilled that she asked if it could work out that they could do it. That she was excited to spend time with him and willing to work her schedule around it.

Monday and Tuesday weren't a problem. Sunday and Monday nights, they'd stay at Egan's condo. The rest of the week, he'd bring her over in the morning, but couldn't guarantee he'd be the one to bring her home.

Maybe it'd give them an idea of what it'd be like to almost live together. He'd suggest that he'd go to her house after work each night so they could ride to the airstrip together. He didn't have a problem being at her house while she was working. It'd give him time to do a few things for her too.

He felt bad that in the months they were together, she was always the one cooking for him. The only thing he'd done was build all those shelves for her herbs. But she'd been talking about other things she wouldn't mind having. Just in passing. He could do that and surprise her.

Yeah, that was what he'd do. Repaint her bedroom a calming blue like she'd brought up several times. That would only take a few hours to do.

Or new paving stones from her patio to stairs that would walk down to the beach. Maybe that would be a better choice. She wouldn't even notice him doing that until it was done.

And when his mind was thinking of those things, it brought back memories of him wanting to take care of Lara and he realized that Grace didn't need anyone to take care of her.

"Everyone ends up being a good catch for someone," he said. "You just need to find the right person."

"Guess you're thinking that you did that, aren't you?" Roxy asked.

He shrugged. "It's early yet and I'm not one to plan out my future."

"Please," Roxy said. "You've always had a plan. At least in life. It used to drive me insane that you had things figured out. Not that you thought this job would happen, but you had plans and your plans had backup plans. I couldn't even pick a wedding date. It drove Pete nuts."

"Why didn't you?" he asked. "Just curious. You were high school sweethearts. Most people marry quickly in the service so they can live together in better quarters."

Roxy shrugged. "I guess deep down he wasn't the one. I wanted him to be, but not being able to pull the trigger made me realize it. When I left the service it was the same. He wanted kids and I wasn't sure. It put a strain on things."

"You don't want kids?" he asked.

"I don't think so," Roxy said. "Some guys don't like that."

"I want kids," he said. "I always did."

"You never said that," Roxy said.

"It'd never been a conversation."

"Do you think Grace is someone to put her career on hold for kids?" Roxy said. "It's harder for women than men. But again, she's had her career handed to her so I guess she won't care."

"Nothing was handed to her," he said more firmly than he meant. "I've got to get ready to go."

He had to leave before he said even more than he had. It wasn't like him to get into a spat with a coworker, but he wasn't going to let his relationship with Grace be knocked down either.

He liked what they had. He knew there could be more—he just had to convince Grace of that.

34

JOY OF COOKING

"How was the first day of the clinic?" Lincoln asked Grace when she walked into Egan's condo at one.

They'd come over last night after she was done working and relaxed. This morning she got up and drove to one of the Bond family hotel restaurants. She'd told him they were letting her use the facilities for the mornings.

"It was great," she said. "There are only eight students for the clinic and we were out of the way. Part of the clinic is helping with prep to show the students what it was like to work in a restaurant kitchen so it helped the staff out too."

"I can see it on your face how much fun you had."

"I forgot what it's like to do this," she said. "It's like I've got this whole month to experience the joy of cooking again. Actually more than the month."

"How's that?" he asked.

He was sitting on the balcony looking at the view of the harbor in the distance. Egan had a sweet place here. It was not like his rented home on the island, but it was nicer than anything he could afford.

Lincoln could buy the place he rented, but he knew that Mitchell would never sell it to him. In exchange for living there cheaper than they would rent to anyone else, he did all the lawn work and snow removal. He did repairs inside too.

They knew he wouldn't contact them for anything so they'd send someone over to check out the house once a year. The big things like windows and roofs, even the appliances.

He'd gotten lectured when he'd replaced the washer and dryer one year and was told it wasn't his responsibility. He laughed at Mitchell and said it was already done.

"I've always found enjoyment in my job, even when I'm running around issuing orders and stressed. On my time off, I cook for pleasure, but it's really just cooking for me or finding new recipes. But since I've been dating you, there is another excitement in it for me. Or another enjoyment."

He grinned and reached his hand for hers. She was standing behind him and he'd had his head turned.

She moved closer and put her hands on his shoulder and started to run them around his muscles in a soft caress.

"What enjoyment is that?"

"Trying to make you happy," she said. "I've always wanted people to enjoy my food. But with you, I want more. I guess I never thought of it before or that it could be different. I was told it's my love language, feeding people. I used to laugh at that."

"I love when you feed me," he said. "I'd eat anything you give me, but it feels good to hear you say what you are."

Sometimes he wondered if he was the one feeling more than he should.

That she held more back, but he realized it was him that was holding back and he wished he could just break that cycle. But the whole issue of Lara was stuck like a block of ice inside him and he could not get it to budge. And what would Grace think of him if he told her?

"I know you would eat anything. I'm thrilled that you are eating less fast food."

"Because you keep me well stocked," he said.

He almost always had some kind of food he could bring to work or heat up. She made a lot when they were together to give him leftovers.

Days she went to work late, she was up earlier and cooking something for him and Egan that she'd drop off, then go about her day.

Things his mother used to do.

He never thought he'd want to end up with someone like his mother. Nor did he think Grace was really like his mother, but there were caring nurturing parts that were.

"That is what I'm trying to say. I found that I enjoyed the competition. Next week for the premier we will see how I look on TV. If they showed me in a good light or made me out to be a villain."

She was laughing when he pulled her around to sit on his lap. "I don't think you did or said anything that could showcase you that way. Do you think they want to turn anyone into that?"

"I'm not sure. Other than Destiny behind the scenes, no one was really bad. Some more competitive than others. There were joking comments made, but I believe they don't want any resort to get a bad name."

"Then you've got nothing to worry about," he said.

He'd only witnessed the one day on the beach and from what he could see in the distance was Grace sacrificing her own time and cooking to help Pierre and give him water and make sure he was fine.

She ended up in the bottom that day and if the producers were looking for ratings, they'd show that. They'd show that there was a human side even when people were fighting for a prize. That life wasn't all cutthroat.

He needed Grace to be showcased that way. Having been born into wealth didn't mean she didn't care for others.

And Grace needed to see people didn't only see her as someone from the Bond family too.

"I don't think so," she said. "But I'm not getting worked up either way. It's over with and there is nothing I can do at this point and nothing to change it."

"Nope," he said. He was hugging her tight to him, his mouth on her neck. "You know I love you, right?"

"I do," she said. "What did you do?" She was laughing when she asked that.

"What do you mean?"

"My father always said that phrase to my mother when he did something wrong. Or when he was going to surprise her with something she might not like."

"Oh," he said. "I just wanted to say the words. But I can surprise you." He stood up and had her in his arms. "We can go to the bedroom. That is where I do my best work."

"Please do," she said. "I love surprises."

"You do?" he asked.

"Yep. I know you're a planner and all. But surprises are fun too."

"You like to know everything too," he pointed out.

"I do, but I'm learning not knowing everything isn't a horrible thing either. I'd say I've had a few curve balls thrown my way that I've hit out of the park."

Which meant he could go ahead and do some things at her place this week since she agreed to what he'd suggested. It'd give them more time together in the process.

"Don't hit anything in this room," he said, laughing and dropped her on his bed.

"Nope," she said. "I'm not into any of that kinky stuff in the bedroom. No slapping or hitting."

He flipped her on her stomach and started to pull her clothes off. Since she was in her workwear, they came off quickly with a tug.

Her bare ass was flashing to him, so he leaned down and gave it a light kiss. "Not even this, though I do love it."

"I appreciate it," she said. "Slapping bare flesh isn't much fun."

He'd never thought so. Maybe because he had more strength to him and was always worried about hurting someone.

"No," he said. "It's better to show my appreciation of your body."

He rolled her fast and had her on her back now, the sound of her laughter as he yanked her top off.

"You're not showing much finesse with the way you're tugging and yanking me around like a sack of potatoes."

"You want finesse?" he asked. "How about I just treasure you the way you should be?"

"Oh boy," she said. "I think you mean torture rather than treasure, but I'm up for it." Her hand reached for his crotch and cupped him. "Looks like you are too."

"Stop talking, Grace, and just enjoy."

She lay back on the bed, and his mouth started at her neck, little soft pecks while his hands traveled to her breasts.

He wanted her to feel like she was being worshiped.

He was massaging and lightly running his fingers over her nipples, his lips moving over the collarbone and down her chest. Touching everywhere but where she wanted it.

Since she was bucking her hips up against him, he knew where she wanted it.

"Your shorts are rough. Take your clothes off too."

"Nope," he said. "This way I can't let you talk me into stopping my agenda and moving to yours."

She growled and he was trying not to laugh that he called her out on that.

But he did move his mouth down to her breast and pulled one puckered hardened nipple between his lips, swirled his tongue around, then applied some suction.

"That's it," she said. "Just like that."

He let her say her words and wasn't going to talk back. He had his mouth full anyway.

She continued to rub against him and he didn't want her to get off like that either.

He moved to the other side, did the same to that little hardened beauty and had her cursing on the bed.

When her hand moved down to get between her legs, he pulled it back and pinned it to the bed.

"No, no," he said. "Only I get to touch there right now."

"Then do it," she said firmly. "I'm not known for my patience."

"You say that a lot, but I've seen otherwise," he said.

He did shift and started to place a trail of kissing down her belly, over her hips, past her swollen bud and to her inner thighs.

Why not tease her some while he was at it?

Working her up was part of the fun.

The pleasure.

The enjoyment.

Didn't she say she'd found those things in her cooking the past few months since she'd met him?

It's like he found those things in his life since he'd met her.

He thought if he voiced it, he'd come off like a wuss. Better to just show her.

She was wiggling around on the bed so much that he was finding it hard to keep her pinned down.

Might as well give her what she was waiting for.

He settled between her legs, his hands under her hips lifting her up close to his mouth.

He didn't do anything though. Was just breathing and looking at her.

"What are you waiting for?" she asked.

"You to tell me what you want," he said.

"I want your mouth on me."

"Where?" he asked, kissing her lower hip. "Here?"

"No," she growled.

"Tell me where," he said. "You're vocal, so tell me."

"I want you to lick my pussy," she said. "Right now. All of it. Taste it and eat it as if it was food I put on the table and you haven't had anything in days."

"Fuck!" he said. Guess she could push his buttons and move him past his agenda.

He hadn't expected her to talk like she had and it was more erotic than he'd thought it'd be if he imagined it.

He dove right into her tender flesh and did exactly as she'd said.

He was licking her. Kissing her. Nibbling. Tasting everything he could.

She was squirming even more but in an effort to get closer. To get more.

He held her still and found her swollen bud and laid his lips on it like a vacuum finding its target and going full force.

She let out a scream of pleasure, the sounds of it echoing off the walls, her body thrusting up into his face again and again and then just falling back on the mattress in a heap.

He jumped back fast and started to undress.

"I'm on the pill," she said.

"What?" he asked.

"Birth control. Do what you want with that knowledge."

He was going to ask if she was sure, but he looked at her face and saw her eyes closed, a soft smile on her lips and her legs apart, her hips lifting up and down as if she was waiting for him.

He didn't hesitate to climb on the bed, slide between her legs and enter her fast.

She sighed at the movement, his body screamed for a release.

If he wanted to take it slow, he couldn't with her moving up and down almost urging him to get to the end.

He started slamming into her harder and faster than ever before.

"Slow down, I don't want to hurt you."

"You aren't. Just let go, Lincoln, and give me what you want to."

He had no choice after that, his body taking over, his emotions with it.

He collapsed on her a minute later, his breathing heavy to his own ears.

He heard her laughing and didn't even have the energy to ask why.

He almost didn't want to know.

He thought he had control over this but realized he might not have had any control since the day Grace asked him for a drink and he brought her to the dive bar he'd never shared with anyone before.

35

HER LOVE

The following Monday night, Grace and Lincoln pulled in front of her parents' house on the island. She saw her brother's car there along with her grandfather's, Emma's, Roark's and Hunter's.

She wasn't expecting this many people to show up for dinner.

"What's going on?" Lincoln asked her. "Is there a party we don't know about?"

"No," she said. "Or not one I was told about. You know my parents wanted us to watch the first episode with them tonight. Looks like they might have gotten others to do it too. It's kind of embarrassing."

She'd put off the family dinner as much as she could. Some of it wasn't by choice. The other was she didn't want Lincoln to feel any pressure.

For someone who didn't move fast in life when it came to her dating life, she wanted to move faster than she was now.

That might be why she agreed to have him stay with her all last week.

When he'd shown her Saturday morning before she went to work that he'd put pavers in the backyard, she'd been stunned and thrilled.

He listened to her. Exactly what it was she wanted. He'd said he bought them in Boston, flew them over and then dropped them off when she was working on Wednesday. Now she understood why he didn't want to go out by the beach Wednesday when she'd gotten home. He wanted to sit on the patio and relax.

Where they'd sat, she couldn't see the pavers piled against the house.

Then Thursday and Friday she'd gotten home after dark and they just got ready for bed together. Saturday morning before she went to work was the first chance she'd get to see it. He'd pulled her out there before he left and she found herself crying and him panicking.

She wasn't someone who cried often and least of all when she was happy.

But the fact he did this for her because he listened and remembered was more than anyone else ever had before.

He even found the exact stone she'd pointed out on TV one day when they were watching some show. If that didn't tell her how much Lincoln loved her, she didn't know what did.

And forget about her trying to pay him for the materials. He'd cut her off before she had a chance and she dropped it.

He wanted nothing from her but her love. She actually believed it.

He'd even told her about the conversation with Roxy and she realized if she'd felt any jealousy, it was gone. He'd admitted what Rob had told him and he explained he'd never felt that way and was sorry she might have, but he wanted Grace to know there was nothing to be worried about.

Did she think about the fact that she knew he'd been burned? Yeah, she had, but it was in his past and nothing for her to be concerned about. At least he'd told her that enough and she was starting to believe it. And him. Why wouldn't he be honest if it was more?

"There isn't anything to be embarrassed about," he said.

"I guess you're right. I've been more worried about this than anything. I feel as if I've hidden enough on this island and who I was and now it's going to be that thirty seconds of fame."

"More than thirty seconds," he said. "Remember, you're on every episode."

"Don't remind me," she said.

They walked into her parents' house and to the back where everyone was gathered in the family room. "I didn't know there'd be so many people here."

Jack came running to her. "Do you have cookies?"

"No, buddy. I didn't cook anything. Aunt Melanie is doing all the cooking. I had to tell Lincoln not to compare or judge. It won't be as good as mine."

"Thanks," her mother said. "I taught you how to make your first chocolate chip cookie."

"And I've only improved since," she said. "Really, is there a reason everyone is here?"

"Moral support," Kayla said.

"We knew you were nervous about this," Hunter said. "I appreciate you doing it."

"I don't think I had much of a choice," she said dryly. Her eyes shifted to her grandfather. "Just like Lincoln didn't about going with me."

"I would have wanted to anyway and everyone knew

that," he said. "This way I didn't have to stress over it and I would have never asked for the time off last minute."

"Which we all knew," her father said. "It was a win for everyone."

She wasn't sure where her father was going with that statement but decided to let it drop for now.

"What are you making for dinner?" she asked her mother.

"Dad is throwing steaks on the grill. He's got it lit now. I made a few salads to go with it. Just keeping it light. No reason to do anything fancy and have Lincoln feel as if he has to choke it down."

"Thanks a lot," he said, bumping his shoulder into hers.

"My mother is just joking with you. Is there anything I can do to help?"

"Nope," her mother said. "Sit and relax. You do enough cooking."

"Tracy was excited you took her shopping," Ashley said.

"Who's Tracy?" Lincoln asked.

She turned and looked at him. "Tracy that flew over with me a few weeks ago. I didn't tell you about her?"

"No," he said.

"Tracy was in foster care in Boston," Ashley said. "Grace brought her to the island and gave her a job and Melanie found her housing so she could finish high school and now she works for Grace full time and lives here. Grace is kind of training her. I wish she could go to school with me. Then I'd know someone."

"You'll be fine," Chelsea said. "You're only in Boston and can come back when you want. But you can't commute. And driving in Boston traffic daily would be difficult."

Ashley didn't even want to live on campus, asking if she could stay in Roark's condo. Since Chelsea worked on the island full time and Roark in Boston but could split his time, they spent more time on the island and Roark in Boston a few days a week.

There was no reason Ashley couldn't stay at Roark's from time to time but the traffic to get to the school and back might be too much and she understood Chelsea wanting her sister to experience college life in the dorms.

"What did we talk about?" Roark said. "If you need me to come get you to give you a break, I'll do it. Or you can drive to the condo when you want. You're always welcome. But give this a try. You might love it."

Ashley's shoulders dropped. "It's so hard to fit in."

Grace knew that. Though Ashley was coming at it from another side.

When Chelsea and Ashley first moved here, Ashley didn't have much. Chelsea gave her younger sister a better life and taught her hard work and appreciation for it.

Roark gave them both an amazing life and Chelsea had fought hard against what her new husband could give her.

Grace looked over at Lincoln and realized that was not so different from her situation and she learned to accept that everyone had their pride.

What was better was knowing the person you loved didn't want anything but that love.

"It will all work out," she said. "And you know you can call me anytime too."

There was more talk around the room, her brother and Lincoln talking about sports. She hadn't realized Lincoln watched many sports, but it's not like they had that much time together either.

"I hear Lincoln did some work at your house," Emma said to her thirty minutes later. Grace, her mother, Kayla, and Chelsea were all getting the food out. Ashley was with the kids and the men either in the living room or on the deck. "Talk about sweet."

"And he built shelving indoors and out for my herbs," she added.

"Do you hear the change in your voice?" her mother asked.

"What? No," she said.

"Yes," Kayla said. "Amanda and Sidney said my voice did the same thing when I was dating Hunter."

Amanda and Sidney were Kayla's best friends. The three women had all lived together when Kayla moved here and now they were all married to Bonds.

"Maybe it's love," Chelsea said, laughing.

"I don't think your voice ever changes like that when you talk about Roark," Emma said.

"Roark had to wear me down," Chelsea said with a smirk. "I'm not as easy as Kayla and Grace."

There was a lot of laughter to that statement. No one in this room thought she was easy.

And two hours later when they were sitting around waiting for the first episode to start, Grace turned to the room and said, "Listen, don't hold anything against me and don't pick on me either. I did the best I could, but I've got no idea what they are going to air."

The first episode was going to be ninety minutes long while they spent some time showcasing the venues that each chef worked at. She found it nice that everyone was willing to have a late night knowing they most likely had to work tomorrow. Even the kids were lying on the couch calmly now. They'd get to bed late.

"We are all proud of you," her father said. "I'm sure you did wonderfully."

"It's starting," Emma said. "This is so exciting."

Grace wasn't so sure she felt that but would let it go.

She watched the same as everyone else when they showed the contestants and then she was last.

The Retreat was first shown up above by several shots from the helicopter. Production had done a wonderful job showcasing all the venues. No one would complain about that.

It started with her climbing out of the helicopter and Lincoln being in the shot but no comments on who he was or why she was there. Talk about embarrassing. As if she arrived at work that way every day!

Then there was a thirty-second reel of her in the kitchen cooking the plate they asked of her, then showing it by her face as she'd said what she felt was a forced comment they made her say about why she loved her job.

She wouldn't say she loved it because it was family and carried so much pride for her to do her best. She didn't want that aired so she came up with something else.

At the first commercial, Hunter said, "Lucky you getting a lift to work from your boyfriend daily."

"That was overkill," she said. "Why would they do that?"

"I'm pretty sure no one is thinking what we are," her mother said. "They also got you saying you loved living on the island. You wouldn't need an airlift to work if you lived on the island."

"I guess you're right," she said. Grace knew she was reading more into this.

After an hour, they were going to move to the judging after the commercial. Her grandfather said, "So far, so good. They aren't focusing on more than one person at a time but spreading the viewing around."

"They kind of are," she said. She noticed the camera was

more on the two people who'd end up on the bottom along with the two people who'd be on top.

She wasn't either of those four on the first day and was fine riding the middle.

She wasn't going to say that to the group either. They'd figure it out themselves. Most reality shows did that.

"Your dish looked great," Hunter said. "Are you going to use some of them on the menu? That might be asked."

"We'll see," she said. "I had thought of that too, but some of them I'd tweak or not use. You'll see when we get further along in the show."

When the episode was done, she breathed a sigh of relief that it was over.

"You did great," her father said. "Very professional and relaxed. I thought you might be stiff."

"Me too," she said. "I think I was at times, but they do a good job finding the right angles and what to show. Again, not much was on me. Just judging my plates."

"And you got positive comments on it," Ashley said. "I think they were nuts saying you needed more seasoning. Your stuff never needs salt."

She grinned and loved how Ashley stood up for her. "Actually they were right," she said. "I didn't have a chance to put a finishing touch of it on at the end. The clock ran out. But I'd stand by that dish every day of the week. I appreciate you all being here for this."

"We wouldn't be anywhere else," her mother said. "I know you're worried about work on Wednesday, but don't be. It will be fine. Just take it as another day."

"I will. As I've said more than once, not much I can do but hope they do our business justice."

"I still can't believe you won't tell us the results," Emma said.

Only Hunter, her grandfather, her parents and Lincoln knew she made it to the finale. No one else was privy in this room. No one but Lincoln even knew she didn't win. They'd all find out soon enough.

"You get to wait with the rest of the world."

"I bet Lincoln knows," Ashley said. "You always tell those you love everything."

She turned and winked at Lincoln. "I'd like to think that."

He smiled, but it was forced and she didn't know why.

36

MAKE THE ROUNDS

Lincoln's phone was ringing two weeks later as he was getting ready for work.

When he saw it was his mother, he panicked. She never called this early. Ever.

"Hi, Mom. What's wrong?"

"Nothing," his mother said. "Sorry to scare you like this. I just know you're busy and then with your notoriety and all."

"Very funny," he said.

Two days ago the third episode had been aired.

Grace said she was going to be embarrassed over all of this, but it ended up being him.

Egan wouldn't let it end that people were calling and asking to get a ride with the sexy pilot dropping off Grace.

No one watching the show even knew he was Grace's boyfriend yet.

In one confessional, she'd commented on cooking for him and used his first name, but that was it. He'd been touched she'd said it and she blushed when it was aired.

They'd watched every episode together. Since they were both off on Mondays it was easy enough.

And though the summer was over and Labor Day just passed two days ago, they were both still pretty busy.

Another month or so and things would slow down some, but it normally didn't hit until late November that Egan stopped booking as many tours.

He said right now the demand for them had increased and not just from those visiting the island but people staying in Plymouth, Boston and Cape Cod wanting tours. They didn't pick up as many in Cape Cod and Plymouth but were going to have to start changing the schedule now.

"You look so handsome," his mother said.

"Enough that people are requesting me for flights. Egan is jealous. I never thought I'd see the day. They didn't show him on camera, only me. But they did get some nice shots of Egan's ride and he's proud enough of that. When people call to schedule a ride on that, they are told it's not with me."

"That must make him feel better," his mother said. "He's equally as handsome and charming."

"I'm not charming and you know it."

"You can be," his mother said. "Grace is doing a great job."

"She is," he said.

"I know you can't tell me how it works out."

"I can't," he said.

"Do you know?"

"Of course I do," he said, laughing.

"You love her, don't you?" his mother asked.

"I do."

"I can see it in your eyes."

"I have sunglasses on," he argued.

"You have them off when Grace is climbing out. I see you behind her."

"They made her climb in and out enough times I got sick of sitting there with them on and put them in the front of my shirt like I normally do."

It was funny how on TV no one saw how many takes it actually took for them to get that ten seconds worth of film. Talk about a job he'd never want.

"I've had so many people stop me around here asking if that is you."

"I didn't know that many people knew where I worked," he said.

"You haven't changed all that much," his mother said. "And those I work with know who you are. The same with your father. It doesn't take long to make the rounds. I know you're not on social media."

"No," he said.

Though he knew all the island's social media accounts were blowing up with Grace's appearance. It wasn't just good for The Retreat, it was for everyone.

Grace had told him that there had been over thirty calls for weddings in the past two and a half weeks. Guess that was a lot. Not only that, vacation reservations there and everyone else's properties.

He knew the casino had an uptick in guests too and that Bella was booking more acts.

He'd never paid much attention to so many things on the island as he was now.

"Well, it made the local news outlets here."

"Huh?" he said. Not what he wanted.

"I thought I'd let you know. They aired a piece two nights ago about you and some of your story. They wanted your father and me to do an interview and we declined. I thought that might be the end of it, but it wasn't."

"Why?" he asked.

"One, we didn't think you'd want that. That is the most important thing. And second of all, we didn't want to embarrass you. Your father and I aren't the type to get on TV."

"Stop," he said. "No, I wouldn't want that. But if it's something you want to do, I'd never tell you no. And I don't ever want you to worry that I'd be embarrassed over anything."

"I didn't want to upset you. I'm not telling you for that. I just wanted you to be aware."

"I'm not upset. I'm glad you called me too. Really, I am."

"There is something else," his mother said. "I doubt anything will come of it. Or I don't think so."

He didn't like the sound of her voice. "Let me guess. Lara?"

He knew that he'd be noticed once his face was on TV, but he'd hoped maybe Lara or her family weren't watching. It's not like everyone watched reality shows or cooking shows.

But since there was a piece on the news or it was making the rounds he was on it, that hope diminished.

"Yes," his mother said. "When I went to work yesterday, there were some whispers. It took me a while to hear them all. You know I stay out of things."

"You do," he said.

He remembered when he had his accident years ago. There was a lot of talk about it around his mother. His mother worked for the school district. Even though she was an aide in one of the elementary schools, many knew Lara and her family. The accident and the outcome were big news.

He knew he'd get blamed and her family tried to do it and slander him as much as they could.

But as Egan had said, he was a passenger and there were no drugs or alcohol involved. It had nothing to do with him other than it changed his life forever. Lara's too.

"It finally got back to me at the end of the day. Patty, she's nice and all. We're friends. Someone told her and she felt I should know. It could be nothing."

"Or it could be something. What is it, Mom?"

"Some are saying that Lara and her family are going to reach out and let the news know you're not the hometown hero. They played you up that way. Your background in the Air Force. They did interview some of your friends from school."

Shit. He'd kept in touch with some while he was in the service. Those that stayed local. It was giving him the part of life he was missing.

Maybe he was using it as a reminder of why he left too.

What he'd had with Lara was done and over with and he'd been hurting on so many levels.

As his mother had said before, they talked of getting married.

He loved her. He thought she loved him.

"Not much I can do to control that," he said. "I'm not sure the news is going to care all that much. If they know or do their job there isn't much they can say."

"No," his mother said. "Not about the accident. But they can talk about your relationship with Lara. And the one you've got with Grace."

"They haven't said anything about me and Grace having a relationship on the show," he said.

"Lincoln. Come on. Aside from the way you looked at her, she said your name in an interview. Sure, it could be another Lincoln, but it's not that common of a name. And those that know it's you, know your name. What many haven't figured out yet is that Grace is part of the Bond family."

"Which won't be hard to figure out," he said. "If they do dig and I'm sure Lara and her family are doing that." It would come out later on the show anyway.

"They are only going to make fools of themselves," his mother said. "You and I both know that. Nothing will come about it."

Or something could and he didn't want to take that chance.

"Thanks for calling, Mom. Let me know if you hear anything else, but don't worry about it either. I'm not."

"Good," his mother said. "I didn't call to worry you."

He hung up and went to the airstrip. His fear was exactly this happening and he had to at least let Egan know.

He couldn't very well tell Grace without her asking more questions, but Egan would talk to his father and then maybe it'd be taken out of his hands.

It could be nothing and he'd have to do what he lied to his mother about and pretend that he wasn't worried.

Maybe if he just came clean with Grace she'd understand, but he was embarrassed that she'd find out and think that he was with her for money even when he said that was the reason he didn't want anything to do with her in the beginning.

But if she saw some of his past, would she believe otherwise?

He'd even tried to relieve her mind about Roxy and felt he had. But would she think he was doing that so that she wasn't mad and he was trying to hang onto her?

He never felt this unsure of so much in his life, but he knew that the first step was telling his best friend.

"You're here early," Egan said. "You don't have a flight for an hour."

"I need to talk to you," he said. He told Egan about his mother's call. "I don't think it's anything."

"But you're worried," Egan said. "No reason to be. I'll talk to my father, but better yet, Hailey will be here with the baby in ten minutes."

His shoulders dropped. The last thing he wanted to do was bring in the family attorney, but hadn't Egan told him already that was their shield?

"Not ideal, but I'll leave the decision up to you," he said. Once again in his life there wasn't much he could do about things.

When Hailey showed up a few minutes later, Egan was just hanging up the phone after talking to his father.

"Do you have a few minutes before we take off?" Egan asked Hailey. "We need to tell you something that is going on. Just inform you."

"Sure," Hailey said. "J.B. is sleeping. He won't care."

Lincoln looked at the baby in her arms. J.B. would be a year old in another month, but he was out cold. Egan was putting the car seat in the helicopter for the baby. They had a few at both locations.

"I'll start," Lincoln said. He filled her in on what was going on.

"I don't understand," Hailey said. "You dated someone in high school. You broke up. You were a passenger in the car for the accident."

"I told him the same thing," Egan said.

"But it's what happened to Lara and after the accident," he said. He explained more.

"Grace has no idea, does she?" Hailey asked.

"No. I never saw the reason to tell her."

"It's in his past," Egan argued. "What's the big deal?"

"Nothing from a business standpoint. There are a few things we can do. We can sit tight and see if they attempt to do anything. I can make sure we are watching if they want to do anything and nip it in the bud prior."

"Might be best," Egan said.

"That can be done. I'll talk to Hunter and my grandfather and Mitchell. This is a business decision. But from a woman's point of view...you might want to man up, Lincoln. I'd be pissed if I found this out about Rex. Even if it's out of your control, there is a human element to this. One that you're carrying with you. I know my cousin. Trust me when I tell you, we are a lot alike in some ways."

Which meant he better figure it out fast.

37

LIKE A SISSY

"Hey," Grace said on Saturday morning. "I thought you had flights this morning."

"I do," he said. "But I've got an hour yet before I've got to be to the airstrip. I'm glad you could make time for me."

She laughed at him. "Anytime."

"Why are you laughing?"

"I don't know. You seem off. Your comment sounded so professional. You know, make time for you, like have a meeting."

He ran his hand through his hair. His sunglasses were in the front of his shirt like he normally kept them when they weren't on. His body was tense though and that wasn't like him.

"You could call it that. I know you're going to be upset."

"Upset?" she asked. "Is everything okay? You're not breaking up with me, are you?"

She was grinning when she said it, but he was still pacing. "No! It's not that. You're going to be pissed. Not upset. I know you are."

"I'm starting to feel that way now because you're not getting to the point. Spit it out, Lincoln. It's not like you."

"I should have talked to you earlier in the week, but you've been working and I wasn't sure if anything would come of it. I let Egan know right away and then Hailey was at the airstrip and she told me she was taking care of it. I figured it was fine. I guess I was wrong."

"Hailey?" she asked. "If my cousin is involved it's a legal matter. Did you break the law or something?"

"No," he said. "Nothing like that. Come sit down."

He guided her to the living room and sat in the chair across from her. "If it's not a legal matter then why is Hailey involved?"

"Let me start at the beginning. Or at least go back in time. You've slipped in comments before about me saying I've been burned in the past."

"I have," she said. "And you never talk about it. I was frustrated with it before, but I figured when you were ready you'd let me know if it mattered. I guess I started to assume it didn't and that is my mistake."

"Honestly, I'm not sure I'd ever be ready and didn't want to say anything now, but I don't have a choice."

She held back grinding her teeth over his statement. That he didn't want to *ever* tell her. "Tell me now."

"When I was in high school I was dating this girl, Lara. She was way out of my league, but she had approached me."

"Okay. We've all had bad experiences in high school. More so with dating."

"This is different. It was different. She came from money. Her mother's father had it. Her grandfather had some business and her father worked there. Lara's parents were strict with her. Or so she said."

"You didn't think so?" she asked.

He shrugged. "Looking back, they might have been more so than my parents, but I don't think they were outrageous. She was a girl. Their only child. They spoiled and sheltered her. When they started to give her some more freedom around sixteen she rebelled. She didn't like being home at curfew, she'd talk back. She wanted to move away. I was her first."

Grace was trying to absorb all of this as he rapidly fired facts at her. "Some people hold onto their first. That it's special or something. I can't say mine was. I remember it not being horrible or anything, just a fact of life."

"She wasn't my first, but I loved her. She loved me. She could be jealous of the girls that talked to me. She had a temper. But I didn't mind so much. I was flattered. I guess it went to my head."

All she heard was that Lincoln loved this girl. The one he was telling her about that burned him.

Someone who seemed somewhat like her.

Had money.

Showed a bit of jealousy.

Had a temper.

This wasn't going well in her eyes.

"That is probably normal for most teenage boys."

"Her parents hated me. I wasn't good enough for Lara. They didn't like her spending time with me. They felt like all her rebelling was because of me. They had no idea Lara didn't plan on going to college and was going to move with me."

"Didn't you say you'd have to be married for her to live with you in the service?" she asked.

"That was the plan," he said. "My parents knew it. I had no problem with it. But I didn't like that she wouldn't tell her parents. It didn't feel right to me. Here her parents were planning this life for her in college. She was leading them on that she was going and then she said maybe she'd go one year while I was in training, then drop out to be with me when I was stationed."

"I don't think I could do that to my parents," she said. "Whether money was an issue or not. Did she go and then decide she wanted a different life? Is that why you felt burned?"

Maybe he was led to believe one thing and Lara just ghosted out of his life.

"No," he said. "I thought that would happen. I almost expected it. I planned on being with her. Protecting her from her parents whom she didn't like all that much. Deep down I knew it was fabricated, but love clouds things, especially when you're a teenager."

"So what happened?"

"Her grandfather gave her this Mustang as her first car. I liked speed, but she was reckless. I didn't even like driving with her, but she'd laugh and tell me I could handle it."

Testing his manhood. Not something you did for someone you loved.

"Sounds immature to me," she said.

"She was that. A few months before graduation, we went out to the movies. It was dark when we were leaving and she hit the gas to pull out in front of a car that she shouldn't have. It was a big truck. It hit us in the driver's door. I just remember her body being thrown and the seatbelt snapping her back. I lost consciousness after that. It was like this slow-motion thing you see in the movies. I felt this pain in my arm and shoulder, across my chest and nothing at all."

"How badly were you hurt?" she asked.

Grace knew her jaw was open. She couldn't believe he'd never mentioned this. Never mentioned anything when she pointed out scars on his body. She assumed they were from being in the service.

"I broke my left collarbone and my wrist. I had surgery on my collarbone; my wrist was fine. I thought for sure I wouldn't be able to get into the service then and all my plans were gone. I felt like shit when I woke up and my parents told me what happened, that it was my first thought my career was gone before it started."

"I'd think that was natural," she said. "More so if you were using that to get away with someone."

"Yeah," he said.

"What happened to Lara?" she asked.

"She broke her back. She's in a wheelchair. Her parents have blamed it all on me."

"You weren't even driving," she said.

"No. No drugs or alcohol or anything. Just Lara being reckless as I said. The guy that hit us died. He didn't have his seatbelt on. There were no tickets issued. Lara's family knew people. I don't know. I think they looked at the fact this teenage girl was in serious condition, I wasn't in any better shape. The guy that hit us, he would have been ticketed for no seatbelt. He'd had some run-ins with the law. Drugs and alcohol. He was clean that day, but I think no one cared all that much about him and that made it worse for me."

"Do you know that for a fact?" she asked.

"No. It was just the talk from Lara's parents after. Again, I was a kid."

"And her parents blamed you even though you weren't driving? Because she was in a wheelchair she couldn't go with you? Did she blame you?"

Grace was trying to understand this. Did Lincoln feel as if he let Lara down?

"She blamed me. She was even more pissed when I

healed and was still going to leave. She said I was nothing more than a piece of shit abandoning her, but it's not like I'd seen her much before I left. Her parents wouldn't let me in to see her."

"She had to be able to reach you via text or something," she said.

"She did. She was." He looked up at her, his eyes a little glossy. "Grace. She'd been pregnant."

"Oh," she said. She was hurt just as he'd said she'd be. She was ticked off too.

Why wouldn't he say this to her? She wouldn't have thought poorly of him. She would have had sympathy for him.

Which of course he wouldn't want and some of it was now making sense. Someone as prideful as Lincoln wouldn't want pity or sympathy, even from a loved one.

"We didn't know," he said. "I believed she didn't know. She would have told me. She would have used that as another reason to get married right away. Her parents would have pushed it to save face. But they'd taken blood work before surgery and found out."

"What happened to the baby?" she asked. "If you tell me you've got a child out there..."

"No," he said. "I don't. She lost it. She was only a few weeks along. Her parents were told. They wanted the doctors to terminate the pregnancy."

"That's horrible," she said.

"They didn't. They told her parents they wouldn't do that. They were going to try to see if they could repair all the damage to Lara. They didn't. They couldn't. She had a spinal cord injury. Chances are she wouldn't have carried the baby to term anyway. It wasn't meant."

Grace wanted to argue with him about that statement

but didn't. "Fast forward to why you're telling me now," she said.

"Lara hated me after that. She'll never walk again. She'll never have a child. She lives at home and works for her grandfather. The life she wanted far away from all that she didn't get. She won't because she won't push herself to do anything. She wanted someone to take care of her."

"You were going to be her savior?" she asked.

"That is what she always said. But I left."

"You wouldn't have been able to care for her at that point in the service," she argued.

"No. Although, I probably wouldn't have gone if she didn't end things with me. It was just her reaction when I told her I was still trying to go. She didn't even ask me to stay, just hurled everything at me that her parents had always said. If maybe I wasn't treated the way I was… I don't know. I carry that guilt still. I've got this life and she didn't get anything she wanted."

"Nothing is stopping her from getting it now except excuses, by the sounds of it," she said. "I wouldn't sit back and feel sorry for myself."

"No," he said. "You wouldn't, but that is how she was. The guy that died, his family sued Lara's family in a civil suit and won."

"More insult to injury," she said.

"Yep. My parents still get treated like crap by those that know Lara's family. They are used to it and let it go."

"But now they've seen you on TV," she said. This was all adding up now. And though nothing had been aired yet about Lincoln being her boyfriend, she had said his name. People who knew him would most likely put it together.

"They have. My mother called me Wednesday morning

before work to let me know there was a local news piece on me."

She listened to what he said, everything up to Hailey saying she'd take care of it. That it was a business matter.

"What has happened that you're telling me now and not days ago?" she asked, crossing her arms. Now she was pissed. Her cousin knew intimate details about her boyfriend's life before her.

"Yesterday morning Egan got a call from Lara. She was threatening to go public with all of this. She was trying to get me fired."

"Which Egan wouldn't do," she said.

"No. But she wants money to not do it."

"Jesus, she's blackmailing my family?"

"I guess that's a good word for it. I'm supposed to let Hailey deal with it, but last night Mitchell told me Hailey was going to send some official documents threatening back. Getting the police involved."

"Which she should do," Grace said.

"I don't want my parents to have to go through this again," he said.

She wasn't thinking of that. "I don't know that there is anything you can do," she said.

"I'm flying to see Lara this afternoon. Hailey is going with me. So is Hunter."

"What!?" Grace stood up and started to pace. "I guess I could see Hailey as the family attorney and all. But even then I'm ticked off I'm just finding this out now. But why Hunter and not me?"

"This has to do with The Retreat. She's threatening not just Egan but Hunter. Egan isn't worried and isn't doing anything. So she's going after your employer."

"But it's my cousin," she said, laughing.

"She knows that," he said. "And she knows the family wealth."

"This is ridiculous. We wanted to get publicity for The Retreat, but not this."

"I told Egan all of this beforehand. I didn't want to be on camera."

She felt her eyes fill. "Even Egan knows. Everyone knows but me. The woman that you're supposed to be in love with."

"I *am* in love with you," he said.

"You've got a great way of showing it," she said. "Telling everyone what is going on but me until the last minute."

"I'm sorry, Grace. I handled this wrong."

"Yep," she said. "You did. And now you've got to go to work and so do I."

"That's it?" he said. "That's all you've got to say?"

"Oh," she said, "I've got a lot to say, but if I do I'll regret it. For now, I need you to just leave."

She watched as Lincoln stood up and walked out of her house and she burst into tears like a sissy.

It didn't seem like there was anything else she could do so she sat down and sobbed over the fact that he felt he could trust everyone but her with this knowledge.

That she didn't even know the man she loved.

38

MOVE ON

"Can I do the talking?" Lincoln asked Hunter and Hailey when he shut the helicopter off. They'd just landed at his parents' house and he was going to take his mother's car to see Lara. She knew he was coming. He'd reached out and asked if they could meet.

"I'd prefer to do it all," Hailey said.

"I know. The fact you're with me and Hunter, she thinks she's getting something out of this."

"Why would she think that?" Hunter asked, frowning. "I know what it's like for someone to try to blackmail my family."

Lincoln remembered when Kayla's mother attempted to cause problems years ago too. He supposed this was just one more thing that Grace's family had to go through.

"I know," he said. "But it's the only way I could get her to see me. Was to allude to the fact we were willing to negotiate."

"She's not getting a dime," Hailey said. "She's lucky I don't show up with the police. And you know damn well I'll be recording this."

He sighed. "Yeah. You told me the plan."

Griffin had put recording devices on Hailey's purse and another on Lincoln's sunglasses. He was never without them. He hated that the family would know what was being said, but there was no other way to end this in his eyes.

All he wanted to do was move on with his life. It seemed as if the past was always running on his heels though.

His mother came walking over to him and gave him a big hug. "Here are my keys," his mother said. "Are you sure you want to do this?"

"Mom, Dad, this is Hunter Bond and his sister, Hailey Bond Knight. They are Grace's cousins. Hunter is also Grace's boss."

"Her cousin," Hunter said, shaking his parents' hands. "The boss is a formality."

"I'm so sorry to have caused any trouble," his mother said.

"You didn't cause any trouble," his father said. "All we've done is mind our own business. The same as Lincoln. Things like this happen in life and there isn't much we can do about it."

"No," Lincoln said. "I wish there was. I'm hoping to end it now."

"If there are more problems after we leave," Hailey said, handing them a card, "I want you to call me directly. We'll make sure you're taken care of."

Lincoln shouldn't have been surprised by that offer, but was. His mother nodded her head and he kissed her on the cheek.

"We'll be back soon," he said.

He took the keys to his mother's SUV and then drove them the twenty minutes into town and to Lara's parents' house.

It didn't look so big and grand to him now. Not after being accepted into the Bond family.

He was so lost in his own world as a kid and where he lived that it never occurred to him how much bigger it was outside of Scranton.

The three of them got out and went to the door. He rang the bell and expected Lara's mother or father to answer. He didn't expect it to be Lara in the wheelchair.

He wasn't prepared for the sight of her.

She hadn't changed much other than there were lines in her face from years of bitterness.

She was still thin. Her nails were professionally done; her makeup was applied thickly like always. Her hair was done too as if a stylist attended to her daily.

After the call with her, he'd expected her to be someone that let herself go. That didn't care about life or anything. The way she kept spewing hatred toward him made him feel as if he had ruined everything.

But what he saw was a girl who was still in fashionable clothing and had expensive jewelry on her hands.

"Come in," Lara said. She hit a button on the wheelchair to back up. He shut the door thinking that maybe she didn't have much movement in her arms.

"Thanks for agreeing to meet with us," he said.

"Of course," Lara said. "Let's go do business in my father's office. My parents are out of town this weekend. My father won't care."

He looked at Hailey as they followed Lara down the hall. She was far from helpless if she was in the house alone. It was not the impression he was made to feel by their earlier conversation.

He looked around her father's office. He'd never been

allowed in here as a kid. He was barely allowed in the front door when he picked her up.

Lara wheeled over to her father's desk, picked up her laptop and set it on her lap, then opened it up. She had full use of her arms and hands.

"Listen, Lara. You do know what you're doing isn't legal, right?" he asked. "You're trying to get Grace's family to pay you money so that you won't cause problems for something you did when we were kids."

"It's *your* fault," Lara snarled.

"You were driving," he said. "You always drove too fast. I even tried to warn you not to go."

"You see it your way and I see it mine. You walked away free and clear from everything. You can walk. You got the career you wanted. You even got out of here."

"I'm sorry you ended up in a wheelchair," he said. "No one wanted that. No one wanted any of this."

"That's right," Lara snapped. "I've been stuck here at home while my mother babies me because she doesn't want me to live alone."

"But they left you alone for the weekend?" Hailey asked curiously.

Lara narrowed her eyes at Hailey. "There is a housekeeper. She'll be over later tonight so I'm not alone at night. You know, in case I want to get drunk and they think I'll fall out of my chair."

The way she was laughing told him that it might have happened more than once.

"What is it you want?" Lincoln asked. "What are you trying to accomplish here?"

"I want the payday I never got. I want to get the hell out of this town and start over."

"No one says you can't do that now," Hunter said. "You've

got a job. Looks like you're living here, so probably not a lot of bills."

Lincoln was thinking the same thing, but he could tell she was probably spending her money on material possessions like she always did.

One big payday would take care of that in her eyes.

"Nope," Lara said. "I want what I never got. I can get it from you. I think it's fair. Lincoln gets to go on and have a family. Not me. I'll never walk again. I'll never have kids. All those things normal people get, I won't."

"And you think blackmailing my girlfriend's family is going to give you that?" he asked. "All these years you could have come after me and never did."

"Why would I?" Lara said. "As far as I knew you were in the service. You probably didn't have a pot to even piss in. Isn't that a saying your father used to use?" She was laughing at her own comments.

She'd always cut his parents down when she was around them. Not to their face but behind their back. He'd stick up for his parents, but she'd smirk at him and say he was too sensitive.

"What if you didn't figure out I was dating Grace? Would you even do this?"

"It has nothing to do with who you're dating," Lara snarled. "It's embarrassing you and making you feel some of my pain. I'm hoping you lose your job over this."

"Not happening," he said. "Why would it? It has nothing to do with them. With any of them."

Lara was just as vindictive as he'd thought. Talk about feeling like an asshole that he was bringing this to Grace's family.

It did have to do with Grace. If he weren't dating her, he

would have never been filmed. None of this would have come down on her family.

"If they won't fire you, the next best thing is to see if I can get some money out of this before I start going to the press or social media. I doubt you want bad press when you're getting so much good right now."

"It's not the first time we might get bad press in our family," Hunter said, shrugging. "We are almost immune to it."

"All of this could go away with one little deposit. I'll pretend you were never here. I've got my bank information all ready."

"How much are you looking to get out of this?" Lincoln asked. He wanted as much detail as he could get. He hated what they planned on doing, but he knew it was the right thing.

"Two million sounds like a good number," Lara said. "I can pick up and move. Get me a nice house fitted for someone in a wheelchair."

Hailey was walking around the room looking at pictures while Lara talked. She was a cool one.

"This picture looks somewhat new," Hailey said. "You're standing on crutches."

"That's old," Lara rushed out to say.

He moved closer to the picture and looked. No, it wasn't old. "Are you walking?"

"No," Lara said. "I'm in a wheelchair. Are you blind?"

"But you're standing on crutches here," he said. "I've known you most of my life. You weren't on crutches before the accident. Ever."

"I had surgery a year ago," Lara snapped. "For a short period of time I had the strength to stand with crutches but not walk. I can't anymore."

He looked into her eyes and knew she was lying. It wasn't worth arguing over. They had more than enough.

"We are sorry for your accident," Hunter said. "We wish you well."

"Two million will go a long way," Lara said. "So, thanks."

"Sorry," Hailey said. "You're not getting any money from us. This was just a courtesy call to find out what your end game was. Now we know."

Lara's face almost twisted with anger. "For that, it's up to four million. You're going to regret playing me, Lincoln."

"As you've said, I don't have a pot to piss in. You won't get anything out of me. But I will give you a word of advice. You'll find yourself in a shitload of legal trouble if you try to go anywhere with this. You should do a bit more research into who you are trying to blackmail. I'm sure you'll be in touch."

The three of them left after that.

"Damn," Hailey said. "She's greedy."

"Always been that way," he said. "Wish I'd seen it before."

"Stop beating yourself up over this," Hunter said. "It's not on you."

"Yeah," he said. "It is. If I weren't dating Grace I wouldn't be on film. I brought this to your family. I should have just kept my distance like I'd told myself. I'm not meant to mix with you guys on anything more than being an employee."

There was silence in the car after that. He was glad. He didn't want to hear anything they had to say.

He'd do the right thing soon. Grace was just better off without him. He'd just have to learn to live without her, but it was going to be much harder than what he'd gone through with Lara and the guilt he carried there.

39

SUMS IT UP

"What are you doing here on your day off?" Hunter asked.

Grace looked up from her desk. She couldn't stay home. It hurt too much.

Maybe she shouldn't have given Lincoln such a hard time about what he'd told her, but she'd been hurt and pissed. Exactly as he predicted.

Staying home alone on a day they always spent together would have only made it worse.

"I've got things to do," she said.

He moved into her office and shut the door. "Have you talked to Lincoln?"

"Not since Saturday morning," she said.

Hunter sighed. "I figured as much. So you have no idea what happened?"

"Nope," she said. "If he wanted me to know he'd tell me. He's good at keeping secrets. Besides, you or Hailey could have told me and didn't either."

"Hailey and I decided it would be best if Lincoln did it."

"Don't hold your breath. I'd have to see him for him to talk to me, and even then, as I said, he's good at secrets."

"Just like you," he said. "You haven't told us the results of the show and you could."

"Don't go there, Hunter. It's not the same thing and you know it."

"No," he said. "It's not. I get it. You're hurt and upset and pissed off at him. And the combination is confusing and frustrating."

"That about sums it up," she said.

"Don't blame him. This was nothing he did."

She leaned back in her chair. "Is this a bro code thing? You standing up for him? I thought for sure it'd be Egan coming to me."

"It's not that," Hunter said. "Not at all. You weren't there and I was."

"That's right," she said. "He didn't want me there."

"No," Hunter said. "Hailey and I said no."

This was news to her. "He said it was him," she argued.

"I'm sorry he lied to you. Maybe he thought if you knew it was me and Hailey, you'd try to call Grandpa or someone else and appeal your case to go."

She would have. "Do you think Grandpa would have let me?"

Hunter lifted an eyebrow. "Most likely. I think Lincoln could have used your support. Maybe he would have been embarrassed over what happened. I was for him, but it's not his fault and out of his control."

"Lincoln wouldn't want anyone to feel that way about him," she said.

"No," Hunter said, "he wouldn't. But when people are in love they don't make the best decisions. They don't think things through."

"Tell me what you think I need to know," she said. "I can tell you want to rub my face in something."

"I wouldn't do that. But you need to know she was a nasty woman. I don't know everything Lincoln told you about their relationship, but I got the feeling that he loved her at one time."

"He said he did. Then he felt guilt. She pushed him away when he would have stayed, but her family wouldn't let him anywhere near her."

"She played the helpless card, but there was more going on. Griffin was able to get some information on Lara. She had surgery a year ago and is learning to walk again. She had a bunch of posts on social media but then deleted things before this all started."

"And Griffin found them?" she asked.

"The internet is forever," Hunter said. "I hear that enough. My point is, she wants someone to take care of her by any means necessary. She was trying to play off his emotions again."

"I don't think he has many," she said.

"You're wrong, Grace. Don't do that because you're hurt. It's your pride talking. If you could have seen him or heard him, you'd see how little he thinks of himself and tries desperately for people not to see it."

She knew that and wasn't surprised her cousin spotted it.

"What did he say?"

"I shouldn't play this for you. I'm only going to play the last part. Nothing else. We were quiet afterward and Hailey and Lincoln shut the recorders off after."

Hunter pulled his phone out and she listened to Lincoln say he wasn't meant to mix with her family. That he should have kept his distance.

The sadness in his voice brought tears to her eyes.

"He's an idiot."

Hunter laughed. "You should tell him that rather than sitting here stewing. Maybe he's keeping his distance and hoping you end things with him."

She grabbed her purse and stood up. "I'm going to give him a piece of my mind now."

"I expected no differently," Hunter said.

She marched out of the building, to her car and drove to Lincoln's. His truck was nowhere to be found. She went back to the airstrip and didn't see it there, which meant he wasn't working.

She was going to drive home and try to call him when she decided to check out the bar he brought her to months ago.

Jackpot, there was his truck.

She parked her SUV, got out and stormed to the front door with more purpose than ever before, whipped it open and started to look around. The bartender noticed her and nodded her to the corner.

There was Lincoln sitting by himself in a corner booth with an empty whiskey glass in front of him looking like he hadn't slept in two days.

"Getting drunk?" she asked, moving onto the bench across from him.

He looked shocked to see her. "What are you doing?"

"Trying to find your sorry ass and see what the heck is going on."

He lifted an eyebrow at her. "Nice to see you too."

"If you think avoiding me is going to tick me off enough to break up with you, then you've got another thing coming."

"Really?" he asked. He stood up to leave and she ran to keep up with him.

"Yep. Don't walk away from me. You're not keeping this in like you do everything else. It's all out in the open and we are going to clear the air so we can go back to the way things used to be."

"You're making a scene," he said.

"So?" she said. "I don't care. Everyone knows who I am. They knew who I was before that damn show and now they know more. What's a little bit more attention?"

Her voice was rising and people that were walking around outside stopped to look at them.

"This is crazy, Grace. Calm down."

"Nope," she said. "I've got a temper and I'm showing it to you. If you don't want everyone else to see it, then agree to talk to me."

He looked around at people staring at them. "Fine. We can go to your house."

"Works for me," she said, walking to his truck.

"Your car is back there."

"It is and once we talk you can bring me back to get it. This way you can't ditch me."

He frowned. "Do you think I'd do that?"

"I don't know what to think," she said. "The man I love wouldn't be wallowing in self-pity that he wasn't good enough. I'm going to prove to him that he is. Actually, I'm kind of shocked that my family sticking up for him for months wasn't enough, but I guess he's blind as well as stupid."

"Stupid," he said. "This is how you think we are going to clear the air and go back to normal? By insulting me?"

"It's getting you to talk to me, isn't it?"

She was grinning, but it was forced. She hated saying

what she was, but some of it was coming out without thought at this point.

He climbed in his truck and they drove to her house.

When they were in the house, she kept walking until they were sitting outside on the beach. She needed it to calm down and she knew he would too.

They both took a seat and she just stared at him.

After two minutes of silence, he asked, "What do you want me to say?"

"Tell me what happened on Saturday," she said.

"You don't know?"

"I know that Hunter came to see me in my office because I was there and not here. I'm not going to keep secrets. He told me I was being a fool. Then he said how nasty Lara was and that she was playing on your emotions."

"I knew that," he said. "I knew she was lying when Hailey saw the picture of Lara on crutches."

"And you still felt like shit?"

"It's hard not to," he said. "She had her life turned upside down."

"She did," she said. "But so did you. Did you ever stop to think about that? You made something out of it. That's the tattoo, isn't it? It's over your scar. I know you've got one there. You wanted it covered with something to remind you family was what was important."

"Yeah," he said.

"Well, you've got more than just your family. You've got me and mine unless you are going to throw it away. I figured you'd at least fight for it."

"I don't need to bring this into your life," he said.

"Please," she said, waving her hand. "This is nothing. I'm a Bond. We weather shit like this all the time. That's why we've got Hailey."

"She is pretty scary. She was so calm she wasn't even paying attention half the time."

"She is always paying attention. Just like me. I just wish I'd seen more. Or asked more. Maybe I should have pushed you to tell me all of this with Lara beforehand."

"It wouldn't have changed a thing that happened."

"Nope," she said. "I'm glad you can recognize that. But it would have changed my reaction. It would have changed your feelings of self-worth."

"I doubt that," he said quietly.

"I can be pretty persuasive. Didn't I get you to date me?"

"You did," he said, grinning.

"And I got you to fall in love with me too."

"I might have done that on my own."

She smiled. "Then I can get you to forgive yourself for something you shouldn't take the blame for to begin with. No one in my family is blaming you for anything. They never have and they never will. But if things don't work out with us, then are you going to blame me? I'm the one with the temper. Not you. You walk on water to most in the family."

"Janet and Mitchell do think fondly of me," he admitted. He was slowly coming around.

She got up and moved into his lap. "Am I getting to you now?"

"A little," he said.

"Good," she said. "I'm going to keep it up until we are back to normal. If it takes a day, a week, a year. I'm not giving up."

"Don't," he said. "Don't give up on me."

"Never. I expect you to never give up on me either. Because we know I'm going to lose it again with you on something. Why else do you think my family sent you to California with me? To keep me under control."

"You've got great control," he said. "You would have been fine."

"But I was better with you. I'll always be better with you. Do you believe that?"

"I do," he said, kissing her.

"Good. Then we are finally getting there."

He laughed and picked her up. "We can go anywhere you want. Just tell me and I'll take you."

"As long as you're with me, I don't care where it is!"

EPILOGUE

F*ive Weeks Later*

"WE CAN'T WAIT to see how this ends," Hailey said.

The family lawyer looked at him and grinned. He had to say he was thrilled Lara would finally be out of his life and he could put his past where it belonged. In the past.

Thanks to Grace's family.

He'd apologized to the woman he loved repeatedly. He said he was a coward, a fool, and embarrassment and pride kept his past where it was hoping he'd never have to explain. He should have known that wouldn't be the case.

More so, he was worried she'd be disappointed in him.

Hailey had sent the recordings to Lara's family who had no idea what she'd been doing. Since Lara had always said her family controlled her, it was the plan they would now too.

Lara's parents knew the ramifications if the police were brought in and they handled it. It appeared to be over.

"I know," Grace said. "I've been hearing this for weeks."

She looked at Lincoln. He wasn't surprised the finale was being watched on a big screen at The Retreat with half her family here and a ton of employees. It was set up like a movie theater.

"Do you feel weird having everyone here watching this?" he asked. They were sitting at a table with her parents, Hunter and Hailey and their families, her Aunt Nicole, Uncle Charlie, Skyler and her grandfather.

In the past few weeks, Grace and he had worked it out.

They were right back to where they were before he was...stupid.

She'd put him in his place and told him no more secrets. Not again.

She'd reminded him she'd never be disappointed in anything he did and hoped he'd felt the same way about her.

"Nah," she whispered. "We know the results. I'm just more concerned about what is going to be aired on what they'd asked of me. So far, everything has been very positive."

"You won over everyone's heart a few weeks ago on the beach," Skyler said. "Even I was shocked by what happened. You were on the bottom and never even blamed it on the time you lost with Pierre."

"It wasn't about that," she said. "Not sure why everyone was so shocked I helped him and made sure he was fine."

"Anyone who knows you knows that you've got a heart of gold," Steven Bond said, looking at Lincoln.

"She does," he said. "I'll never forget. But I saw it that day."

Production got a better view. They even captured her words that she'd said standing there with him. She needed a drink anyway.

She didn't want the guy to feel like he was alone.

Again, a good reminder for him.

He'd never feel alone or not worthy again as long as he had Grace by his side.

"Anyone hungry?"

He looked up to see Tracy come over with a large tray of snacks.

"Hi, Tracy. Let me introduce you around to everyone," she said.

The girl that Grace helped to get on her feet. Yeah, anyone who thought she had a heart of...stone was clueless.

When Tracy left, the room got quiet as the show started.

For the next hour they watched Grace and Pierre working in the kitchen, sweat dripping down both of their faces, exhaustion visible. But she never faltered, she never cursed someone who almost dropped a plate that she had to fix.

When both of them were done plating, Grace gave Pierre a hug. "You've got this," she'd said to the Frenchman.

"I don't think so," Pierre said. "Those were some great dishes."

"But you did a French menu. Completely French. Do you know how many people want to have themed cuisine like that at a wedding? Your bosses better get ready."

Pierre had laughed and winked.

"That was nice of you to say that," her father said.

"I'm a nice person."

A commercial came on and everyone was chatting, then they returned and did a few interviews with both of them on how they felt.

The camera was panning in and out as everyone ate their main meal in the room and the judges listened as both Pierre and Grace explained their dishes.

"I'm so nervous," Melanie said. "Grace, I'm so proud of you. You handled yourself so well. You made the family proud."

"What do you think, Grandpa? Am I bringing in the bucks or what? I don't even have to run the place to do it."

There was a roaring of laughter over that comment from most of the Bond family in the room. He knew Grace didn't want any part of running The Retreat, but damn, what she did, she should get a ton of credit.

"Since reservations for the off season are up thirty percent already and we've got more wedding consultations lined up than ever before," Hunter said, "you're the one doing most of that work."

"Totally worth it," she said and leaned back to put her head on Lincoln's shoulder.

That move had a lot of eyes on them and he had to say he never felt more accepted than he did in that moment.

It only got better though.

Pierre was announced as the winner and there were boos in the room, but Grace said loudly, "He earned it. Quiet. One more interview to go."

Everyone was quiet as they listened to Pierre in the confessional in tears thanking his wife for letting him have a week away from the kids. The Frenchman laughed after that statement.

Grace's face came up on the screen. "What are you going to do now?" the producer asked her.

"Go home and start thinking of my own wedding now that I've got all these wonderful ideas."

"Are you and Lincoln engaged?" the producer asked.

They'd shown him and Grace together two episodes ago, confirming the relationship and Bond Charter phones all but blew up after with his background. Just like they'd done a two-minute section on Pierre's wife and kids back in Florida.

It was a nice touch if he did say so himself.

Now he was waiting to see what Grace said, as there was silence in the room.

"Not yet," Grace said. "Maybe after this airs, he'll get the hint."

There were a ton of cheers in the room, clapping too. Talk about being put on the spot.

Too bad he wasn't prepared for this night. If he'd known he would have been.

He heard a whistle and turned his head to Egan. "Heads up," Egan said and tossed something in the air.

He reached out and snagged it.

The ring box of Grace's engagement ring that he'd bought two weeks ago. What the hell? How did Egan get this and why did he bring it today? Of course, his buddy knew he'd bought it, but still.

"How did you find this?"

"Let's say I had an idea something was going on and for a guy that always plans ahead you didn't this time. Sorry about the mess. You hide things well."

"What's going on?" Grace said.

"Well, you did put me on the spot. Might as well let everyone know I got the hint. Funny thing is, I had no idea you were going to say that."

There was a loud gasp and he got down on one knee.

"Oh my," she said.

"Yeah, well, you asked for it," he said.

"I just had to make that first move. Everyone in this room remember that."

"You won't let me forget it," he said. He flipped the lid on the ring box. Inside was a thick band with two large baguettes on each side meeting to a square diamond in the center. "Grace Stone, will you be my wife?"

"You know it," she said. "I only had to feed you to get here."

There was more roaring that had the room almost vibrating in laughter, him standing and pulling her up and into his arms.

"I guess we've got a wedding to plan," he said. "I'll leave the menu to you. I'd say you've got it covered."

She reached up and framed his face in her hands. "I've had it covered from the first day I met you, just needed to wait for the fate of this island to come into play."

"Oh, now you are going to say you believe in it," her mother said.

"Seems to be working in my favor now," Grace said and gave him a big kiss. "Didn't Lincoln say something about that at Egan's wedding? Works for us both now."

"Yes, it does!"

The End!

Check out the next in the series...Family Bonds- Kelsey & Van

While recovering from a life-threatening injury, Van Harlowe is given the chance of a lifetime to start over and do anything he wants. All he has to do is accept an inheritance from a man he's never met and grew up hating. Most of all, he just wants the truth, which means the decision isn't all that hard to move to a small island. It's not like he has anything he's leaving behind other than horrible memories.

Kelsey Raymond has made some poor dating decisions in her life but her humor keeps it real and allows her to push on with a shrug of her shoulders. When fate intervenes and she runs into the man that helped to save her dog, she decides to ask him out. What could go wrong? The fate of the island Gods jump in and throw it in her face he is the one? Or that he's a stranger that she finds out isn't really a stranger to her family after all? Sure, why not? She rolls with the punches. But can she stay serious enough to help Van find his way or risk losing him altogether?

ABOUT THE AUTHOR

The Road Series-See where it all started!!

Lucas and Brooke's Story- Road to Recovery
    Jack and Cori's Story – Road to Redemption
    Mac and Beth's Story- Road to Reality
    Ryan and Kaitlin's Story- Road to Reason

The All Series

William and Isabel's Story — All for Love
    Ben and Presley's Story – All or Nothing
    Phil and Sophia's Story – All of Me
    Alec and Brynn's Story – All the Way
    Sean and Carly's Story — All I Want
    Drew and Jordyn's Story— All My Love
    Finn and Olivia's Story—All About You
    Landon Barber and Kristen Reid- All Of Us

The Lake Placid Series

Nick Buchanan and Mallory Denning – Second Chance
    Max Hamilton and Quinn Baker – Give Me A Chance
    Caleb Ryder and Celeste McGuire – Our Chance
    Cole McGuire and Rene Buchanan – Take A Chance
    Zach Monroe and Amber Deacon- Deserve A Chance
    Trevor Miles and Riley Hamilton – Last Chance

Matt Winters and Dena Hall- Another Chance
Logan Taylor and Kennedy Miles- It's My Chance
Justin Cambridge and Taryn Miles – One More Chance

The Fierce Five Series

Gavin Fierce and Jolene O'Malley- How Gavin Stole Christmas
    Brody Fierce and Aimee Reed - Brody
    Aiden Fierce and Nic Moretti- Aiden
    Mason Fierce and Jessica Corning- Mason
    Cade Fierce and Alex Marshall - Cade
    Ella Fierce and Travis McKinley- Ella

Fierce Family

Sam Fierce and Dani Rhodes- Sam
    Bryce Fierce and Payton Davies - Bryce
    Drake Fierce and Kara Winslow – Drake
    Noah Fierce and Paige Parker - Noah
    Wyatt Fierce and Adriana Lopez – Wyatt
    Jade Fierce and Brock James – Jade
    Ryder Fierce and Marissa McMillan – Ryder

Fierce Matchmaking

Devin Andrews and Hope Hall- Devin
    Mick McNamara and Lindsey White- Mick
    Cody McMillian and Raina Davenport – Cody
    Liam O'Malley and Margo West- Liam
    Walker Olson and Stella White – Walker
    Flynn Slater and Julia McNamara – Flynn
    Ivan Andrews & Kendra Key- Ivan

Jonah Davenport & Megan Harrington- Jonah
Royce Kennedy & Chloe Grey- Royce
Sawyer Brennan & Faith O'Malley- Sawyer
Trent Davenport & Roni Hollister- Trent
Gabe McCarthy & Elise Kennedy – Gabe
Ben Kelley & Eve Hall – Ben
Dane Grey & Sloane Redding – Dane

Paradise Place

Josh Turner and Ruby Gentile – Cupid's Quest
Harris Walker and Kaelyn Butler – Change Up
Philip Aire and Blair McKay- Starting Over
Nathan Randal and Brina Shepard – Eternal
Ryan Butler and Shannon Wilder – Falling Into Love
Brian Dawson and Robin Masters – Mistletoe Magic
Caden Finley and Sarah Walker- Believe In Me
Evan Butler and Parker Reed – Unexpected Delivery
Trey Bridges and Whitney Butler – Forever Mine
Dylan Randal and Zoe Milton- Because Of You
Cash Fielding and Hannah Shepard – Letting Go
Brent Elliot and Vivian Getman – No More Hiding
Marcus Reid and Addison Fielding- Made For Me
Rick Masters and Gillian Bridges – The One
Cooper Winslow and Morgan Finely- Back To Me
Jeremy Reid and McKenna Preston- Saving Me
Christian Butler and Liz Carter- Begin Again
Cal Perkins and Mia Finley- Angels Above

Amore Island

Family Bonds- Hunter and Kayla
Family Bonds- Drew and Amanda

Family Bonds – Mac and Sidney
Family Bonds- Emily & Crew
Family Bonds- Ava & Seth
Family Bonds- Eli & Bella
Family Bonds- Hailey & Rex
Family Bonds- Penelope & Griffin
Family Bonds- Bode & Samantha
Family Bonds- Hudson & Delaney
Family Bonds- Alex & Jennie
Family Bonds- Roark & Chelsea
Family Bonds- Duke & Hadley
Family Bonds – Carter & Avery
Family Bonds- Egan & Blake
Family Bonds- Carson & Laine
Family Bonds- Grace & Lincoln
Family Bonds- Kelsey & Van

Blossoms

A Love for Lily – Zane Wolfe and Lily Bloom
A Playboy For Poppy- Reese McGill and Poppy Bloom
A Romantic For Rose – Thomas Klein and Rose Bloom
A Return For Ren – Ren Whitney and Zara Wolfe
A Journey For Jasmine- Wesley Wright and Jasmine Greene
A Vacationer for Violet – Violet Soren And Trace Mancini
A Hero For Heather- Heather Davis and Luke Remington
A Doctor For Daisy- Daisy Jones And Theo James
An Investigator For Ivy- Ivy Greene and Brooks Scarsdale
A Date For Dahlia- Dahlia Greene and Hugh Crosby

A Surprise For Sage- Sage Mancini and Knox Bradford

Looking For Love

Learning To Love – West Carlisle and Abby Sherman
  Love To The Rescue – Braylon Carlisle and Lily Baker

Love Collection

Vin Steele and Piper Fielding – Secret Love
  Jared Hawk and Shelby McDonald – True Love
  Erik McMann and Sheldon Case – Finding Love
  Connor Landers and Melissa Mahoney- Beach Love
  Ian Price and Cam Mason- Intense Love
  Liam Sullivan and Ali Rogers - Autumn Love
  Owen Taylor and Jill Duncan - Holiday Love
  Chase Martin and Noelle Bennett - Christmas Love
  Zeke Collins and Kendall Hendricks - Winter Love
  Troy Walker and Meena Dawson – Chasing Love
  Jace Stratton and Lauren Towne - First Love
  Gabe Richards and Leah Morrison - Forever Love
  Blake Wilson and Gemma Anderson – Simply Love
  Brendan St. Nicholas and Holly Lane – Gifts of Love

ABOUT THE AUTHOR

Sign up for my newsletter for up to date releases and deals. Newsletter.

Follow me on:

Website
   Twitter
   Facebook
   Pinterest
   Goodreads
   Bookbub

As always reviews are always appreciated as they help potential readers understand what a book is about and boost rankings for search results.

Printed in Great Britain
by Amazon